NUMBERS NEVER LIE

A Romantic Suspense

Diane Burton

Copyright © 2018 by Diane Burton

Excerpt from *The Case of the Meddling Mama* copyright © 2017 by Diane Burton

Cover design by The Novel Difference

ISBN-10 0-9966374-9-4

ISBN-13 978-0-9966374-9-7

Praise for

The Case of the Meddling Mama

What a fun read . . . Ms. Burton had me biting my nails by the end of the book. ~ Maris Soule, author of *A Killer Past*

The Case of the Bygone Brother

"...plenty of action and sexual tension that kept me turning the pages. I loved this book and these characters. I'm glad this will be a series. I can't wait until O'Hara and Palzetti are back together again." ~ Marilyn Baron, author of *Landlocked*

". . . a wonderful modern love story made sweeter with humor, family values, and Sam Spade suspense." ~ Rolynn Anderson, author of *Fear Land*

One Red Shoe

". . . fast-paced, super suspenseful, run-for-your life action. . . . mixed in perfectly with that action, like the bubbles in a gin and tonic, is humor."
~ Kristen Brockmeyer, author of *Lucky in Love*

Also by Diane Burton

Dedication

To my amazing daughters, Liz and Katy

To my terrific sons Doug and Matt

To my grandchildren who bring so much love into my life

And especially to Bob, my best friend and hero

Acknowledgements and Thanks

To Doctor Matthew Carr, MD, whose answers to my medical questions keep me on the right track. Errors are mine.

To Alicia Dean for her invaluable advice and terrific editing. She always makes my story better. And to Florence at The Novel Difference for the amazing cover art. Thank you, ladies.

To the members of the Mid-Michigan chapter of Romance Writers of America® and Holland Writers Group for their continued support and advice.

Most importantly, I want to thank my family for all their support. Liz & Matt, Doug & Katy, I'm very proud of you. Thank you for encouraging me.

To my husband, Bob, my greatest supporter, who makes meals, does laundry and all the yardwork so I have time to write. How glad I am that our friends fixed us up on that blind date!

CHAPTER ONE

The garage door rose. All by itself.

Maggie Sinclair's heart shot into high gear as she set down the camping equipment next to her SUV. She hadn't gone anywhere near the button next to the door to the house. And the remote was right where it belonged, clipped to the Suburban's visor. *She* hadn't opened the door.

Someone had keyed in the code.

As the door lifted, a pair of athletic shoes and legs encased in wrinkled khakis came into view. Only one other person knew the code to her garage. The numb-nut scaring her half to death had better be him.

In case it wasn't, Maggie stepped quietly to the rack on the wall where the garden tools hung. Good thing she'd leaned the shovel against the wall instead of hanging it up properly. The awful screech if she'd pulled it off the hook would give the intruder warning. She seized the shovel just as the figure outside bent in half and ducked under the door.

Maggie raised the shovel, ala Detroit Tiger Miguel Cabrera, fully prepared to whack the intruder. His look of surprise almost matched hers.

"Jack Sinclair," she yelled. "What are you doing sneaking up on me?"

"Whoa!" Her brother recovered fast, right after dropping a plastic case on the dusty garage floor. A CD spilled out. "What are you doing here?"

She lowered the shovel. "Gee, I don't know. Ya think maybe because I live here?"

Jack picked up the CD and case. "Are you sick? It's Friday. And only—" He checked his watch. "—one o'clock. Why aren't you in school?"

About to lambaste him for scaring her, she gave her brother a long look. Shadows rimmed his eyes, and his mouth had creases she hadn't noticed the last time she saw him, a couple of weeks ago. Her neatnik brother was never disheveled, yet there he was in wrinkled slacks with only part of his sport shirt tucked in.

"What's wrong?" she asked.

He looked beyond tired, more like he carried the weight of the world on his shoulders, as their mom used to say. "With Ben out, I had to take over his clients on top of my own."

Jack's partner in the accounting firm had a nasty confrontation with the pavement when his motorcycle went one way, and he flew the other. For the past month, he'd been either in the hospital or rehab.

"How's Ben doing?" she asked.

"He came into the office for the first time today, hobbling on crutches and trying to type with one hand. You never said why you're home in the middle of the afternoon."

"School is out for the summer." She returned the shovel to the rack, securing it properly while cringing at the screech. "And you never said why you're sneaking into my garage?"

A cocky grin eased the creases along his mouth and across his forehead. "Can't I visit my kid sister?"

She put her hands on her hips and pursed her lips with an expression that could quell a room of high school seniors full of themselves for being on the brink of adulthood and sophomores, who were just full of themselves. "When you thought I wasn't going to be home? Try again, Ace."

Jack cuffed her around the neck and, with his knuckles, rubbed the top of her head in a noogie. "Okay, you got me. I want to try out a new CD on your system."

She ducked out from under his arm then hip bumped him. "The truth comes out."

For Christmas and her birthday last year, he gave her a sophisticated sound system. After setting it up, he left detailed—printed, no less—instructions for its use. That was Jack. Always covering the bases. Heaven forbid, he leave anything to chance. Even his sister's entertainment center.

"Hang on. I've got something for you in the car." He ran back to his Chevy Blazer, parked in the driveway.

She followed him. "I thought you were going to get a new car. How old is this thing, anyway?"

Jack turned around. "Do not disparage old Betsy here. She got me through college and is still going strong." He patted the hood of the fifteen-year-old SUV then glanced across the street. "Uh, oh. Mrs. O'Malley's standing at her window."

The elderly neighbor kept the curtains open across her large picture window until she went to bed. Nothing got past her. Unless it was Bingo Night.

"She's watching us." Maggie groaned in dismay.

Jack laughed. "Remember how Dad always complained about her?"

"Yes, but he always said she's better than any security system. She'll be coming out any minute with a bucket and mop to scrub her porch, as an excuse to see us better."

Whenever she was introduced, Mrs. O'Malley always pointed out she only *married* an Irishman. She was a DeBoer, poster child for the "scrubbing Dutch."

"Here." He plunked a Detroit Tigers' baseball cap on her head. "A client gave it to me."

"Thanks, kiddo."

"I knew you'd wear it more than I would." He glanced across the street. "We'd better go in, or she'll be over wanting to know why I'm here in the middle of the day."

At the door between the garage and the house, Maggie checked over her shoulder. Sure enough, Mrs. O'Malley opened her front screen door and came out with a broom. Maggie quickly hit the button to close the garage door. "Have you had lunch?"

Jack appeared to think about that. "Uh, no. I, uh, forgot about the time."

"Since you thought I wouldn't be here, did you plan to raid my fridge?"

"I would never mooch off you." His offended expression matched his tone. "I told you, I only came over to give you the cap and to listen to my CD. But if you're fixing . . ."

Maggie laughed at his obvious ploy. "In that case, you can fix your own tea—and one for me—while I wash up."

She pulled the fixings for lunch out of the fridge while Jack went into the living room. When the music didn't come on right away, she called out, "Forgotten how it works?" She couldn't resist a smirk. "Why don't you read the instructions?"

"Nobody likes a smart-ass," he called back.

Because he seemed so tired, his choice of music surprised her. Head-banging rock.

"Could you maybe turn it down?" she yelled to be heard over the music. "The neighbor kids will get the wrong idea about their English teacher."

Jack changed the song to a classic oldie and lowered the volume. When he came out into the kitchen, he grabbed her around the waist and spun her away from the counter. "Maybe those teenage delinquents you insist on trying to educate will think you're a normal person."

He twirled her around the small kitchen in dance moves from the sixties. His antics reminded her so much of their folks dancing in the kitchen, Maggie laughed and matched his steps.

"Normal? Instead of the Wicked Witch of the West?" She gave an evil laugh. "'I'll get you my pretty.'"

"'And your little dog, too,'" Jack quipped as he dipped her over his arm in a flourish. "You gotta work on that image, Mags."

"Hey, it works for me."

During lunch, Jack asked about the camping equipment in the garage. "I thought your camping days were over when Trish moved away."

As it often did, Maggie's eyes teared up at the thought of Trish Morrow. They'd been best friends since kindergarten. A natural born leader, Trish could get anybody to do anything—like conning Maggie into helping with the group of pre-teen campers. Last summer, after eight months of unemployment, Trish's husband took a job in Denver. Trish and the kids followed, and there went the leader of the group.

"We've been meeting," Maggie said around the lump in her throat.

"Suck-er." Jack grinned. "How many volunteer jobs do you have now? Little League umpire, peewee hockey ref, high school girls' baseball coach—"

"I get paid for that one," she interrupted. "Can I help it if the girls wanted to get together to talk?"

4

"From the camping equipment you were loading into your SUV, it looks like you're going to do more than talk."

She shrugged. "They still want to go to Isle Royale. Their theory is if they practice camping all summer and into the fall, Trish will come back for the trip next summer. We're going on an overnight camping trip tomorrow."

"You got another mother to help chaperone?"

Maggie grimaced. "Not exactly."

He dropped his sandwich. "You aren't taking the girls by yourself? That's crazy."

"Add in irresponsible, brother dear. Which I'm not. I'd never take kids on a trip without another adult." She eyed him with an appraising expression.

Jack held up his hands. "Don't look at me. I'm up to my eyeballs in work."

"Don't worry. I wasn't going to ask you, although it did cross my mind."

Despite her brother's usually super-neat appearance, he loved the outdoors almost as much as Maggie. Sports and scouts were his life when they were kids—just like her. While he went from Tiger Cubs through to achieving Eagle Scout status, she'd gone from Daisy Girl Scouts to earning her Gold Award. That made having a group of campers not affiliated with Girl Scouts a little weird. But, Trish didn't like organizations with rules and regulations and, since Maggie hadn't been in charge, she went along with her best friend.

Now her BFF was gone, and guess who was in charge?

"So, who's helping you with the troop?" Jack pulled a couple of grapes off the stems and popped them into his mouth.

"Ellen's dad."

Jack started to choke. She jumped up ready to do the Heimlich until he laughed. She considered whacking him on the back on general principle.

"Drew? Drew Campbell? The guy whose idea of casual is loosening his tie?"

At least, Jack's tired expression was gone. She tapped her short, no-nonsense fingernails on the table. "I'm so glad I could provide entertainment with lunch."

He continued to laugh—almost braying.

"I'm loaning him your sleeping bag and backpack." She worked hard not to smirk.

"What!"

"Consider it *rent* for storing your stuff in my garage. And basement."

Technically, the house was half his, part of their inheritance. After their folks died, she was grateful to leave her one-bedroom apartment. Since Jack already had a condo and didn't want the upkeep of a house, their home was all hers, along with storage for his belongings.

Jack frowned for a second. "My equipment? You're loaning out my camping equipment?"

"He's your friend. I didn't think you'd mind."

Jack started to laugh again, this time a guffaw. "Oh, God. I wish I could be there to watch." He went off again, laughing so hard tears formed until he wiped them away. "Drew Campbell wimped out of Cub Scouts."

When his eyes started watering, and the numbers on the computer screen blurred, Jack knew it was time to quit. He whipped off his glasses and tossed them on the desk he used at Vander Haar Manufacturing. They skidded across the papers and would've fallen on the floor if not for his quick grasp. Damn, he was tired. He rubbed his eyes before glancing at his watch. Twelve-twenty. Time to get home. He interlaced his fingers, reached over his head, and stretched. The cricks and pops told him he'd scrunched his shoulders while crunching numbers.

Jack shut down the company's computer, closed his laptop, and packed the latter into his briefcase, along with his glasses. He locked all the company papers, and his notes, in the desk. Lot of good they did. Thanks to his online classes, he'd recognized the signs of a problem the first day. Problems that became worse the more he investigated.

For the past year, he'd worked on his Master's degree in forensic accounting. He never mentioned that to anyone. Ben was always too busy to just chat. Even before the accident, his partner had been out of the office more than in. He hadn't thought to tell Maggie. They always had so many other topics to talk about. If he'd gotten hold of Drew last night, he would have told him. Damn, he needed his advice. Maybe he should stop by.

Twelve-twenty? Waking up his best friend, along with his daughter in the middle of the night was not a good idea.

Besides, Jack needed sleep more. He'd call Drew in the morning.

Slinging the laptop case/briefcase over his shoulder, he checked the room assigned to him for the audit to make sure he hadn't left anything out. He shut off the lights and locked the door behind him. He still had much to do. This morning, Ben said he would finish the audit. But, that wasn't the way Jack worked. When he started something, he always finished.

"Working kinda late, arncha, Mr. Sinclair?"

Startled, Jack spun around.

The janitor leaned on his mop. "It's after midnight."

"No rest for the weary, Max." Jack pocketed his keys.

"You be careful going home, Mr. Sinclair. Fog was rollin' in off the lake when me and the missus drove in to work."

"Thanks for the heads-up." Jack saluted the affable worker and headed down the hall. The doors to the other offices were closed. Only the cleaning crew remained.

Hazel, Max's wife, stopped dusting the receptionist's desk. "'Night, Mr. Sinclair. You best be careful. Noticed you parked all the way at the end of the parking lot. The light there is out. Saw that when we came in. The company what takes care of our lights won't come out 'til Monday. You want Max to get a flashlight and walk out with you so's you can find your car? What with the fog and all?"

Jack forced himself to smile. In the five days he'd been auditing the books at the manufacturing plant near Muskegon, he often worked late and ran into the older couple. "I'll be fine."

"'Night, then. You be careful, now. Ya hear?"

Even before he pushed open the heavy glass door, he saw that Max and Hazel were right. The solitary light at this end of the parking lot barely penetrated the fog. Maybe he should have taken Hazel up on the offer of a flashlight. He wasn't worried about finding the Blazer in this pea soup. He worried more about tripping on the curbs and breaking his arm.

Wouldn't that be a fine mess? Worse than Ben. A one-armed accountant.

Duh. The flashlight on his cell phone. He should've thought of that sooner. Jack clicked it on, but it shone only a foot or so in front of him. A soft skitter came from near the dumpster. Rats? He shuddered and clicked his remote. From fifteen feet away, his head- and taillights barely penetrated the mist.

It would be a slow drive back to Grand Rapids. He should get a motel room for the night. As his spirits lifted at the thought of a motel nearby, he groaned. Finding a vacancy anywhere along the Lake Michigan shoreline would be next to impossible in the summer and even more so late on a Friday night.

Weary beyond belief, he dragged himself to his SUV. He needed to return tomorrow—make that later today. He had to do more digging in the company's files. He couldn't believe what he'd discovered so far. This went way beyond anything he imagined. The implications—

"Jack?"

Startled by the familiar voice, he dropped the keys. His phone slipped out of his fingers and skidded away. The fog gobbled up the light, and he lost sight of it. He peered in the direction of the sound. A figure stepped away from the dumpster's hulking shape.

"We need to talk."

Fear shot through him. Then a modicum of relief. *Thank God, I stopped at Maggie's.*

CHAPTER TWO

"What do you mean no toilets?" Drew Campbell stopped on the dusty forest path, hooked his sunglasses on the placket of his golf shirt, and stared at his daughter.

"Dad-dy." Ellen groaned. Was she only fourteen? She did exasperation better than his administrative assistant. "I *told* you we were camping."

Drew couldn't reveal that camping was *not* what he remembered her saying. She'd asked him while he was working at home, his mind on the client's paperwork. He was certain she asked him to come along on an outing with her little group of friends. Pleased that she wanted to do something together, he assumed they'd go on a hike, have a picnic lunch, and then be home in time for supper.

With a silent snort, he remembered the saying about *assume.* Surprises kept whacking him in the head.

He took a call on his cell in the parking lot near the trailhead. Surprise #1: the "no electronics rule." No cell phones, no iPods. All were locked in the vehicles. Only the leader carried a cell phone, for emergencies.

Surprise #2 came when he glanced in the open hatch of the Navigator. Five backpacks. Five backpacks with bedrolls. He'd transported *four* girls. It didn't take a law degree to figure out who the fifth backpack was for. He was in deep shit. But what could he say in front of Ellen and her friends?

"Of course, sweetie. I knew we were camping." A lie to save face wasn't wrong, right?

"Yeah, sure, Dad."

She didn't believe him? What happened to the adulation that used to be in her eyes? The "Dad is perfect" look.

He tried again. "Camping, like KOA. You know, kiddo? Shower buildings, restrooms, flush toilets. Right now, I'd settle for a port-a-potty."

Ellen groaned again. "Da-ad."

If he didn't know how dramatic she could be, he'd

wonder if she had a stomach ache.

As he'd done several times in the past three hours, he took out his handkerchief, examined it in disgust, and tried to find a clean spot. He wiped the sweat off his forehead. Hot and sticky, the weather seemed more like August in Michigan than June. Drew intensely disliked sweating. Clean sweat—in a gym—was perfectly acceptable. Not this . . . dirt. More than sweaty, he despised being dirty.

Considering the rain in early spring, the dry path surprised him. Who knew twenty feet could kick up so much dust along a forest path. But, sweat and dirt were not his primary concern. He needed a john. Bad.

"C'mon, Ellen. Isn't there a restroom nearby?" he asked quietly. "Even an outhouse?"

"Dad, this is Prim." Ellen had mastered the art of eye rolling. As he'd learned in the past few months, that innate skill emerged in girls during adolescence.

"Prim? What is that?" Drew gave her the self-mocking grin that always made her laugh. "A new rock group?"

Ellen wasn't smiling. She lowered her voice. "It means Primitive Camping. We go in the bushes."

"What!" He glanced around to find the other girls staring at him. He hadn't meant to be so loud.

"You are embarrassing me." She stomped away, kicking up more dust. Before she got to her friends clustered nearby, she shot over her shoulder, "I wish you'd never come. I knew it was a dumb idea to ask you."

"Hey, come back here, honey. I'm sure this is a little misunderstanding. C'mon, Ellen." In the year since his wife died, he and Ellen had had a lot of *misunderstandings*.

"I think she's mad at you."

Drew turned toward the quiet voice behind him. There she was, leaning back against a tree, her knee bent and her booted foot propped against the trunk. Maggie Sinclair, Director of Camp Hell. He knew Jack's sister was an outdoor nut, but he didn't think she was this bad. Pissing in the bushes, for God's sake.

Maggie was a tall woman, only a few inches shorter than his own six feet. She had the tan of a person who spent time outdoors, not a sunbather, though, with laugh crinkles around her eyes. Blue, if he remembered. With sunglasses covering her eyes, he couldn't tell. Blue, he was sure. And still the rough-neck tomboy he'd grown up with. Who else would want to spend a beautiful summer day backpacking on dusty trails through snagging underbrush instead of out on a perfectly-manicured golf course, where you only ventured into the rough to retrieve an errant ball?

Despite the heat and humidity, Maggie's white T-shirt, with its pink 'Race for the Cure' logo, was still white and her jeans, though faded, remained clean. With her dark brown ponytail pulled through the back of a Detroit Tigers baseball cap, she appeared as cool as when they started on this trek three hours ago. That almost irritated him more than her awareness of friction between him and his daughter.

"Ellen? Mad at me?" He affected mock surprise. "Your powers of observation are amazing. Are you ever wrong?"

She cupped her elbow in her hand and tapped a finger against her jaw. "Let me see now. I was wrong once—fourteen years ago, when I married Roger Dodger."

Roger Dodger. An appropriate name for the jerk. The guy got away with paying her nothing, even though she'd supported him while he got his MBA. Drew blamed Maggie's inept divorce lawyer. It still pissed him off that she hadn't come to him. Never mind he specialized in criminal law. He would've made an exception for her. She was his best friend's sister, for God's sake. Friends helped each other.

"Let me think. Have I been wrong since?" She continued the damn tapping then snapped her fingers. "I've got it. I was wrong to let Ellen's city-soft lawyer daddy help chaperone this trip."

Drew gave her the smile that prosecutors knew better than to believe. "And here I thought it was because nobody else would."

She had the good grace to blush. Damn right nobody would help her chaperone. Those parents knew exactly what kind of an outing this was. The mothers probably gave thanks that he'd *volunteered*, while the dads thought "what a sucker."

"Tell me there's an outhouse around here," he growled.

Maggie straightened away from the tree and brushed the

11

seat of her well-worn jeans. Not a bad looking butt, he thought. If he was looking . . . which he wasn't. He never looked at another woman while Lillian was alive. He still hadn't in the year she'd been gone. And he wasn't starting with his best friend's prickly sister's fine derriere.

"In Primitive Camping, we use nature's facilities," Maggie explained. "We also leave no trace. I'm sure there are plastic bags in your pack for your . . . waste."

Appalled at what she meant, he stared. "You have got to be joking."

Maggie shook her head then nodded to the cluster of girls who were avidly following the exchange between the two adults. "I'm surprised Ellen didn't tell you."

"I did tell him," Ellen yelled back. "He didn't listen. He never listens to me."

She frequently accused him of that. But, damn it, he had so much on his mind these days, trying to finish the last of his cases before—

"Even if she hadn't told you," Maggie continued in the voice she probably used on her high school students. "You would have known had you bothered to attend our planning meeting on Thursday."

There she went again, bringing up that damn meeting. This had to be the thirty-seventh time—no exaggeration—she'd mentioned it. A phone call had delayed him at the office that night. At home, Ellen's terse greeting was even colder than the plate of spaghetti, colder meatballs, and a limp salad on the counter. He certainly didn't need Maggie Sinclair's harping on the importance of that meeting to add to his guilt for disappointing his daughter.

Maggie clapped her hands. "Girls, break time is over."

The Drill Sergeant was back. *Hup, two, three, four.*

Groans from the girls met her announcement. Drew knew exactly how they felt.

His legs ached, a blister—no, make that two blisters—had already formed on both sides of his heels. Ellen had warned him not to wear brand-new hiking boots. But he always wore the appropriate footwear. He had golf shoes, tennis shoes, ski boots, and now hiking boots. A pair of bloody hiking boots.

Damn, he needed to take a leak. He never should have stopped at 7-11 for a Big Gulp of coffee no matter how much caffeine he required to start his engine this morning. Ellen warned him not to. He should have listened.

Jack would be laughing his head off if he knew Drew was actually hiking and camping. Both Jack and Maggie had inherited their parents' enthusiasm for camping. Drew shuddered. Not him. That disastrous Cub Scout campout made Drew vow never again to venture into the wild.

Still, when Ellen begged him, he thought a little hike in the woods would be the perfect opportunity for some father-daughter bonding. This trip was not turning out the way he anticipated.

Ellen surrounded herself with her friends, staying as far away from Drew as possible. With the exception of their brief conversation a few minutes ago—and only after he'd pulled her aside to ask about the *facilities*—she barely talked to him. So much for father-daughter bonding. All he had to show for his efforts were a stitch in his side, a charley horse in his left leg, those bloody blisters, and chafing from his new jeans. Lillian had thought jeans were low-class. Since they weren't allowed on the country club golf course, they hadn't been part of his extensive wardrobe until his quick trip to Meijer's at six this morning. The megastore had everything he needed.

When Drew returned from his *visit* behind a large tree, a couple of girls came out of the woods on the other side of the path. They joined the group, while Drew waited in the background. Maggie caught his eye, and he knew she was about to castigate him again for missing the meeting. She'd bided her time. Here it came.

"Mr. Campbell, you may lead for a while," Maggie directed. "I'll bring up the rear and make sure—" She dropped her sunglasses down her nose and stared over the steel rims at the girls. "—we don't lose anyone."

The girls giggled and lined up. Drew straightened his shoulders despite the backpack cutting into them. He was certain Ellen had loaded the pack with rocks. Leading wasn't that bad.

All right. He could do this. He was a man, not a wus. He

13

could tough it out. He would not embarrass his daughter. He'd make her proud of him. Just put one foot in front of the other . . . and try not to wince.

"Mr. Campbell, it's okay to go faster," one of the girls said. "We can keep up."

Maggie Sinclair wondered for the tenth time that morning why she hadn't had her head examined before agreeing to Ellen's offer. The week before, Maggie called off the trip when not one parent volunteered to chaperone. She hated disappointing the girls who had been crushed when their leader moved away. For the past two months, they talked about camping again. But week after week they returned with the same news. Their mothers refused, and their dads were too busy.

So when Ellen said her dad would help, the girls went wild. And Maggie, who should've known better, believed Ellen who swore she'd asked and her father agreed. Maggie should have followed up with a phone call, but years of avoiding Drew Campbell prevailed. Years of unreciprocated longing—from when her heart first took notice, through the years when he was single, then while he was married. Except for that one time, she never let him know. Avoidance was best. So, she never checked.

Now here she was needing his help with the girls. Preparing them for a week-long camping trip to Isle Royale had been Trish Morrow's goal when she started the group four years ago. The girls loved roughing it. They just needed more hiking and camping experience before tackling the primitive island in Lake Superior.

Though they'd gotten a late start this morning because of the fog, Maggie noticed the girls' energy start to flag after the fifth mile of the hike. That was when she put Drew Campbell at the front of the line. From the rear, she watched him trying to set a faster pace—especially after Gretchen's assurance that they could keep up. The man was in a world of hurt even if he made a concerted effort not to show it. Because he was so trim and athletic, Maggie assumed he was in good shape.

Typical desk jockey. He probably got his exercise in a climate-controlled gym. No, wait. In a health club.

For better or worse—and she was afraid *worse* was the operative word—she was stuck with him for the next thirty hours.

Are we having fun yet? she mocked herself as she tromped through the woods with eight tough little girls on the brink of womanhood and her brother's best friend. From the back of the line, Maggie watched his long-legged stride and the way his navy golf shirt revealed his strong shoulders *and* the way his obviously new jeans conformed to his butt. She lifted the tail of the bandanna knotted around her neck and wiped the sweat from her upper lip. She couldn't blame the sun for the heat coursing through her.

Okay, Sinclair, she told herself, keep your mind on the matter at hand. And not how good Campbell's butt looked in tight new jeans.

Good Lord, she felt fifteen again—instead of thirty-four. Her stomach in knots, her skin on fire. Lusting after the man who said she kissed like a guppy.

Maggie made sure the girls had lunch preparations under control before sitting on a large stone. She arched her back and hoped for a whisper of a breeze. The dense trees sheltered them from the sun but also prevented the air from moving.

"Do you sweat?" Drew Campbell slowly lowered himself to a nearby rock, exhaustion evident.

She thought about, but didn't warn him, he was going to hurt even more when they started up again after the lunch break.

"I'd better sweat," she drawled. "Natural air conditioning. You have to worry when you don't sweat."

He harrumphed then gingerly stretched out first one leg and then the other. A groan accompanied each movement. Oh, yeah. He was going to hurt worse by the end of the day.

Ellen brought over lunch for Maggie and Drew.

"Thanks, kiddo. You didn't have to do that," he said. "I—

We could've gotten our own lunch."

"That's right," Maggie added. "Thanks for being so thoughtful."

Ellen stared down at them. "Are you two still mad at each other?"

"Hey," Drew responded first. "We're not mad." Maggie nodded in agreement.

Ellen gave them a look of disbelief. Drew had yet to realize that kids her age were hard to fool.

"Your father and I had a disagreement about procedure," Maggie said. "I think we've come to an understanding."

"A power struggle? Goody." Ellen grinned. "Oh, Dad, don't give me that look. I know what power struggles are. You both want to be the boss. My money's on Maggie." She walked away with a jaunty skip to her step.

Maggie couldn't help grinning herself. "Guess she told you, hey, Counselor?" She decided she'd tweaked the tiger's whiskers enough. Poor guy, surrounded by women, he didn't stand a chance. She leaned toward him. "Just in case, this might be a good time to take care of your personal needs. The girls are busy eating, and I'll make sure they don't disturb you."

He shot her a look she remembered from when they were kids. It said "don't push your luck." She merely hopped off the stone and walked over to the girls. Then, as an afterthought, she came back. "Beware of poison ivy. *Leaves three, let it be.*"

They reached the campsite around seven. Much later than Maggie had planned. She'd slowed the pace because of the heat, making sure the girls—and Campbell—drank plenty of water. The girls were all seasoned hikers and could have managed. She hated to admit it, but she slowed the pace for Campbell, too. He was having a rough time. He needed a lot more exercise if he planned to continue chaperoning.

She mentally groaned. Needing Drew's help put her in an awkward position. While avoidance had worked in the past, she couldn't because, if he didn't help, the trip to Isle Royale was off. God, she would hate to disappoint the girls.

Every muscle in Drew's body hurt. He had muscles he didn't know existed, and they all protested the abuse.

He was amazed how effortlessly the girls settled into a routine once they stopped at the campsite. Some quickly put up tents, others started dinner. Maggie showed him where to set up his tent. Ellen started to help him, but he shooed her away. What was so hard about erecting a tent? Fifteen minutes later, he found out. You needed an engineering degree to put up the damn thing.

"Need help, Campbell?"

As if he'd accept help from Maggie Sinclair. If kids could do it, so could he. "No thanks. Don't the girls need your help?"

"They know what to do."

He gave her a haughty look. "And I don't?"

Before she turned away, he noted her blue eyes clouded. Oh yes, definitely blue. Wait. Had he hurt her feelings? Nah. Rubbing in what a greenhorn he was seemed to please her. He'd never known her to be sadistic, but then they'd hardly spoken to each other in over sixteen years.

She walked to the edge of the campsite and stared off into the distance. Drew couldn't see what held her interest. Throughout the hike, she pointed out trees and evidence of wildlife—if not the wildlife itself. If she located a bird, she'd motion the girls to come and see. They listened intently to its call. Some of the girls even imitated it. Their delight in the bird's response made him smile.

The third time the tent collapsed, Drew searched for the instruction manual. Standing with the tent draped over his head, he checked the bag from which he'd taken the tent, poles, and stakes. Nothing.

"Mr. Campbell?"

He recognized Beth Oostveen's voice. She and Ellen had been best friends since first grade, and she was often at their house. Just as Ellen spent many nights sleeping over at Beth's.

"Do you need help, Mr. Campbell?" Beth continued.

He didn't think he'd ever heard sweeter words. Yet, how would that look? Ellen would be humiliated that her father couldn't even figure out how to put up a tent. No, he wasn't going to wimp out, even if the girls' tents had gone up in less than five minutes. Of course, since it appeared to be so easy for them, he hadn't paid that much attention. If fourteen-year-olds could manage to raise a tent, a man on the downhill side of thirty—with a law degree—should be able to do it.

"Thanks, Beth," he called out through the cloud of blue nylon. "I've got it."

He heard some whispering and then footsteps that led to the firepit. No fire for safety reasons, just a ring of rocks on which they sat to eat the dinner the girls prepared on a two-burner campstove. He was impressed with their skill and after the thousand-mile hike today—every bone, every muscle aching—he'd been starving. Spaghetti never tasted so good. Little did he know, in his backpack, he'd carried the stove as well as the pasta which had been cooked and frozen at Thursday's meeting, the one he didn't attend. The rest of the dinner was great although he wasn't so sure when they called one item ants-on-a-log. Peanut butter on celery was okay, but he could've done without the raisins.

He sat on the tent floor, still shrouded by the nylon tent, and emptied his backpack. No manual. No rocks, either, though from the ridges in his shoulders, he could've sworn there were. He would just have to figure it out for himself. Maybe, he should've used the stakes first. He scooted to the opening of the tent and reached out for his boots. He did remember that little nugget from his one and only campout. No shoes in the tents.

Drew backed out on his knees.

Beth and Gretchen ran up. "Mr. Campbell, Ms. Sinclair wants you. She's down at the lake."

Drew quickly stood and searched for Ellen. Had she fallen in? No, he heard her voice coming from one of the tents about fifty feet away from his. He couldn't see Maggie.

"Did she say what she wanted?" He shoved his feet into his boots.

"No, sir." Gretchen pushed her glasses higher on her nose. "I think she might want to talk about tomorrow's schedule. She's around the bend, beyond those trees."

He followed her directions, every muscle in his legs screaming. Now he knew how his folks must feel every morning as they shuffled to the bathroom.

Maggie stood along the shore of a lake that was longer than wide and about sixty or seventy feet west of the campsite. Knowing east from west was a no-brainer since the sun was a huge red ball low on the horizon. Still, he was pleased with himself that he knew direction without a compass. Nearby grasses had been trampled. Maggie squatted, intently examining the odd markings in the sand near the water's edge.

"What are you looking at?" he asked.

She stood. "Evidence that this is a water hole. Our campsite is far enough away that we shouldn't bother the animals who will come out for a drink this evening."

She was concerned about them disturbing the animals? Drew worried more about the animals disturbing him . . . and the girls, of course.

"It will be dark soon." She pointed to the setting sun.

"You've been standing here for some time. Is something wrong?" he asked quietly.

She shook her head but didn't glance at him. "I was thinking how proud Trish would be of the girls." She jerked her head toward the campsite where the girls were working and laughing. "They complain about how tired they are, and yet they buckle down right away."

"You two taught them well."

"A compliment? Be still my heart."

He ignored her sarcasm. "I owe you thanks for what you've been doing for Ellen."

"You don't—"

"Would you just be quiet and let me finish? I didn't realize she was still having problems. At the beginning, we talked a lot. And then she seemed to accept that Lillian . . . that Lillian was gone. She didn't say anything, so I figured she was over it."

"A girl doesn't get over her mother's death," Maggie snapped.

Chagrin shot through him. He hadn't thought about Maggie losing her own mother to influenza followed by

19

pneumonia. That wasn't like him to be so callous, even if it was unintentional.

He shoved his hands into his back pockets. "That came out wrong. I didn't realize she still needed help."

"Why would you? You've been wrapped up in your work. How many hours a week do you work, Campbell?" She nailed him with her glacial stare.

Enough of that. He didn't need another lecture. "What did you want to see me about?"

She shook her head. "What?"

"The girls said you wanted to see me."

"No," she drawled. "Hmm. I wonder what those kids are up to." She headed back to the campsite at a quick walk.

He spotted their handiwork immediately. And was mortified.

"Girls?" she called.

A head popped out of the doorway to their two tents. Giggles sounded from inside.

"Yes, Ms. Sinclair?" the two called. They giggled and ducked back inside.

Drew leaned close. "Don't get on their case. They performed an act of charity."

"What do you mean?" She moved away and stared up at him.

He rubbed his hand across the back of his neck. He did not want to tell her that he couldn't even erect a tent, and those girls took pity on him and did it for him. But the way she was suspiciously eying the two tents where the girls still giggled, he knew he'd have to confess before the girls got into trouble.

"They put up my tent," he mumbled.

"Sorry?"

Drew cleared his throat. "The girls erected my tent."

"I'm surprised at you, Campbell." Disgust colored her voice. "Expecting those girls to do your work for you. Haven't you seen anything on this trip? I'm trying to help these girls be independent and you—"

Drew walked away. It was embarrassing enough that the girls took pity on him and sent him on a fool's errand to get him out of the way, so they could do their good deed. Having

Maggie think so little of him brought a surge of anger on top of humiliation.

She'd misjudged him in the past. In eighteen years, nothing had changed.

CHAPTER THREE

Drew walked away from the pit toilet—the new-fashioned term, he'd discovered for an old-fashioned outhouse. By the strong beam of the flashlight—thank you, Ellen—he made his way back to his tent. Twigs snapped under his feet. He tripped on a tree root and stumbled around in the brush, sounding, he was sure, like an elephant on a rampage.

As he returned to the campsite, something didn't look right. What was moving near his tent? He swept the flashlight back and forth. Nothing. Cautiously, he walked around the tent, still sweeping the light in a wide arc.

Two beady eyes caught the light.

"Ye-ow!" Drew stumbled backward, yelling, "Get out of there. Get. Get." He waved the light at the small, furry creature. It took a second before he realized what it was. A raccoon had been trying to get into his tent. The animal had already taken a swipe at it. Three long tears split the nylon tent.

Drew waved his arms, the light dancing wildly, and he yelled again. Finally, the raccoon took off. But not before the entire camp came running. Eight girls and their leader ran out of their tents in their nightclothes, feet jammed into boots, laces dragging in the dirt. Nine flashlights lit up the area, searching for the danger. Intent on rescuing him.

"Stay back, girls," Maggie ordered. "What's wrong? What happened?"

She stood poised to do battle. Armed with a lethal Mag-Lite. Boudica in dark nylon running shorts and a white tank top, sans bra, which he shouldn't have noticed. A mighty warrior out to slay the dragon and rescue the hapless victim.

Christ, he felt ridiculous.

"It's okay." He walked toward the group.

The girls, wide-eyed, stood behind Maggie.

"Sorry I woke you up. I think a raccoon wanted to share my tent." He tried for a crooked grin. "Guess he was cold."

"Stay here, girls," Maggie ordered over her shoulder. She approached the tent more cautiously than he had. Like Drew, she swept the area with the big flashlight.

She found the rips and gasped. "You are so lucky, Campbell. Can you image what those claws could have done to you?" Her voice rose. She marched around to the entrance. "What do you have inside?"

"What? Inside? The usual. Sleeping bag. Backpack."

She ducked in, not bothering to remove her boots, and hauled out his sleeping bag and backpack. She shook out the sleeping bag then eyed him like a criminal.

"What's in your pack? Raccoons are attracted by the scent of food." She tossed the sleeping bag at him, along with her flashlight. "Hold this so I can see."

She opened the top flaps and rifled the contents. He supposed he should be grateful she didn't toss each item on the ground. Pawing through his clean underwear was bad enough. Apparently satisfied with the main pouch, she checked the smaller ones. On the third, she extracted the power bar he'd brought to give him a needed boost in the morning.

"What is this?" She dropped the pack and held up the bar as if she'd found a drug stash. She grabbed the flashlight from him and shone the light squarely at his face, blinding him, just like a prisoner in an interrogation room.

He heard a soft "Oh, Daddy."

"Take it easy," he said to Maggie.

"Easy? Easy? Didn't you see the girls hang the food bag on the line? Didn't you hear Gretchen say it was to prevent animals from getting into our food? Didn't you think this was food?" She waved the power bar in front of his face.

That close he could smell the chocolate.

"Raccoons have a keener olfactory sense than humans. They can smell food almost as good as a bear. They don't let tents or citified lawyers stand in their way. Your arms, chest—" She glanced at his T-shirt covered chest then quickly looked away. "—the rest of you would have been ripped by the raccoon's razor-sharp claws, just like the tent. And they can be rabid. My God, Campbell. Where's your sense?"

Drew had had enough of her rant. Nobody liked being on the receiving end of a reprimand, especially not in front of his child and her friends. He was an excellent lawyer who commanded hefty fees for his services. In the ten years he'd been with the firm, he pulled in more business than any other partner. He had a two handicap in golf and could still swim the four hundred meter free in under six minutes.

Yet, she made him feel like a total incompetent.

He put his hand on her Mag-Lite and lowered it. "Stop." He used the quietest, fiercest voice he could muster when he really wanted to rip her head off for humiliating him in front of his daughter.

Maggie snapped her mouth shut. She'd been startled waking up to his yell. She feared for the girls' safety. Stories of campers being attacked by crazies had raced through her mind while she shoved her bare feet into her boots and raced toward the sound. When she discovered the raccoon damage, she'd lost it.

She thought she'd learned years ago to control her temper, to make her point then drop it. Instead, she ranted until she pushed too far, and the man became furious. Oh, yes, he was furious at her. She'd belittled him in front of the girls, especially in front of his daughter and destroyed whatever standing he had as an adult authority on this trip.

She'd made him look like a fool.

Yet, as hard as she pushed, he hadn't taken a swing at her, until he grabbed the flashlight. Fear had jolted through her. Fear of retaliation, a fear she still couldn't stifle despite years of distance and therapy. She'd breathed a small sigh of relief when she realized he only wanted to lower her light.

Salvaging this debacle was going to take more finesse than she thought she was capable of. "I guess that's enough excitement for one night," she said to the girls. "Let's take down this tent. That'll fool Mr. Raccoon." She forced a laugh. "Girls, while I get my sleeping bag, make room for your new tentmate. Mr. Campbell will sleep in mine."

As she strode toward her tent, she heard Gretchen say

quietly, "She's not really mad at you, Mr. Campbell. She only yells like that when she's scared for us. One time, I went for a walk by myself and got lost. She yelled at me until I wanted to cry. And then she hugged me."

"Yeah," Madison chimed in. "Remember the time I made a fire, and it got way too big. Boy, did she ever yell about that. And then she was sorry and hugged me."

"She'll probably hug you, too," added Beth. "When she stops being scared."

Drew rolled out of his sleeping bag the instant he caught the scent. Nectar of the gods. He crawled out of the tent and would've belly-crawled all the way to the firepit where Maggie sat on a log, holding a cup of heavenly brew. Surprised at the cool morning air, he threw on his shirt.

He could barely walk. Crawling would be better. If he never hiked again, he would be a happy man. Then, he remembered they had to hike back to the lot where they left the vehicles. *Just shoot me.* He was prepared to wait for the ambulance, but the scent wafting toward him beckoned.

"Is that coffee?" he asked softly as soon as he came near. "Please tell me there's more, or I'll have to wrestle you for the rest of that cup."

She didn't look at him, just pointed to the campstove. Wisps of steam rose from a small pan of water. Next to the stove, on the make-shift table, sat a small jar of instant coffee and a larger can of hot chocolate mix. No cups.

He retrieved his mess kit from the backpack he'd hung on the foodline last night. Because he wasn't about to ask how to turn on the stove, he just used the less than steaming water then joined Maggie on the log.

"Since I didn't get a hug, I assume you're still mad at me," he said. At her arched eyebrow, he explained what Gretchen had told him. Silently, she drank her coffee.

His first swallow made him shudder. "This is almost as bad as the stuff I made with tap water in the dorm, so I could stay awake for an eight o'clock class."

"Well, golly gee." She actually spoke. "We don't have espresso machines on a *primitive* camping trip."

"I don't—" Why did he bother to explain he preferred 7-11 to Starbucks? And homemade to both. "I see you still wake up grumpy. Just like when you were a kid. Forgive me if I need my morning wake-up juice."

"You? Mr. Work-from-Dawn-to-Midnight? You need coffee to stay wake? My, how things change."

Ignoring her, he took another swig, waiting for the caffeine to kick in.

He watched the beginning of sunrise to the east. Good, he was getting the hang of this outdoor stuff. East, west. He could even figure out north and south. As long as the sun stayed where it was. A pink-gold glow colored the sky.

"I can't remember seeing dawn unless it was driving to the office in the winter," he said. "It's really peaceful here, isn't it?"

"It was." She gave him a droll look. "This is my favorite time. The girls still asleep. Just me and nature."

"Which I interrupted." He started to get up.

"You don't need to go." She grabbed his arm, jostling his cup. Coffee sloshed on his jeans. "I am so sorry." She tried wiping off his pantleg.

The feeling of her hand on his thigh caused his jeans to tighten. He swallowed and shifted away. "Good thing it wasn't hot."

A light blush colored her cheeks as she jerked away her hand. "So, Campbell, how did you sleep last night?"

Sleep? What was that? The girls giggled and whispered most of the night. Again, he marveled at their energy and endurance. He'd thought they would crash as soon as they hit the tents. Wrong. But, he could have slept through the whispers—even the giggling—when his tent was a good distance away from theirs. After the debacle with the raccoon, he lay awake hyped on adrenaline and curiosity. Why did she shrink away from him when he reached for her flashlight? Had he frightened her? Why—

"Tell me, Sinclair." He used her last name with the same tone she used his—with just a hint of mocking. "Did you put those rocks under my sleeping bag? Before we switched tents?"

Her narrow stare should have alerted him. "You had

rocks?" She waited a moment. "If you had attended the informational meeting—"

God, he was tired of her throwing that missed meeting in his face.

"—you would have learned how to check the area before pitching a tent. Of course, the girls know all that because they've been camping since fourth grade. And . . . since they erected your tent, they would have made sure there were no rocks."

"Damn it." He kept his voice low, even though he wanted to yell at her. "That's called hyperbole."

Before she turned away, he caught the faint pink in her cheeks. About time he embarrassed her instead of the other way around.

The morning, though cooler than the night before, promised another hot, sticky day. He'd slept in the clothes he'd worn yesterday. No way was he undressing down to his skivvies with eight girls fifty feet away. His clothes stunk of sweat and were still damp.

The trees provided some shade, but he knew once they were hiking again, the sun would shine through the trees and fry his brain. He rolled his shoulders, trying to ease the aches. His legs felt like they were filled with lead. He scrubbed his hand across his beard and gave thought to wrestling Maggie Sinclair for the rest of the coffee she was drinking rather than get up and make more for himself.

She gave him a long look then handed him her cup. "Here, you look like you need this more than I do. Sorry, gourmet coffee isn't on the menu."

"I don't—aw, shit. Never mind." He grabbed her cup and finished it. He wasn't proud.

The girls stumbled out of their tents, some with more enthusiasm than others. With no directions from Maggie, they gathered their breakfast, trail mix and oranges. One of the girls brought him a little plastic bag with trail mix and an orange.

He thanked her—Madison?—then waited until she joined the others. "Do they always serve the leaders?"

Maggie smiled, a hint of sadness in her eyes. "They loved Trish so much that was their way of saying thank you. Since she let them, I did, too. I guess they want to thank you."

"You miss her." He let the words hang.

"She's my best friend. What do you think?"

Surprised at her snippy tone, he asked softly, "Do you think we could be civil to each other for the rest of the trip? I don't remember you being this bitter when you hounded Jack and me to let you tag along."

Again, her cheeks turned rosy. "Yeah, well, what did I know? I was a kid, and you guys were a whole three years older. I thought you two were cool."

"And you don't now?"

"I used to think my brother's best friend was a stand-up guy—until he didn't have time for his daughter." She shifted away then, before he could protest, she took a deep breath. "I'm sorry I yelled at you last night."

"Do I get that hug now?"

"You wish."

They sat in silence until the girls finished their breakfast. Two began packing the food while the others headed for their tents. Maggie set her cup on the log next to her. She wore the jeans and T-shirt from yesterday. He preferred seeing her in the running shorts and tank without her bra from last night. But, lust was not on the menu this morning. Then he remembered her flinching from him.

"You thought I was going to hit you."

She jerked.

"Last night, I saw fear in your eyes. You thought I was going to hit you."

"No, I—"

"I don't hit women. Don't hit guys, either."

Scrambling off the log, she clenched her teeth. A muscle ticked along her jaw. "An equal-opportunity non-hitter, hey, Campbell?" She took two steps and turned back to him. "By the way, the girls told me how they suckered you into leaving so they could put up your tent. I'm sorry for thinking you asked them to do it for you."

An apology? He kept his mouth shut. He was more concerned about that look of fear. In fact, he'd stayed awake long after the raccoon incident wondering why she would think he was about to hit her.

28

"Okay, girls." She clapped her hands. "Let's break camp."

While she strode toward the tents, Drew poured the rest of his coffee in the empty firepit. His stomach churned too much for any more acid. "Not the first time you've misjudged me," he muttered. "Probably won't be the last."

Maggie wanted to slap herself for her snarky remarks to Drew. She had misjudged him and regretted that she'd mentioned his daughter. As she'd done during the night, she wondered why he provoked her. She'd joked with Jack about being the Wicked Witch of the West to her students. Not that she was. So why had she turned into W^3 during the weekend? With Drew.

He wouldn't think she still held a grudge because of his mocking her when she asked him to teach her how to kiss. He probably didn't even remember. She wasn't that petty to hold teenage behavior against him. But she did admit that she'd wanted him to ask her out back then. Her teen imagination had them dating and even marrying. Instead, he'd married perfect Lillian, and she eloped with Roger Dodger, king of lies, affairs, and abuse.

God, she needed to forget the past.

On the way back to the parking area, she let Drew lead while she brought up the rear. The girls were flagging so his pace was about right for them. Even though they'd hiked through the neighborhood regularly, the girls needed to build up their stamina. The day hikes—for which she'd gotten a couple of moms to walk with them—hadn't been enough. They'd have to work harder, hike more. Since those same mothers as well as their spouses weren't always available to help, she'd have to make sure Campbell joined them.

Although she would never admit it out loud, his speed worked for her, too.

In her driveway, Maggie stood back and watched the girls haul their gear out of Drew's Navigator and her Suburban late Sunday afternoon. He'd started to help them until Gretchen set him straight. They didn't need help. They were tough. So, he stood off to the side, allowing them to fend for themselves. Not an easy thing to do, she knew.

She'd jumped to too many conclusions the night before and didn't much like herself for it. Despite her apology over the tent episode, she sensed more tension between them. She didn't want to leave things that way.

"Well, Campbell," She punched his upper arm. "For a desk jockey, you didn't do too bad.

"What?" The man had shadows on the bags under his eyes and still moved slowly. As the girls raced in and out of Maggie's garage then down to their parents' vehicles, he said, "Where do they get all that energy? I want to lie on your cement driveway and go to sleep, and they're still running around." He made a self-mocking sound, somewhere between a laugh and a snort.

Drew Campbell didn't have a monopoly on aching muscles. It wasn't just the girls who needed to toughen up. But she kept that little tidbit to herself. All she wanted was a long hot shower, a quick shampoo, and something to eat that didn't have dirt adhering to it. Despite loving the outdoors, she never liked gritty teeth.

The girls lugged their sleeping bags and backpacks to the curb in front of Maggie's house where minivans and SUVs waited.

"Hey, look on the bright side. You survived a weekend of primitive camping." She smirked.

He leaned toward her and said quietly, "I finally understand Ralph Cramden's 'to the moon, Alice.' Because, *Alice*, if I weren't so tired that I can't lift my arm, you'd get to see Neil Armstrong's footprints up close and personal."

"Ralph Cramden? Alice?"

"*The Honeymooners*. Old TV show. My dad loves to watch shows from the fifties. Ralph always said 'To the moon—'"

"I get it." Maggie patted his bristly cheek. "Poor baby. Admit it. You had fun."

"Yeah, sure. Fun." He plastered on a smile. "Never had such a terrific time."

"Hey, that's great." She slapped him on the back.

"Jesus, Sinclair, flatten me, why don't you?"

"Wus." Good grief, they'd reverted to their childhood bickering. Back then, all she wanted to do was cool stuff with the guys, and they proclaimed girls had cooties.

Ellen and the rest of the girls raced back. They insisted that Drew clasp hands with them in a friendship circle, the traditional ending to their meetings and trips. Contrary to her behavior over the weekend, Ellen actually held her father's hand. Maybe there was hope for the two of them, yet.

Afterward, Maggie said, "Don't forget to air out those sleeping bags. You did well for your first time out in almost a year." She smiled her approval. "Are we ready to do this again next weekend?"

The girls cheered.

"*If* Mr. Campbell is agreeable." She raised her eyebrow. She'd be in a fine fix if he refused. So, she played nice and smiled.

"Tell me you're joking," he said out of the corner of his mouth.

The girls eagerly looked at him. "Please, Mr. Campbell. You have to come."

He didn't answer right away, and she feared his refusal. Not for herself, for the girls.

Then, he smiled brightly. "Right. Next weekend."

Again, the girls cheered. Maggie gave him credit for not disappointing them. "Our next planning meeting is at Ellen's house on Thursday. Seven o'clock." When she noticed his gaping mouth, Maggie added, "She said she cleared it with you."

"I did. He never listens," Ellen said, a sullen twist to her mouth.

"Of course, I heard you." He recovered quickly. "Milk and cookies, right?"

"It's my turn to bring snacks, Mr. Campbell," Beth Oostveen said. "You don't need to bother. We are very self-sufficient."

That they were. Maggie experienced a sense of pride. The girls could take care of themselves in the outdoors. And they did it by cooperating instead of voting each other 'off the island.'

"Bye, Ms. Sinclair. Bye, Mr. Campbell. Thanks for the

great trip." The girls ran down the drive to their waiting parents. Only Ellen and her father remained.

He turned to Maggie. "Are they related to the Energizer Bunny?"

"You need to get in shape. Start walking every day." Advice she'd better take. She thought coaching the girls' baseball team all spring and now umping Little League games that had her racing from one base to another was enough. But with the end of the school year and all that entailed, she'd stopped running every night. Now, she was paying the price with aching muscles.

"Right," he drawled. "I'll do just that. As soon as I get feeling back in my legs."

She glanced at the legs in question. He'd never pass for a *GQ* model today. His new jeans were rather worse for the wear—snagged from underbrush and dust-covered from the trail and the coffee stain near his knee from the jostled cup. As she remembered trying to brush off the coffee, feeling his strong thigh beneath those jeans, heat shot through her veins.

"Ellen?" Beth called from the curb. "What's taking so long? Did you ask?"

"I'm try-ing." Ellen rolled her eyes. "They're still talking, and I can't get a word in edgewise."

Relieved by the interruption, Maggie realized she'd been so absorbed in her memory of his reaction she failed to notice Ellen's impatient shifting from foot to foot. Drew reacted first, by raising a questioning eyebrow.

Ellen shot him a *finally* look. "Can I go to Beth's for dinner and sleep over? Beth's mom said it was okay with her if it's okay with you."

"Not on a school night," he said so quickly it sounded automatic.

"Da-ad." Ellen brushed aside her father's dark, straggly hair and knocked on his forehead. "School got out on Thursday."

Maggie shook her head. Didn't the man even know when school ended for his daughter? What provisions had he made? How was he going to make sure Ellen stayed safe if he didn't even know she would be alone all day?

32

Then his shoulders slump, and she thought twice about berating him for his lack of awareness of Ellen's schedule.

"As long as it's okay with Beth's mother." From his weary tone, Maggie surmised he was doing his own berating and didn't need help from her.

"Thanks, Dad." Ellen stood on tiptoe to give him a quick kiss on the cheek. "Ooh, scratchy." She grabbed her backpack, ran down to the curb, and jumped into the minivan with her friend.

For a moment, he stared at the vehicle pulling away. He gave Maggie a half smile. "Alone, at last."

Disconcerted by his quip, she punched his upper arm. "Surely, a silver-tongue lawyer can come up with a better line than that."

"Good God, Sinclair." He nursed his arm. "Would you quit beating up on me?"

"Wus."

Perhaps she was taking the just-one-of-the-guys routine too far, the way she'd done when they were kids. He shoved his hands in the pockets of his jeans but made no effort to drag out his keys. Why he wasn't leaving? Silence stretched between them.

She broke it. "I appreciated your help this weekend. I won't hold you up. You probably want to get home and get some dinner."

"I think my dinner date just left." He nodded at the minivan disappearing around the corner.

Another long silence ensued.

"That hang-dog expression does not become you." She had to wonder—when he avoided her eyes—if he was lonely. Was that why he wasn't leaving? Because he didn't want to go back to an empty house?

Oh, crapola. She knew she was going to regret what she was about to say before the words even left her mouth. "I guess the least I can do for helping me this weekend is offer you a peanut butter sandwich."

He levered away from his vehicle, his hang-dog expression gone, replaced by enthusiasm. "The *least* you can do is grill steaks."

Had he just conned her?

"And give me a back rub, considering you lined my sleeping bag with rocks." He arched his back and rolled his shoulders.

"Dream on, big boy." She would be a Good Samaritan and feed the man. Then he would go home. Half hour tops. After thirty hours with him, what was another thirty minutes?

He followed her through the garage dodging, as she did, the lawn mower and her bike. Now that school was out she should attack this mess. At least, the girls had stacked the camping equipment properly—the same way they used to stack the equipment at Trish's. God, she missed her friend. Camping this weekend brought her sadness to the fore.

She channeled Scarlett O'Hara and promised to think about her loss tomorrow. Now, she had to deal with her brother's best friend.

"You can earn your dinner by helping me spread out the tents."

She piled the three tents into his arms then grabbed her sleeping bag and Jack's. Ellen had come over late Friday to borrow Jack's equipment for her dad. Maggie wished she knew then that Drew hadn't known what he volunteered for. Maybe it was better she didn't know.

They walked through the side door of her garage into the backyard.

"I thought I earned my keep," he said, "by helping you chaperone those gluttons for punishment, euphemistically known as teenage girls."

"Just because they walked rings around you?" She gave him a wicked smile. *Poor guy.* He'd had a rough time this weekend. Yet, he never quit. She had to give him points for that.

"We can stretch out the tents over the deck railing." As she spoke, she pulled each lightweight nylon tent out of its bag. With his help, they quickly draped the tents and sleeping bags over the railing. Too bad Jack worked so many hours. He would've enjoyed this weekend in the wilderness.

"I'll replace this." He held up the tent with long rips from the raccoon's claws.

He didn't know how lucky he was that he'd been

34

answering nature's call when the animal tried to get into the tent. He could have been badly clawed. As it was, his outraged yell woke not only the girls but the entire forest population and scared off the raccoon as well as five years off her life.

"Jack will appreciate that."

Hand on his heart, he staggered dramatically against the deck railing. "That was Jack's tent? I will never hear the end of it."

"I warned—" She broke off. "Sorry. I hate when people repeat 'I told you so.'"

"Now, she realizes." Again, he made a dramatic gesture.

Heat burned her cheeks as she entered the house. She had to quit harping on that. A wave of heat from inside almost knocked her over. Even though her neighborhood in a Grand Rapids suburb was as relatively safe as any community these days, she never left windows open when she was gone.

She hooked her keys on the rack just inside the door from the garage and pulled off her baseball cap. When she sailed it into the combination laundry room/lavatory, the cap landed on top of the washer.

"Nice." Drew leaned against the doorframe to the garage to remove his boots—an unexpectedly thoughtful gesture. "You never could sink a basket, though."

"Didn't matter." She unknotted her bandanna, wadded it up, and tossed it overhand. The ball landed neatly inside the upturned cap. "Baseball was my game."

"I know. MVP your senior year. You had an arm that put many guys to shame. You used to fire the ball from outfield to home so hard I'd wonder if the catcher's glove was smoking."

She laughed, surprised—and pleased—at his memory. "Al Kaline was my hero."

"Kaline was long before your time."

"You know how your dad loves old TV shows? Mine made me watch the games from the fifties and sixties." She bent over to remove her dusty boots.

"*Made* you?"

"Okay. I loved watching those old games as much as the

recent ones. Kaline was everyone's hero back then. Mr. Tiger."

"You know," Drew mused. "I've seen a side of you this weekend I've never seen before."

As he padded in his socks down the short hall into the kitchen, she asked, "In what way?"

"You were never this mouthy when Jack and I let you tag along with us."

"*Let* me tag along?" She snorted. "You guys tried everything you could think of to lose me." She followed him into the kitchen.

"It's been a long time." He exhaled loudly. "I haven't been here since your dad's funeral."

Unexpected tears burned her eyes. Must be from lack of sleep. The girls giggled and whispered until well past two. And she truly was exhausted from the hiking. Maggie hadn't cried for her parents in long time. She'd lost them too close together. Six months after her mom died, her dad's heart gave out. She often thought he couldn't bear to live without her mother and died of a broken heart.

Seeing Drew in the kitchen where she'd grown up, where he spent so many hours with her brother, brought back many memories. Mom baking cookies for them—

Maggie cleared her throat. "Why don't you open some windows?"

Moments later, he came back from the living room. "I remember your mom making snickerdoodles. She let Jack roll them into one-inch balls, since he was so precise." Drew laughed. "My job was to roll the balls in cinnamon sugar."

Maggie smiled. She remembered, too, and wondered why she never made those cookies. Jack loved them. Since school was out, she had the time. She would surprise him. Maybe tomorrow. Definitely not tonight when it was going to be a monumental task just dragging herself into the shower.

"Speaking of Jack," Drew said. "He left a message on my voice mail Friday. I haven't heard from him in over two months, then out of the blue, he wanted to meet for lunch."

She stopped cranking open the window above the sink. "Jack called you on Friday? He was here that afternoon."

"He wasn't at work? Jack? The workaholic played

hooky?" He walked around the kitchen table to open the slider to the deck.

"Is that the pot calling the kettle black?" She stared hard at him. "The man who was too busy to come to a meeting for his daughter."

"You've made your point as tactfully as ever." He returned her stare. "I thought we were discussing Jack."

She regretted her remark nearly destroyed their relaxed attitude. "Jack surprised me, too, not being at work. I couldn't believe it when he said he wanted to try out a new CD."

"A CD, really? I thought everybody downloaded tunes these days." He shook his head. "But what do I know? I saw your sound system in the living room. Sweet."

Relieved Drew had put his irritation aside, she pulled salad fixings out of the fridge. "That was his gift last year, birthday and Christmas. You know Jack. Always the latest in technology."

"Did he give you written directions on how to use it?"

She shot him a droll look. "What do you think?"

Drew laughed. "That's Jack. He never leaves anything to chance." He glanced at her blinking answering machine in the corner of the peninsula counter that divided the kitchen from the eating area. "You have a message."

"I'll get it later," she said over the running water as she rinsed the lettuce. Unlike her mother, she didn't let the phone rule her life. No matter what she was doing, Mom always ran to catch the phone. As if afraid she would miss a call.

"What if it's important?" He studied the machine again with its flashing red light.

"My friends would call my cell. And the only person I *need* to hear from is Jack. He knew I was going on the camping trip. If it was important, he would've called my cell. As I told you before, I check for messages on that phone while we're on a trip—in case it's one of the parents."

"I'm surprised you still have a landline. Most people don't."

"My folks had it. I should disconnect it since I only get robo-calls." She dried the lettuce then set it on the counter.

Drew prowled the kitchen, making her trips from the refrigerator to the sink worse than dodging an obstacle course. "I can't get over Jack wanting to listen to a CD in the middle of a workday."

While she washed and chopped veggies, she told him about Jack's visit on Friday. "I couldn't believe how tired he looked. He didn't say much—you know Jack."

Drew nodded. "Never complain, never explain." Which pretty much described Drew, also. She thought it prudent not to make the comparison out loud.

"I guess he's putting in a lot of hours making up for Ben being out." She explained about Jack's business partner's motorcycle accident. "Jack's doing an audit over in Muskegon. I gather it isn't going well."

"Muskegon? Seriously? I'm working with a client over there. In fact, I was there all day Friday." Drew slanted his eyes at the answering machine. "I can't believe you're not curious enough to listen to your message. I'd never not check."

"I'll bet you never *not* answer your cell phone, either. Did you go through withdrawal this weekend?"

"Of course, I'd answer the phone. It might be important."

Slowly, she wiped her hands on a towel. "Some things are more important than the phone. Like family." She took a deep breath. "You have to pay more attention to Ellen than your work."

"Excuse me?" His usually soft gray eyes resembled granite.

She'd seen him in different moods this weekend . . . frustrated, irritated and angry—at her, not the girls—self-deprecating, and even teasing. But never hostile. Until now.

"I would suggest you stop right there." His voice was as hard as his eyes.

Maggie tossed the towel on the counter. As a high school teacher, she saw too many kids floundering. This was the age when they needed their parents the most. She could no more stop lecturing Drew Campbell than she could the parents of her students. "Ellen needs you—more than ever since her mother's gone. You need to pay attention now or, when you do have time for her, she won't have time for you."

His piercing stare probably made battling litigants quail. She didn't back down. She was made of sterner stuff. After all, she'd taught teenagers for more than twelve years.

"You appear unwilling to accept that I had a good reason for missing that damn meeting of yours." His voice was tight, controlled. "A client called—"

"A client who is more important than your daughter."

"No, damn it." He wasn't so controlled now.

Maggie took a step back. She had good reason not to trust a man who stayed perfectly controlled, perfectly reasonable. Though his anger was aimed at her, she trusted emotional outbursts more than controlled condescension.

"It's because of my daughter," Drew continued in a hard voice, "that I'm working long hours. I have to finish up my cases before leaving the firm."

Maggie closed her gaping mouth. "You're leaving the firm? But you're a partner."

She recalled the party Lillian threw for her husband when Drew achieved that milestone. His wife made sure all their friends knew about it. Actually, Maggie thought the woman's boasting over the top.

"A partner who has no time for his family." Drew's anger changed to frustration. "I'm going to open my own office. I want to control my hours. I want to spend the little time I have left with Ellen before she goes off to college. Now, get off my case about neglecting my daughter."

Taken aback by his outburst, she finally understood. Why hadn't he explained—

He glared at her answering machine. "I can't stand this." He punched the Play button.

"You have a lot of nerve—"

"Saturday, one-fifty-three pm. This message is for Maggie May Sinclair. Please call the Muskegon County Sheriff immediately." A phone number followed.

Maggie stared at Drew. Her heart thudded in her chest. Alarm plummeted into her stomach like an icy weight.

"Jack?" Drew voiced her worst fear.

She grabbed the receiver and dialed the number. "This is Maggie Sinclair. I'm returning a call I received."

"One moment," the operator said. A minute later, a man answered. "Ms. Sinclair? I called about your brother, Jack Sinclair."

Alarm shot through her veins. She heard bits and pieces through the roar in her ears. "Regret to inform you . . . accident . . . early yesterday morning—"

She slid to the floor, the kitchen cupboard at her back. The phone clattered on the white vinyl.

"Ma'am?" the man on the phone said. "Can we call someone for you? Ma'am?"

Maggie pressed her forehead against her knees and shook.

"Maggie? What is it?" Drew picked up the phone.

She could still hear the deputy. "Ma'am? Are you all right?"

When she didn't answer either of them, Drew talked to the deputy. She barely heard his words. After he replaced the receiver, she raised her head. "Jack is dead."

His face reflected the anguish crawling through her. "I know."

CHAPTER FOUR

"I-I can't believe he's—"

Drew helped Maggie into a kitchen chair and forced her head between her knees. Talking to the deputy sheriff created such pain in his chest Drew feared it might be a heart attack. A tremendous heartache, instead. No wonder Maggie slid to the floor, ready to pass out. She always appeared so confident, strong, capable and now she looked . . . vulnerable.

Maggie sat up, her expression haunted.

"Take deep breaths. C'mon, Maggie May."

He deliberately used her full name, the way he did when they were kids. She hated to be reminded that she'd been named after a song. His own breath hitched. He tightened his jaw and swallowed past the thickening in his throat. His best friend was dead. Killed in a single-car accident near Muskegon in the early hours of Saturday morning. While he was grousing about the inconveniences of primitive camping, Jack lay dead. Thrown from his SUV that had rolled down a river embankment. Undiscovered until late morning, after the fog burned off.

Drew forced his grief to the back of his mind to concentrate on Jack's sister. Her pony-tail flopped over her shoulder, while wisps of dark brown hair framed a face that had gone whiter than her T-shirt.

"Stay put." He grabbed the teakettle resting on the back burner, dumped out the water, and refilled it. "Tea. Be ready in a minute."

As he set the kettle to boil, he tried to think what to do next. His First Aid class had been ten years ago—or longer. Think, he told himself.

She had to be in shock. Warmth, that's what she needed. He rushed through the archway to the living room, grabbed a blue and red flannel quilt off the couch, and wrapped it around her. Then he stooped to rub her shoulders while her hands dangled between her knees, her head bowed.

With his knuckle, he raised her chin. Her eyes appeared unfocused.

"Come on, Maggie. Look at me." *Come back from whatever abyss you're standing too close to.* He stopped rubbing her shoulders and started on her hands. He held onto those icy, limp fingers as if he could pull her back from the edge.

She blinked several times and slowly peered at him through her dark bangs. Another moment passed before she pulled her hands away from his. "It's a hundred degrees in here and you're wrapping me up in a quilt?"

At first, he was taken aback by the abrupt change. Trust her to camouflage her shock with sarcasm. As she sat back in the chair, the quilt drooped from her shoulders. Her eyes, as blue as Lake Michigan, shimmered with tears.

Tears disconcerted him. He never knew what to do. Lillian always brushed aside his attempts to comfort her. He stood with all the grace of an elephant with four left feet. "I, uh, I think the water is hot enough."

He rummaged in her cupboards until he found the tea bags. Dunking one up and down several times in the mug, he finally thought the tea looked strong enough. What did he know about tea? He was a coffee man. He stirred in two spoonsful of sugar, and then dumped in one more for good measure. If he concentrated on details, he could hold his own grief at bay.

"Drink." He held out the mug. "I might not know how to pitch a tent, Maggie May, but I can handle shock."

As she accepted the mug, she gave him a wobbly smile. "I must really look bad for you to call me *Maggie May.*"

She seemed to be coming out of it. Relief swept through him.

"Scared the hell out of me." He matched her tone. "I've never seen Super Woman collapse before."

She took a sip of the hot drink and grimaced. "Did you slip kryptonite into my tea?"

Maybe he'd overdone the sugar. He didn't bother to point out that she'd collapsed *before* he gave her the tea. He wondered if she, too, were holding back grief by talking about tea and kryptonite—anything other than Jack.

If that worked for her, Drew would follow her lead. "Wonder why I didn't think of kryptonite this weekend when you were ragging on me because I didn't know an ash from a hole in the ground."

That got no response other than a quirk of her eyebrow. Feeling awkward standing over her, he grabbed one of the kitchen chairs, twirled it around and straddled it. "I'll take you up to Muskegon."

She squared her shoulders. "No need. My brother. I'll deal with this." She set the mug on the edge of the table, where it wobbled until he pushed the mug away from the edge.

"My best friend," he declared. "You don't have to deal with this alone."

"I said you don't need—"

"I do." Drew took a deep breath and squeezed the bridge of his nose. "I told you I haven't heard from Jack in a while. I haven't had time—no, I didn't *make* time to call him." He clenched his teeth. "Friday, I'd turned off my cell while I was in a meeting. Later, I checked my messages, and I didn't even try to call Jack back."

That's what made Drew sick inside. He'd had one last chance to talk to his friend, and he hadn't taken the time. Too busy. He'd do it later. Now, he couldn't.

"You probably wouldn't have gotten hold of him anyway."

Her eyes filled with such understanding his own stung. He had to swallow . . . hard. He practically leaped out of the chair before she could tell his feelings simmered close to the surface. He took her mug to the sink and rinsed it out. If he concentrated on little things, he could keep his grief from spilling out.

Someone knocked on the front door. *Not now.* Maggie didn't need visitors. But when the knocking continued, even louder, he couldn't ignore whoever was there.

He yanked open the front door and barked, "What?" at the same time.

Mrs. O'Malley backed up so quickly, she almost fell off the small porch. The elderly neighbor gasped then peered up at him. "Andy? Little Andy Campbell? Oh my, you've grown."

He worked to recover the patience he needed to deal with the busybody from across the street. Too many times, she'd tattled on him and Jack when they were kids, resulting in Jack getting into all sorts of trouble. Thank goodness, she hadn't lived across the street from his house.

"Did you want something, Mrs. O'Malley?" He forced a small smile to temper his abrupt words.

"Well! If you must know, I came to talk to Maggie."

"She's, uh, indisposed. I can deliver a message."

"It's okay, Drew." Maggie edged around him. She tried to open the screendoor. It stuck for a moment, then she wrenched it open. "Come in, Mrs. O'Malley. What is it?"

"Oh, dear." She wrung her hands but stayed on the porch. "The sheriff came to your door on Saturday afternoon. Muskegon County Sheriff, not Ottawa County, which I thought was odd. Is everything all right?"

Maggie dug a tissue out of her pocket and wiped her nose. "No. My brother . . ." She backed into Drew. He clasped her upper arms holding her steady against his chest.

"We've had bad news, Mrs. O'Malley." He swallowed hard. "Jack died in a car accident Friday night."

"Oh, no." The old woman gasped. Her hand fluttered to her throat.

"We were just leaving for the sheriff's office. I'm sure you'll excuse us."

"Yes, yes. Oh, my. I am so sorry." She backed away. "Let me know what I can do to help, Maggie."

She nodded. "Th-Thanks." Maggie twisted away from Drew then headed for the kitchen.

Drew closed the screendoor. Again, it stuck, and he had to force it to close. "Thank you for your offer of help. I'm sure you can see how upset Maggie is. We need to leave. Now."

"Of course, of course." Mrs. O'Malley stepped off the porch then turned around. "Tell Maggie I'll organize the neighbors. Just let me know the funeral arrangements."

He nodded as he closed the front door. The lock seemed to stick, so he put his shoulder into the door until he felt the lock snick into place. Maggie stood in the kitchen, staring but not focusing.

"Do you want to change before we go see the sheriff?" he asked.

"No. I need to—" Her voice broke. She still wasn't in control. "I need to wash my face."

She scooted past him, sliding in her socks on the vinyl floor. "And get my shoes," she added before closing the door to the lavatory.

At the garage door, he stopped to put on his boots. He heard a muffled sob above the sound of water running in the sink. She would be embarrassed if she came out and caught him listening. He walked out to his Navigator in the driveway and propped his arm on the edge of the roof. He rested his forehead on his wrist.

God, this was as almost as bad as when Lillian died. A call from the police, the stunned horror of dealing with the aftermath of a car crash. Especially since it was his fault. Even her folks said so, despite the police's assertion that it was indeed an accident. Nobody's fault, they said. He knew, though. They'd argued again about the neighborhood and a bigger house. She'd taken off. In a hurry and distracted. His fault.

Maggie's hand on his arm dragged him out of his painful thoughts. "If you need a shoulder, Drew . . ."

Her gentle touch, unlike the jabs and playful punches earlier, surprised him. He hesitated for a moment. After closing himself up when Lillian died, he was just starting to feel alive again. Now Jack's death threatened to pull him under again, into that black abyss of abject grief. With effort, he stepped back. He pinched the bridge of his nose before answering.

"I'm not sure if I can handle kindness from you, Mags."

Was that a flicker of hurt in her eyes? She glanced away too quickly to tell. "If we're going, let's go." Her tight voice revealed her anguish. She jiggled her keys.

He had hurt her feelings. But he was too raw to do more than say "Yes" before walking around to open the passenger door. "We have a lot to take care of."

"*I* have a lot to take care of. I'm just letting you tag along." Because that sounded so much like Jack when they were kids, he relented, giving in to her. As they always did.

Her eyes were still red, her hair damp around the edges. Though she'd tucked the wisps behind her ears, she hadn't taken time to change out of her camping-soiled T-shirt and jeans. Lillian, who cared too much about her appearance, would have changed and put on make-up. She would never have worn jeans and a T-shirt, let alone gone camping with her daughter. In fact, she often encouraged Ellen to give up the group.

Despite his own aversion to camping, he knew how much Ellen enjoyed the camaraderie with the other girls, as well as their leaders, Trish and Maggie. Trish's departure had left a hole in Ellen's life too soon after losing her mother. Even though the girls still got together, Ellen complained it wasn't the same. Witnessing their boisterous enjoyment this weekend had been an eyeopener for him. He credited their enthusiasm to Maggie. She made them feel special and capable.

While he dawdled, lost in thought, she'd walked to her Suburban. "Let's go."

"I'll drive." He continued to hold the door open for her. "I'm blocking your car. Close the garage door and get in."

Maggie wasn't sure why she let Drew drive. She could have made him move his vehicle. Maybe she was just too tired to argue, better than admitting she appreciated his company. Her hands still trembled as she wondered what would happen when they got to the sheriff's office. She had no idea what was in store for her. Jack had taken charge after their parents died. He'd done his best to shield her and, in her grief, she'd let him. Now, she was close to letting Drew do the same thing. It would be so easy to let him take charge. He was a forceful man. But, she couldn't let him. When a man took over small things, he graduated to much larger ones. Something she couldn't let happen again.

As she stared out the window, she focused on her thoughts instead of seeing the industrial scenery blurring past. The weekend had taken its toll on her. Two full days with Drew Campbell had kept her on edge. Despite hiking in the primitive forest, she got next to no sleep as she lay in her tent, thinking about the man on whom she'd had the world's largest teenage crush.

She reluctantly admired his perseverance when three hours into the hike he didn't turn around and walk right back to where they'd left their vehicles. She gave him even more points for not complaining despite his obvious discomfort from brand-new hiking boots and new jeans. New jeans? She shuddered. It was a wonder the man could still walk.

"Thinking about Jack?" Drew's baritone, which always reminded her of velvet threaded with steel, barged into her thoughts.

She continued to stare out the window so he wouldn't see the heat in her face. Her brother had just died. Why, in heaven's name, did her thoughts center on Drew? "Uh, no. I was thinking about how good the girls did this weekend." *Liar, liar, pants on fire.*

"You taught them well."

"Kudos, Campbell?" Then she caught herself. His comment was genuine, and she'd thrown it back into his face. She cleared her throat. "Trish deserves the praise. She knows more about the outdoors than I ever will."

"It's a shame she moved. Ellen has really missed her this year."

"We all have."

"You and she were good friends, weren't you?"

"The best. Like you and Jack."

Silence settled between them. She shifted in the buttery-soft leather seat, regretting that she'd brought up Jack. Yet it had seemed so natural to refer to their friendship. For as long as she could remember, Drew—Andy back then—and Jack had been best buds. Inseparable from second grade through college. Roommates, even. He must be suffering, too.

"Mrs. O'Malley said she'd organize the neighbors," he said.

She snorted. "She must be thrilled to be the bearer of news." Remembering her parents' funerals, she almost smiled. "We'll have more casseroles than we can eat in a month."

"She remembered me. Called me 'little Andy Campbell'." He chuckled. "Haven't been called Andy in years, though

Mom forgets sometimes and slips."

"Nothing gets past Mrs. O'Malley. She's eighty-two, and her mind is still as sharp as ever. Our own Neighborhood Watch. That's what my dad called her. Nothing and nobody got past Mrs. O'Malley."

Talking about her busybody neighbor kept her grief at bay . . . for the moment. Nothing overshadowed what was to come. Fear gripped her. Considering she'd broken down trying to tell her neighbor about Jack, she worried how she would deal with the sheriff. If the deputy expressed any sympathy, she'd lose it.

"Ellen enjoys the camping." Drew interrupted her thoughts. "I don't know where she gets it from. Lillian was very fastidious. She abhorred getting dirty or sweaty—unless it was playing tennis at the club."

"Hmm. Sounds like you're describing yourself." To remove the sting, she gave him a small smile. He was probably avoiding his grief, too.

"Excuse me. Tennis is not my game. I enjoy being out in the sunshine and fresh air. But I prefer a civilized game of golf rather than tromping along dusty trails."

"Chasing a little white ball around a golf course isn't exactly exercise."

"I do swim, you know."

She did. He'd been captain of the high school and college swim teams. He'd even come within fractional seconds of making the Olympic team.

"In a pool full of chemicals?"

"Better than a lake or pond full of God only knows what kind of organisms." He shuddered.

The man certainly disliked parts of the outdoors. Poor guy didn't know what he was missing. For someone uncomfortable with dirt and sweat, he did well this weekend. Jack would've been proud—

Jack. Stifling a sob, she swallowed hard and hoped Drew hadn't heard. She couldn't bear sympathy. A squeeze of her forearm told her he'd heard. She was thankful he didn't say anything. Just that small squeeze.

Several moments passed before she broke their silence. "I wonder why Jack was working so late Friday night. He must have gone back to the plant after he left my house."

"Didn't you say he was working long hours to fill in for Ben?"

Oh, God. She'd have to tell Jack's partner. Something else to do. She should make a list.

"After the accident, Ben was in a medically-induced coma, and then he had a long recuperation. Jack said he tried to keep what he was doing—all the extra work—from Ben so he wouldn't worry."

"Nasty accident, motorcycles."

"Ben was lucky he survived." She took in a ragged breath.

Survived.

Why hadn't her brother survived? He was a good guy. A pain in the butt sometimes, typical older brother. She cleared her throat, trying to get past the lump lodged there.

She sniffed back tears. "Jack said Ben came into the office for the first time Friday, looking like death warmed over." *Oh, God, why had she said that?*

Drew glanced at her but said nothing about the ghoulish expression. "So, Jack was working on his own clients as well as Ben's? It makes sense that he'd work late. You know Jack. He was like a terrier. He never let go of anything until he got the job done."

Responsible Jack. Dependable Jack. Tenacious Jack. Terriers had nothing on her brother. He was good at his job because he paid so much attention to detail. *That* was putting a polite spin on his anal-retentive ways. If he discovered discrepancies, Jack's work ethic wouldn't let him rest until he found an explanation. If the explanation wasn't ethical or legal, he blew the whistle. For Jack, issues—like numbers— were black or white. Right or wrong. No gray areas in between.

You always knew where you stood with Jack Sinclair.

"We're a family of terriers." She felt her mouth curve automatically. "Dad called him Russell sometimes. Like a Jack Russell terrier?"

A corner of Drew's mouth turned up. "I remember that. Your dad was right."

"Dad knew. He was the same way. Mom tempered the

guys. She was so laid back."

"I always liked your mom for that reason. Night and day difference between her and my mom."

Out of the corner of her eye, she caught his grimace. Drew's mom had "standards" as she called them. The Sinclair kids didn't quite measure up, and she let them know it. Maggie never appreciated her mother more than after an encounter with Drew's mom.

They lapsed into silence for the rest of the trip.

When they got to the county sheriff's office, Drew tried to take charge in his usual forceful manner. "We're here about Jack Sinclair," he told the woman at the desk. "This is his sister—"

"Maggie Sinclair." She held out her hand to draw the woman's attention to her. If she let him, Drew would take over. She'd had enough of that in her short-lived marriage.

The woman called a deputy who ushered them into a small office with one visitor chair. The deputy and Drew nodded to her to take it. She'd had her moment of exerting her independence. Now that she was about to hear how her brother died, her knees lost their stability. She sat.

Even though he leaned against the wall next to the chair, she felt Drew hovering over her. The deputy sat behind a desk. He opened a folder and handed her a picture. "Is this Jack Sinclair?"

She took it, but when she looked at his face—eyes closed, slashes across his forehead and right cheek—her hand shook so much she dropped the photo. Drew retrieved it, gave it a quick glance, and returned it to the deputy.

"Yes," he said. "That's Jack." Maggie nodded in agreement.

The deputy handed Drew a clear plastic bag. Inside was a brown trifold wallet. Jack's was a brown trifold. "We compared his body with the driver's license in his wallet before we called you, Ms. Sinclair. Thank you both for confirming his identity." He then began a recitation of facts.

Because of the fog or falling asleep at the wheel, Jack had missed a curve approaching a bridge and went over the embankment. She clenched her teeth, refusing to blink. If she closed her eyes even for a moment, she would *see* in her mind the car rolling over and over.

Only after the sun burned off the fog was a passing motorist able to see the Blazer. And only because of a momentary flash of light from the sun hitting a window.

Maggie let the grisly details swirl around her—speed too fast, a guardrail damaged in a previous accident, an SUV's vulnerability to roll-overs, no seatbelt, thrown from the car.

Her ears perked up on the last. "Wait. That's not right. Jack always wore his seatbelt. And not just because it's the law."

The deputy shrugged. "When the car was found, his seatbelt wasn't fastened. It's possible, with the lateness of the hour, he was so tired he didn't think about buckling up."

She remembered the shadows under Jack's eyes Friday and his uncharacteristically disheveled appearance. It *was* possible, she supposed, that he forgot the seatbelt when he got into the car. Possible but not likely. Since they were kids, buckling the seatbelt was automatic. Mom might have been laid back about most things, but not about seatbelts. She refused to put the car in gear until everyone had buckled up. It had become automatic, even when they were thinking about something else. No matter how tired Jack was, he always buckled up.

"He could have been thinking about the fog, too," Drew told her gently before turning back to the deputy. "Didn't the airbag deploy? That should have given him some protection from—" A fifty-foot drop down a river embankment.

She was glad he hadn't said that out loud.

"Airbags must have been stolen, and he didn't get them replaced," the deputy said.

"Wait. How would you know that?" she asked.

"The cover was off and no deflated airbags." The deputy spoke as matter-of-factly as describing a minor incident. "I'm sorry to say he might have survived if he had replaced them. Or at least worn his seatbelt. When will people—"

"Your point is well-taken," Drew interjected. "What else does Ms. Sinclair need to do here?"

For the first time since they arrived at the sheriff's office, Maggie was grateful for Drew's interruption. Even though she knew the deputy was probably right, she didn't want to hear that Jack could have prevented his death. She took care of the rest of the details. When she finished and the deputy conveyed his sympathy again, she began to shake again. With his arm around her waist, Drew escorted her outside where she bent over and retched into the closest flower bed. She was so embarrassed.

He didn't let her go. Leaning against his sturdy body, she gulped in fresh air. For a few moments, she let him comfort her. It would be too easy to let him take over. Then she remembered her short-lived marriage with a control freak. She'd learned to stand on her own feet, to take charge of her life. A painful lesson in standing up for herself.

"We can go now," she announced.

Inside the Navigator, he gave her a bottle of water. "Are you okay now?"

She nodded. "I want to go to the lot where the Blazer was towed."

He shook his head. "You know what the deputy said."

Of course, she knew what he said. *Too distressing for you.* The deputy only told them the location because the insurance adjuster would need to know. Call the insurance company. Something else she needed to deal with.

"You don't want to see the Blazer. The insurance company will take care of—"

She shot Drew a mutinous glare. "I *want* to go."

"Not a good idea."

"I have to go." She had to *do* something.

He held her hand, rubbing his thumb across the top. "Please, Maggie, for your own peace of mind, don't do this."

The comforting warmth of his touch threatened the tight control she had over her emotions. She wasn't going to let Drew deter her from her goal. Automatically, she buckled her seatbelt. "Then, take me home so I can come back before it gets dark."

He walked around his vehicle, muttering about stubborn women. She didn't care. She needed to see Jack's car.

"The junkyard. Please." She tacked on the latter, as if that would make a difference. "Then, the hospital. I want to get Jack's belongings."

"Didn't you hear the deputy? The coroner won't do the

autopsy until tomorrow. Then all of his effects will be given to the funeral home when they pick up the body." He must have noticed her cringe because he squeezed her hand. "That's what happened when Lillian was killed."

"All right." She hadn't heard much after she saw Jack's picture. For all her wanting to handle everything herself, she was grateful for Drew's presence.

"Are you sure you still want to go to the junkyard?"

"Yes," she said through clenched teeth.

They rode in silence, which was fine with her. But the hard line of his jaw and his white knuckles on the steering wheel bore witness to his disapproval.

Whatever she expected was wiped from her mind when they walked through the field of wrecked cars and trucks. Nothing the deputy said prepared her for the sight of her brother's battered SUV. She sucked in a breath. Every inch was dented, scraped, or broken. The worst was the driver's side where—

Drew touched her elbow. "That's it. You've seen it. I'll take you home."

Shrugging off his hand, she marched up to the driver's door, broken and bent backward but attached with one hinge. Jack's normally scrupulously clean vehicle was muddy and scattered with the detritus of the accident. Careful to avoid the mud, she bent inside and picked up her brother's belongings. Emptying the vehicle kept her mind off the destruction.

Drew stopped her when she began gathering up the trash. "The insurance company will total the vehicle. There's no need—"

She had to do this. Needed to pick up. Not that there was much. A few toothpick wrappers, an empty blister pack from antacids. CDs and their cases were strewn throughout the car. She picked up the CDs and tried returning them to their proper cases. Her hands shook in the process.

"Don't be so fussy," Drew growled at her. He'd returned from the Navigator with a plastic grocery bag. "Just toss everything inside and let's go."

"I knew it was a mistake letting you come." With the inside of her arm, she brushed her bangs off her forehead . . .

along with the tear that leaked out of her right eye. "If you don't have the patience to stand here quietly and let me finish, go sit in your car. Jack cared about his music. I can't just jumble them all together." She had one case left over. A blank one, probably for a CD he'd burned. He did that often, burned CDs with collections of his favorite songs. He'd made some for Maggie, too.

Drew cleared his throat. "I don't think Jack—"

She shot him a *back off* look then felt under the driver's seat. Where was the CD? She brushed glass and dried mud off the seat then lay across it to check under the passenger seat. No CD.

Maybe it was in the player. She tried to retrieve it. She wanted—no, needed to know what he was listening to when he . . .

"Come on, Maggie." Drew urged her out of the car.

Again, she brushed away his offer and managed to eject the CD. She stacked all the CDs in the bag. She nearly wept thinking about Jack's last visit when she complained about his horrible taste in music until he changed it. After backing out of the Blazer, she let the bag fall open on the front seat.

Drew gently took her wrist and turned her to face him. "You're wigging out on me, Mags."

Even if she explained, she knew he didn't understand. "I have to finish. I have to—"

She needed to get away from him before she broke down. Biting her quivering lips, she stepped back. Taking a deep breath, then another, she fought to find calm. Elusive calm. She clasped her elbows and stared out across the lot filled with wrecked vehicles. The evening sun cast long shadows on the hulking carcasses. A graveyard for—

She wouldn't think about that. "Let's go, Campbell."

"Quick recovery, *Sinclair*." He matched her tone. "Are you okay?"

"Considering the circumstances?" She tucked a loosened strand of hair behind her ear then took a deep breath. "I won't wig out on you. I promise."

"Good. Let's go home."

"I'll just . . ." She leaned into her brother's vehicle and checked over the back of the driver's seat to see if anything had flown into the rear. Satisfied that she hadn't missed anything, she picked up the plastic bag.

"Don't say anything," she warned with her foot on the Navigator's retractable step. "Just drive back to Grand Rapids."

"As . . . you . . . wish." While he drew out the words, his mouth curved into a wry smile. He was trying to help her, making an effort to take her mind off Jack. Not that anything could. But she appreciated his attempt and responded in kind.

"*The Princess Bride*? How many times did we watch that movie?"

"'My name is Inigo Montoya. You killed my father. Prepare to die.'"

With a groan, she lightly slapped his thigh. "Don't start. You and Jack spoiled that summer for me with all those quotes."

"Wasn't that the summer you broke your leg? And your mother let you watch movies all day?"

She chuckled. "Yeah. You and Jack hung out in our family room to keep me company then insisted we watch *The Princess Bride* over and over."

"'Inconthievable.'"

That was the summer she fell in love with Drew Campbell.

For several miles, Maggie stared out the side window. Her brother was gone. Why did the people she love have to die? Her parents—first her mom then her dad. Now Jack. Her family was gone. As she realized she was alone in the world, her breath hitched. She leaned her elbow on the door and squeezed the bridge of her nose. She would not give in to weakness and cry. Not in front of Drew Campbell, anyway. He would take advantage and, meaning well, take over.

She tried focusing on something, anything other than the fact that her brother was dead. Still regretting her near loss of control in the junkyard, she went over what she needed to do when she got home. *Make a checklist. Focus on the details.* That was more Jack's way than hers. Normally, she was a paper-and-pencil list-maker. But if she didn't write down tasks as she thought about them, she would forget. She pulled her phone out of her purse.

"Jack's cell phone," she mused. "I wonder why the deputy didn't give me his cell."

Drew glanced away from the road at her. "Maybe they didn't find it. Or if it was in his pocket, the coroner will find it, and you'll get it back tomorrow."

"Or it could've flown around in the crash. We have to go back to the Blazer. It might be underneath the seat."

"No. You searched it thoroughly. You took everything there was out of his car. You even took the owner's manual out of the glovebox, for God's sake."

She stared out the side window, wishing he hadn't seen that. "Jack would've understood."

A sound halfway between a snort and a laugh escaped his mouth. "You're right. God, that guy was so anal. He drove me crazy when we were roommates."

That was Jack. Obsessive compulsive described him perfectly. A lump formed in her throat.

Drew clasped her hand and gave it a squeeze. "I'm sorry. You have to do whatever helps you deal with grief."

Oh God. She'd forgotten he'd been through this before. "I guess you would know."

"Yes, I would. It's taken me a year to deal with Lillian's . . . death." He blew out a breath. "That's the first time I've called it that. Usually, I use a euphemism—like her passing. So, believe me, I do know. I'll help you as much as I can, but you're the one who has to work through it."

"Thanks. I know you mean well."

This time, he did snort. "Isn't that what you and Jack used to say about The Aunts?" Since they were at a stop sign, he took his hands off the wheel and made air quotes around the last two words.

Dear Lord, her aunts. She had to call them. Something else to add to the To-Do list she'd better start. She opened her cell and wrote notes. She finished quickly.

"I hope you're right about his cell phone. He had it Friday afternoon before he left my house. He always carried it."

She remembered the last time she saw Jack. How antsy he'd been during his visit, pacing from the kitchen to the living room, fiddling with her sound system. At first, she thought he was anxious to leave, to get back to work. Yet he'd lingered in her drive, chatting with the door to his Blazer open, his foot on the step. He'd even taken her picture with his cell. Always uncomfortable having her picture taken, she goofed around, striking a vampish pose. Then she'd turned the tables on him and taken his picture.

It suddenly hit her that was her last picture of Jack. As she swallowed past the lump that never seemed to go away, she scrolled through the pictures of the campout until she got to Jack.

She pondered that, staring at his picture. Until she saw—"Oh, my God." She bobbled the phone. She'd spent so much time obsessing over putting CDs in their cases that she didn't realize what else was missing.

"What now?"

"Jack's computer and briefcase weren't in the Blazer."

"So?"

"His briefcase. Jack always had it with him. It's a special case for his laptop computer. I gave it to him for Christmas the year he and Ben went into business together. It should have been in the car."

"He must have dropped it off at his condo or his office before going to Muskegon." Drew sounded entirely too logical.

"No. I know my brother. He always took his own computer when he went to a client's."

"Look." She turned her phone around to show Drew the picture of Jack. "You can see the corner of his briefcase on the passenger seat."

Drew glanced at it. "And that proves . . ."

"He had his briefcase with him when he left my house. Yet, it wasn't in the car when he—" She broke off. *Damn. Don't let me cry.*

"I didn't see it in the Blazer," he said. "You would've picked it up. Hang on." He forestalled her protest. "I'm sure there's a logical explanation. Same with his phone."

"He always carries his phone on that thingee on his belt."

"Thingee? I thought English teachers were more precise."

"Oh, stick a sock in it, Campbell. Cell phone holder. Satisfied?" She glared. "Hang on. Why did the sheriff call my landline and not my cell? Jack labeled both my home and cell numbers on his cell marked ICE, In Case of—"

"—Emergency," he finished. "I know."

"Right. Anyway, in his contacts' list on his cell, I know my cell number is labeled ICE. He made me do the same on my phone. So why didn't the sheriff call my cell?"

"You just said Jack's phone wasn't among his possessions, and it wasn't in the car."

"How did they know to call me then?"

Drew blew out an exasperated breath. "Because Jack carried an emergency card in his wallet?"

Damn, she hated his logic.

Hers was better. "No briefcase, no cell phone. Something isn't right."

"You do realize you're going off on several different tangents at once." Drew had to point out the obvious.

She leaned her head against the window, watching the trees and houses go by in a blur. "Stop." She bolted upright. "Stop the car."

Drew slowed, put on his emergency signals, and pulled over. "What is wrong? Are you sick?"

Twisting around in her seat, she pointed behind them. "That's it. That's the bridge. I'm getting out."

Drew grabbed her arm. "No. You are not getting out here. Too much traffic."

As soon as she opened the door, the sounds of rushing traffic assailed her ears. With Drew pulling her arm, and her desire to visit the scene warring, Maggie didn't know what to do. Her body reflected her indecision, one foot in the car and the other on the tarmac.

"Maggie." Drew's soft voice pierced the roar of passing traffic. "We can come back at a later time."

"No. I don't . . . know. I'm scared to look, yet I feel I must. Please don't stop me. Maybe his phone is done there." She had to make him understand. "I must . . . I need . . ."

"I know. Close your door."

"But—"

"I want to back up closer to the bridge when traffic

58

clears. Now, will you please close the door?"

She complied then he waited for several moments before backing up yet staying on the shoulder.

"Stay put." Drew turned off the engine, pocketing the keys as he got out of the car.

Damn him. He was going to go back there himself. Without her. And it was her idea. Suddenly, he opened her door. "Are you coming or not?"

She scrambled out of the car. They walked along the bridge to the other side. The guardrail hadn't been repaired yet, so it was obvious where it had been hit and broken off. Deep gouges in the embankment marked the descent of Jack's Blazer.

"Okay, you've seen it." Drew's tight-lipped expression mirrored his terse words. "Let's get back in the car and leave this area."

"No. I'm going down."

"Damn it, Maggie. No."

Grateful she still wore hiking boots with a deep tread, she started down the steep embankment. Drew clambered after her. If it had rained, the ground would be slick and treacherous. She avoided the gouges until she got to the river's edge. As she scanned the area, she hoped something would jump out at her. Something to indicate this was more than an accident.

Several branches of varying lengths lay scattered along the edge, some in the river. Other than that, nothing. With the drought, the river was low, and the bank much farther out than usual. Marks in the mud indicated where the Blazer had rolled on its side. She stooped to get a closer look at the indentation in the soft bank. Again, nothing.

Maggie tried to be analytical, objective. As if what she examined had happened to a stranger. That lasted about ten seconds. Her throat swelled, tears burned behind her eyes.

"All right, Mags. Time to go. You are making it harder on yourself."

When he tugged on her arm, she stood, facing away from him. For several seconds, she closed her eyes and fought for control. Drew was right. She was making it harder on herself. Something compelled her to examine the scene up close. Not that she learned anything new. Glass and other debris lay scattered in the mud. No cell phone, though. And no briefcase, even though she scanned the area thoroughly.

"Are you satisfied? You can see how he drove too fast, missed the curve, and plowed through the guardrail." Drew sucked in a breath and slowly let it out. "We should leave."

"Hey, folks." The loud voice got their attention. A sheriff's deputy stood at the broken guardrail. "Need help?"

"No, sir," Drew called out. He clasped Maggie's hand and started upward.

Not wanting to explain why she was at the river's edge, she climbed with Drew.

"Bad accident here Friday night," the deputy said. "With the guardrail out, you could be in danger." He narrowed his eyes. "What were you doing down there?"

Maggie dug a tissue out of her pocket rather than answer the deputy. Drew released her hand to walk closer to him. "Her brother died here Friday night."

Though he spoke softly, she heard every word. And every word shot into her heart like an arrow from a crossbow. Looking at the river sluggishly flowing southwest on its way to Lake Michigan, she tuned out the men and tried to make sense of Jack's accident. Though she heard the engine of the patrol car start up, she didn't look. Drew had to touch her elbow before she turned to him.

"Ready now?"

With a nod, she accepted his support as they walked across the bridge to his SUV. Once inside, she didn't break her silence.

"Wanna tell me what that was all about?"

"No."

They rode in silence for several miles. Jack's briefcase and phone. She dug in her purse until she found the deputy's card. "I'm calling the deputy."

"What? Why?"

"Maybe he can tell me about the briefcase."

She'd punched in three numbers when Drew covered her hand. "Maggie, settle down. You are freaking out."

"I am not. Freaking out would be screaming and crying."

"Not necessarily. I'm sure there are reasonable

explanations for the briefcase, cell phone, and the call to your landline. Let's give it more thought before you call the deputy."

"Why?"

"Because he'll think you're freaking out and won't take you seriously."

With a quick glare that he missed because of his attention on the highway, she turned off her phone and stuck it in her purse along with the deputy's card. "Damn. I hate dealing with *reasonableness*. And logic. You'd make a regular Mr. Spock."

"I consider that a compliment."

His pleasure irritated her so much she wanted to stick out her tongue at him. *That* would have been childish. After several miles, she pointed to a large green sign overhead. "Turn off at the next exit." Jack lived just a few blocks off I-96 on the north end of Grand Rapids. "I want to stop at his condo."

"Now listen, Maggie—" Drew took his attention off the road again to give her an exasperated look. He probably thought she was wigging out again.

She didn't care. "It's on the way. It'll only take a minute."

"Maggie." There was that exasperation again.

"Okay, forget it. I knew I should have driven. Just take me home."

"You're going to come back, aren't you?" He flicked on his turn signal and exited the highway. "If you gloat because you got your way, I will take you straight home."

She knew better than to push her luck. "Thank you," she said quietly.

A few minutes later, Drew negotiated the twists and turns of the condo complex where ranch-type single dwellings were grouped into cul-de-sacs. Jack's was in the back, far away from the entrance and noisy thoroughfare.

"You could do this in the morning," Drew pointed out as he parked in the short driveway in front of Jack's garage.

"I need to see for myself. Besides, I need to take one of his suits to the funeral home tomorrow morn—"

"Have you always been as obsessive as Jack?"

She ignored him. "And I need his address book to call his

friends."

"I'll call his friends, damn it." He sounded like he'd reached the end of what little patience he had. He didn't understand that focusing on details was what held her together.

Even though the sheriff had given her Jack's keys, she automatically opened the condo with the ones on her own keyring. Odd, the things we do out of habit, she thought. The way Jack always used the keycode to her garage instead of the key to the front door. The key they'd had since they were kids.

Her shaking hands made her fumble with the deadbolt lock. She should have gone in through the garage. Of course, then her fingers would've probably slipped off the numbers.

"Need help?" Drew reached for the keys.

Just then she heard the lock snick. "Got it." She unlocked the knob and opened the door.

Air conditioning kept the closed-up house from smelling stale the way hers had. Glancing around Jack's perfectly neat living room, she remembered complaining that he'd taken minimalism to new heights. Nothing, not even dust, marred the surface of the lamp table. No knickknacks, no forgotten glass or coffee cup. Magazines lay neatly stacked on the coffee table. The yellow *National Geographic* provided a splash of color next to copies of *The CPA Journal*.

All perfectly normal, perfectly Jack. Except— She studied the living room, unable put her finger on what was wrong. "Something's not right."

"What?" Drew wandered across the room.

Maggie sniffed. "Strange smell. Not Jack's cologne."

Sniffing, Drew shook his head. "I don't smell anything other than stale coffee." At the bookcase across the room, he pulled out a DVD and put it in a different place.

"What did you just do?"

He shrugged. "One of the DVDs was out of order. I put it back."

"Out of order?"

"Yeah. They're in alphabetical order. I'm surprised that Jack . . ." He shrugged. "It's nothing. He must have been in a hurry."

Possible, she thought. Even her brother wasn't totally perfect. Still . . .

Drew walked toward the kitchen. On his way past a lamp table, he pushed the drawer closed.

"Hold it. Was that drawer open?" She hadn't noticed when they walked in.

"Just a bit." He gave her a sheepish look. "Ellen is always leaving drawers and cupboard doors open, and I'm forever going behind her and closing them. Bad habit, I know."

She scurried past him into the kitchen. The coffee maker sat on the counter, decanter empty, grounds thrown out, yet the smell lingered. Under the sink, the wastebasket contained the grounds. That explained the smell.

As she turned to leave, she saw that the pantry door wasn't firmly shut. Nothing inside appeared to be disturbed. Everything looked the way it always did, cans and jars lined up perfectly straight, an inch from the edge of each shelf. Categorized. Vegetables with vegetables, pasta sauce next to alfredo sauce. She didn't bother to check the spices. They'd be in alphabetical order. Her OCD brother wouldn't have it any other way.

She checked a partially-filled brown paper bag lying on its side on top of other full, flat paper bags on the floor. Jack subscribed to the Grand Rapids *Press*, the Detroit *News* as well as the *Wall Street Journal*. She'd have to remember to cancel them and get his mail from the box at the curb. And another thing—forward his mail to her house. She'd better start writing things down or she'd never remember. She pulled out her cell and made notes. Again, she checked the pantry.

"He took the time to put Friday's newspapers in the bag for recycling but didn't close the door tight." That puzzled her.

"You said he's been overwhelmed by all the work on his plate. He could've been distracted."

She acknowledged that with a raised eyebrow. "Maybe. I need to get that suit." She headed to the bedroom. The neatly-made bed, no blanket dangling below the maroon and gray comforter, sat directly across from the door. She never— almost never—made her bed. The edges of the tailored pillow shams lined up perfectly straight with the edge of the bed. She wasn't sure she even knew where the pillow shams that matched her comforter were. Her closet, maybe?

A 35mm camera rested on top of his armoire, next to a mahogany box with an engraved "S" on top.

"I didn't realize he still had that camera," Drew said. "I remember him using that in college." He picked it up and examined the back then put it back. "No film. I'm not surprised. Nobody uses film anymore. Not with digital cameras on their phones."

"I'd better take this." She picked up the box.

"What is it?"

"My dad called it his 'bits and bobs' box. He said you couldn't call the container for a man's tie tacks and pins a jewelry box." She let herself smile in remembrance. "Jack kept his own bits and bobs in here, along with Dad's. I think he used it more as a catch-all. I have one on my nightstand, but it's not as nice as this."

She rifled through the contents of the box. Dad's watch that no longer ran, Jack's Boy Scout Eagle pin, tie tacks and bars, souvenir pins from conventions he'd gone to, a couple of small batteries, two little memory cards, and coins.

"Would you hold this?" She shoved the box into Drew's hands before going to the closet, looking for clothes to take to the funeral home.

Jack organized his clothes the way he organized everything. Suits were separate from shirts, casual from business attire, all organized by color. For several moments, she stared.

"What's wrong?" Drew came up beside her.

She bit her lip. "I can't decide . . ." *Oh, God.* She was going to cry. *Not now, not here.*

With his hands on her shoulders, Drew steered her away from the closet. "Go check his office for that damn briefcase."

"But his clothes—"

"I'll take care of it."

Because it was easier to let him, she walked down the hall on leaden feet. She'd thought she'd find a clue to what happened to Jack. What made him so careless as to not buckle his seatbelt? Or not get the airbags replaced? She thought about the open drawer in the living room, the misplaced DVD, the door to the pantry ajar. A distracted Jack was making more sense than before.

Standing in the doorway, Maggie scrutinized Jack's second bedroom, which he used as an office. Desk drawers were closed, as were the file cabinet drawers. The desk top was neat, of course, no papers or dust. A sophisticated digital camera sat next to a spindle of writeable DVDs. She turned on the camera and discovered no pictures. Odd. She didn't say anything to Drew. He'd probably remind her of reasonable explanations.

Okay, it would be reasonable to upload pictures to the desktop computer. She turned it on and waited for it to boot up.

Drew came in. "Is everything okay in here?"

"I'm not sure." She opened a desk drawer. Neat, orderly, as she expected. Then, she checked the others. All okay. She opened the top file cabinet drawer. Neat organized. Just like Jack. In the middle drawer, she found neat files, color-coded tabs. Something caught. She pulled the drawer all the way out. In the back, a file was cocked. She pulled out the folder, labeled "security." Empty.

"If I were a conspiracy theorist—"

"What do you mean *if*?" he drawled.

"—I would assume something was taken from this file. I'm trying to be *reasonable*. The folder could be in the back because Jack changed his mind."

"Good girl.

Ignoring his approval, she pulled out the rest of the cabinet drawers. Nothing seemed out of place.

"Were you going to check something on Jack's computer?" Drew asked.

"Yes, pictures." She sat down at the desktop computer and opened the 'picture' folder. "I shouldn't be surprised. His pictures are organized by subject and date." She shook her head. "I gave up years ago. My print pictures are in shoeboxes, and the rest in my phone."

"Why are you checking his pictures?" Drew stood behind her, looking over her shoulder.

"His digital camera didn't have any pictures. I thought

he might have uploaded them into the computer. But, his most recent pictures are from his vacation last winter."

Drew reached around her for the mouse and diminished the screen. "Let's check the trash can." He clicked on the icon for deleted items. Empty. "So much for that theory. Who empties the trash can? Mine is overflowing."

She snorted. "Mine, too. But you know Jack."

"The pictures are probably on his laptop."

She turned the chair around to face him. "Which we can't find."

"Right. There has to be a reasonable explanation."

"Yeah, sure. Someone's been here."

"Whoa. That was a leap. I said *reasonable*. The door was locked, remember?"

Was it? She'd struggled with the key. What if she'd locked and then unlocked the door? She could blame Drew's insistence on helping for distracting her. But she admitted she hadn't paid attention.

"Let's be logical." He was placating her.

"I hate logic almost as much as reasonableness."

He ignored that and went out into the living room. "You've been here more recently than I have. Is anything missing?"

"I—I don't know. But think about all the things we've found. DVD out of place, drawer open, pantry door not closed, the empty file."

"C'mon, Maggie. You're fixating on minutiae. All those things can be attributed to Jack's distraction."

"I know. But what about the missing pictures?"

"In the laptop. You find the laptop, you'll find pictures. It's probably at his office. Let's be sensible. Burglars would've taken the TV." He nodded to the flat screen. "And the cameras and the computer. Jewelry, too. That box was right out in the open on his dresser. Easily portable items, easily fenced. Why would they only take a laptop?"

"You are a pain in the butt, you know that?" Deflated, she picked up Jack's jewelry box. Drew must have brought it out of the bedroom.

"Well, then." He picked up a garment bag off the sofa.

"You remembered his shoes." She pointed to the bag that

sagged at the bottom.

He nodded. "Shirt, tie, underwear. I've done this before."

A stab of guilt cut her heart. He *had* done this before. For his wife, Lillian, a year ago. With her death so recent, and in a car accident, she hadn't considered how Jack's . . . passing must be affecting Drew.

"I'm sorry." She laid her hand on his forearm. "I, uh, you shouldn't have had to do that."

His Adam's apple bobbed. "No problem. I think we're done here."

Following him to the front door, she slowly shook her head then stopped. "I still think someone has been here." She held up her hand to forestall his argument. "The place *feels* as if someone was here. Somebody with bad intentions. Don't look at me like that. Call it my gut . . . or woman's intuition."

Drew all but rolled his eyes. "Far be it from me to question a woman's intuition."

CHAPTER FIVE

The missing briefcase and laptop plagued Maggie most of the night. First, she replayed Jack's unexpected visit early Friday afternoon. That brought her back to seeing his burgundy soft-sided leather briefcase/laptop carrier on the passenger seat when he was about to leave.

At midnight, she wondered if she was preoccupied with the briefcase because she didn't want to accept that her brother, who raised responsibility to an art form, might have been responsible for his accident. That in his fatigue from working long hours, he'd forgotten to buckle up. Because of the pressure of doing his own work plus Ben's, he didn't have time to replace his stolen air bags. That he foolishly drove too fast in the fog.

None of which she believed.

At one-twenty, she reasoned that if she found the briefcase in a normal, logical place, she'd let go of her preoccupation. At two forty-six, she started thinking about the logical, normal places where his briefcase might be. Besides his car and condo, the next logical place was at his office.

Okay, now she had a plan. Check his office then the office at the plant where he had been doing an audit.

At three-oh-seven, she started thinking about illogical places. Like if he hid his laptop.

If the laptop wasn't at either office, she would go back to Jack's condo and check under the bed, behind the couch, anywhere she hadn't looked earlier.

That led to her wondering why he would hide his laptop.

Who wouldn't he want to find it? Was someone after info on it? Why? Since he password-coded everything—and cautioned her to do the same with her phone and laptop—nobody could get in anyway.

Finally, she couldn't stand lying in bed any longer. She

threw on a light-weight robe over her boxer shorts and tank top then strode out to the laundry room off the kitchen where she'd left the bag with Jack's wallet. Though still muddy, she pulled it out. She set it on top of the washer then found a rag to wipe it off.

The wallet held cash—less than a hundred dollars—his driver's license, credit cards, registration and insurance cards for his vehicle, health insurance card, and emergency contact number—her landline. Only her landline.

Why he hadn't included her cell number? The card, though muddy like everything else inside the wallet, seemed new. For sure, he should've included her cell if he just wrote a new emergency card. She puzzled that as she wiped each item and set them on top of a towel to dry.

When she got to the picture at the wallet's back compartment, she lost it. Upon seeing the picture of the three of them—Jack, Drew, and herself—she leaned against the wall next to the dryer then slid to the floor. She had no idea how long she sat there looking at the picture while tears ran down her cheeks.

Maggie pulled herself together. She had to. Nothing would be accomplished if she fell apart and stayed in that state. She stretched to reach the rag and wiped as much mud off the wallet.

Then, she stopped. What if she was wiping away evidence?

Evidence of what? Drew's voice in her head chided her. Because some items were missing didn't mean a crime had been committed. Possibly theft but not what she suspected. If she went to the sheriff, what could she produce that would indicate foul play?

She washed her hands to get rid of the mud then went back to bed. Although it was after four, she needed to sleep. If only she could sleep. She rolled over onto her left side. Her leg cramped. Charley horse. Damn. She'd gotten dehydrated. She stretched out her leg for relief. She tried lying on her right side. Concentrating, she relaxed her toes, then her legs, then . . .

At seven, she startled awake. She remembered dreaming but not the content. Whatever it was left her shaken. Since she'd taken a shower the night before, she only washed her face. The mirror reflected her bad night and lack of sleep. She didn't wear make-up often, but the ravages of yesterday warranted foundation and a little blush. A dab of undereye cream helped with the bags. She dressed and took care with the make-up, but she'd only killed a half hour. Jack's office, ten minutes away, didn't open until eight. She took time to drink a cup of coffee and eat a bagel before driving there. Her stomach churned, and the bagel sat like a lump in the middle of the acid as she anticipated what she had to do.

"Hello, there," Natalie TenBrink, the office manager, greeted Maggie. "Don't you look all patriotic."

Maggie's white slacks, red shell, and navy blazer made her feel pulled together, in control. An illusion.

"Jack's still working onsite," Natalie went on. "Up in Muskegon."

Familiar prickling started behind her eyes. After shedding so many tears last night and early this morning, she should've been through. She swallowed past the thickening in her throat. *Focus on the mission.* "I need to talk to Ben. Is he in?"

Natalie appeared confused by Maggie's abruptness. She usually took time to chat with the efficient older woman who rode herd on the two partners in the accounting firm. "That man." She shook her head in maternal concern. "He just got out of the hospital Friday, and what did he do? He came here. And he's here again. He should be home and not—"

Not waiting for her to finish, Maggie strode down the short hall, smoothing her damp palms along the sides of her white slacks. On the phone, Ben Voorheis waved her into his office with his right hand. His other arm, in a navy-blue sling, supported his damaged shoulder. The call apparently was not going well, if Ben's expression was any indication.

As he hung up, he popped something into his mouth, chewed quickly, and swallowed. "I thought I heard your voice, darlin'. Are you finally going to put me out of my misery and marry me?"

Five years ago, when he and Jack went into partnership, Ben seriously pursued her. She tried to curb his romantic interest, even when he teased that she'd ruined him for other women. She'd gotten used to his joking, although his calling her *darlin'* grated on her nerves. She had to convince him to stop. Today wasn't the day.

Ben hobbled around his desk, a crutch under his right arm and a walking boot on his left leg.

"How are you?" She met him halfway. "Shouldn't you be home resting?"

"You sound like Natalie." He enveloped her in a one-armed bear hug. He smelled of cologne—a heavy, exotic scent—and mint.

Though about the same height as Maggie, Ben Voorheis was burly and about a year older. His blond-white hair, blue eyes, and *apple* cheeks testified to his Dutch ancestors who—like so many—settled in West Michigan.

With one hand, he held her at arm's length. "Hey, girl, I could drive to Chicago on the road map in your eyes. Working too hard? I'll have to talk to that brother of—"

Needing to get this over with quickly, Maggie swallowed. "Jack was killed Friday night."

"What!" He stumbled backward and bumped into his desk. His crutch clattered against his big gray medical boot before bouncing on the carpet. Shock turned his complexion almost as white as the straps of his sling.

"Oh, Ben, I'm sorry I blurted it out like that. I was afraid I wouldn't get the words out." She handed him the crutch he'd dropped. "The sheriff said it was an accident. Fog. He was driving too fast."

"I can't believe it." Ben reached for her again. "I'm so sorry, darlin'."

She eluded him by walking around his desk to the window. On the way, she tucked her shirt back into her slacks, where it had pulled out from his enthusiastic embrace. A little too exuberant at times, Ben hugged everyone. But, she couldn't take his brand of kindness right now. Clasping her elbows, she stared out at the parking lot. The office was at the end of a long line of similar suites. Jack had been pleased to have two corner offices.

"Don't be nice to me, Ben. I'm barely holding it together." She tried for a smile over her shoulder to take the edge off her rebuff.

He backed off, hurt in his eyes. Ben's emotions were always displayed prominently on his boyish face. He hitched his hip on the edge of his desk. "Sit down, then. Natalie," he yelled. "Bring some coffee in here. On the double."

Moments later, the office manager came in with two cups of steaming coffee, both black. A good admin, she knew what the partners and Maggie preferred. "We have a perfectly good intercom. You do not need to—"

"Jack died in a car accident Friday." Ben was as blunt as Maggie.

Natalie dropped the coffee. While tears streamed down her face, Ben marched her out of the office, hobbling as best he could. Even though he spoke softly—or what he must have thought was soft—Maggie heard.

"Now, Maggie's had a real shock. She's barely holding it together." Ben parroted her words. "Don't go blubbering in front of her."

He ushered Natalie to the restroom then returned with another mug of coffee supported by the sling. Coffee sloshed over the rim and stained the material. "What the hell are you doing?"

Maggie had knelt to pick up the fallen mugs. "When I said don't be nice—" As she stood, she gave him a crooked smile. "—I didn't mean you could yell at me like you do Natalie." She set the now-empty mugs on his credenza.

"But—"

She shushed him with an upheld hand. "I'll take that coffee you're holding. And then I want you to tell me where Jack was working." Clasping the cup like a shield, she walked to the visitor's chair and sat down. "The accident happened near Muskegon around midnight. Why do you think he was up there so late on a Friday night?"

"It's all my fault." Ben's eyes teared up.

Good Lord. If he didn't pull himself together, she would start blubbering, too.

He took out his handkerchief and blew his nose. "Jack was filling in for me. If I hadn't had that stupid accident—"

"Hey, no self-recriminations, okay? Jack was doing what needed to be done. Now, please tell me where he was working."

Ben carefully folded his handkerchief and stuffed it in the pocket of his khaki Dockers. "Aw, darlin', don't you worry your pretty little head—"

If ever there was a patronizing comment guaranteed to make her cringe, that was it. How often had her dad said that? Although only a year older than she, Ben had very old-fashioned ideas about the *weaker* sex. The worst part was that he didn't even realize how condescending he sounded. Her previous efforts to change him had been wasted. She finally accepted him the way he was—Jack's friend and business partner. Definitely not a man she'd marry. Not that she had any intention of marrying again. Been there, done that. Had the scars to prove it.

"Ben, I need to learn all I can about what Jack did that last—" Her voice cracked.

"This is not good for you," he said.

She cleared her throat. "I'm fine. Just tell me what I need to know, and I won't bother you anymore."

Guilt flashed across his face. "You'd never be a bother to me. What can I do to help? Just tell me."

"The name of the company where he was working?"

Ben heaved a reluctant sigh. "Jack was auditing one of my clients. It had high priority, and he thought he was helping. I could've managed. He didn't need—"

"The name?" She cut off his rambling.

"Vander Haar Manufacturing. It's southeast of Muskegon. I'll call the president and tell him about . . . about Jack."

Subtilty didn't work with Ben. She had to be specific. "Would you give me the address? I want to go up there and get Jack's things."

Surprise crossed his face. "You don't need to do that. I'll send Natalie."

Maggie shook her head. "There will be enough here in the office for Natalie to do with Jack gone." She amazed herself by how matter-of-fact she sounded. At Ben's nod, she knew she was right about Natalie. Still, he protested so she added, "Going up there and getting his things will help me cope. Okay?"

He heaved another sigh. "I'll go with you, then. This

can't be easy on you." He punched a button on the phone, using the intercom instead of yelling as he did before. "Natalie, cancel my ten o'clock appointment. In fact, cancel everything today."

Maggie reached over and held down the button on the intercom. "Hang on, Natalie." After releasing the button, she stared up at Ben. "You just got out of the hospital. You need to rest. You have a business to run. I'm not being understanding. I want to go and get Jack's personal things—on my own." She gave him a small smile. "Right now, I'd like to get his things from his office here."

"Aw, Maggie . . ." Ben appeared genuinely distressed. "Natalie will do that for you."

She'd had overnight to adjust to Jack's . . . to Jack being gone. She should have called Ben at home last night. But, after all he'd been through, she'd wanted to spare him the shock of a late-night bad-news phone call. In reality, she couldn't deal with telling anyone else about Jack. It had been hard enough calling her aunts—and she dared not call one and not the other, so she did a three-way conversation. Their cries of dismay nearly did her in. Between them, they would spread the news throughout the family faster than a high-speed modem or tribal drums.

Still, she should have called Ben. His blank expression made her think he didn't know what to do next. She placed her hand on his sling. "Just let me do what I need to do. Okay? I'd rather be busy than sitting at home and thinking."

He heaved a sigh then patted her hand awkwardly, giving tacit approval to her plans. "I'll find some boxes for you." He hobbled out of his office with her, then he went into the storeroom and closed the door behind him.

At the doorway to Jack's office, Maggie stopped. It was so . . . Jack. Perfectly neat. Like his home. When she thought of how she'd groused at him about his obsessive neatness, a wave of misery hit her like a punch in the stomach.

She took a deep breath and entered. While Ben's office looked out over the parking lot, where he could see visitors coming and going, Jack's window faced a small forest. If she had such a pleasant view, she doubted she'd get any work done.

With efficiency that Jack would've been proud of, she took the prints off the wall. Photographs of the Mackinac Bridge, Tahquamenon Falls, the lilacs in bloom on Mackinac Island, Whitefish Point Lighthouse. Because Jack loved the Upper Peninsula so much, one Christmas she'd enlarged and framed the photos he'd taken of his favorite places.

Now, don't go ruining that efficiency image, she chided herself as her eyes teared up. She picked up the framed picture that always sat on the corner of his desk. The picture of the three of them—Jack, Maggie, and Drew. The guys had their arms on each other's shoulders. Maggie stood between them, the back of her head even with their crossed arms. She was a gawky eleven-year-old, and the boys looked so full of themselves at fourteen. While staring at the same picture Jack carried in his wallet, another wave of misery flowed through her.

"Excuse me?" Natalie stood in the doorway. "Oh, Maggie. You don't need to do that. I can pack up Jack's—" She cleared her throat and wiped a tear leaking out of her left eye. "I'm sorry. I— Never mind. Sarah Jane DeHoesen is on the phone. I didn't know what to tell her."

"Sarah Jane? I thought she and Jack broke up."

Natalie wobbled her hand. "Not really. They get together every once in a while. What should I say?"

"I'll talk to her." She glanced at the phone. "Do I push this button? The blinking one?"

At Natalie's nod, Maggie answered the call. "Sarah Jane, hi. This is Maggie."

After a moment of silence, Jack's old girlfriend said, "Maggie? What are you doing there?" She hesitated. "How are you?"

Knowing she was about to deliver bad news, Maggie sat in Jack's chair. "Not very well. I have some bad news. Are you sitting down?"

"Just tell me." That was Sarah Jane. Straight and to the point. Just like Jack.

"Jack died Friday night."

"What?" Her anguished cry tore right through Maggie's heart. "Oh, no."

She heard a bump and a thud. "Sarah? Are you all

right?"

A moment later, the young woman cleared her throat. "Yeah. I, uh, slipped and landed on the floor. I'm sitting now. Tell me what happened."

"He had a car accident late at night."

"Friday? And I'm just hearing about it?" Her voice rose.

"I'm sorry. I was away. The police just told me late yesterday. I'm so sorry."

After a long silence, in which Maggie thought she'd hung up, Sarah Jane said, "What are the arrangements?"

"None yet. The coroner hasn't released his, uh, him. As soon as I know . . ."

"Yes, please. I'll come." She gave Maggie her phone number. "What do you need?"

"Pardon?"

"What can I do to help?"

"I don't know. Can I get back to you?" Maggie paused. "I didn't know you and Jack were back together. I would've called sooner."

Sarah snorted. "We weren't. Well, sort of. More like friends. Friends with benefits, if you know what I mean."

Oh, yeah. Maggie knew that expression, but she didn't want to think about her brother and his ex-girlfriend having casual sex. She'd thought her brother too busy for a relationship, the reason he said he and Sarah Jane broke up.

"I need to go." Sarah hung up. Social skills were not her strong point.

Maggie continued to sit, pondering what else about her brother she didn't know.

"I found some boxes. And paper to, uh, wrap his . . . things." Standing in the doorway, Ben studiously avoided her eyes. His were red-rimmed. After that brief glance at him, she took the paper. She wasn't sure she could see the evidence of Ben's sorrow without crying herself.

She thanked him and returned to wrapping Jack's belongings.

"You don't have to do this now," Ben said. "There's no hurry. Why don't you wait until after the, uh, after the funeral?"

"I need to keep busy." She gave him a small smile.

"Remember?"

He nodded. "When is the funeral?"

"Not sure yet. The coroner hasn't released—" She swallowed. "I don't know."

He took his handkerchief out of his trousers' pocket and noisily blew his nose. Then, he folded the white cloth and returned it to his pocket. He took something out of his other pocket and popped it in his mouth. "Okay. I'll, uh, leave you. If you need anything, just sing out."

"Thanks, Ben. I will." She concentrated on wrapping the pictures. "Make sure you keep that ten o'clock appointment."

He mumbled an agreement. "I called Greg Vander Haar. He's the president of the company Jack was auditing."

That caught her attention. She grabbed a sticky note and wrote down the name.

"He said Jack came in early Friday," Ben went on. "And left at noon. He thought Jack was done for the day, so he was real surprised when Jack came back later in the afternoon. Greg figures he must have been working late to make up for his long lunch."

That all made sense. But, it also meant that by insisting on feeding Jack, she was the cause of his *long lunch*.

Good grief. First Ben, now she tried to take the blame for Jack's accident.

She recalled the reason for coming to the office. "I don't see Jack's briefcase and laptop."

"What do you mean?" Confusion crossed his features. "Where is it?"

"That's what I'm trying to find out. I don't see it here. I know he had it Friday afternoon. That long lunch was at my house. He stopped by to see me."

Cocking his head, he stared at her. "He did? Did he do that often?"

"Not often. Sometimes, he'd stop in after work."

"Oh. Uh, Maggie. I hate to say this since he's . . ." Ben paused. "Well, what I mean is, the laptop belonged to the business."

She nodded. "I understand. I gave him that case, though. You know how hard he was to buy for. How fussy he was."

Ben gave her a weak smile. "Yeah, I know."

"I, uh, I'd like to keep the case when we find it. I hope that doesn't sound maudlin." She searched his red-rimmed eyes for a sign that he understood.

He wouldn't meet her gaze. "Jack always took the laptop and case with him. He never left it here . . . or at a client's. It's probably still in his car."

She shook her head. "I checked."

"My God, Maggie. You saw the Blazer after . . ." His voice trailed off.

"I was sure he had the case with him. You know how obsess—particular Jack was," she corrected herself with a wry grimace. "He never deviated from his routine."

"Yeah, that was Jack."

Was that bitterness in Ben's voice?

Before heading to Muskegon, Maggie stopped at the funeral home that had handled her parents' funerals. Even though Jack had taken care of the details, she'd been with him. To her surprise, she recognized the director who'd gone to high school with her. He put her at ease right away, explaining he'd taken over the business from his father. She made the arrangements but wished she'd asked Drew to come with her. So many decisions. So much information her head nearly exploded. She couldn't wait to leave.

Fifty minutes after leaving the funeral home, Maggie pulled into the parking lot of Vander Haar Manufacturing. She would have been there sooner if she hadn't driven right past the plant. With the building nestled in the woods, and the drive surrounded by trees, only a small, discreet sign identified the facility. Large bushes partially camouflaged a dumpster on the right side of the parking lot. She parked in a visitor slot close to the double glass doors at the opposite end.

Before getting out of the car, she surveyed the grassy area between building and forest. In normal times, it probably was a luscious green. Now, it reminded her of her own lawn, brittle and burnt in places by the drought. She sat for a few more moments. What was she doing here? She should have let Ben take care of this. Like packing up Jack's office, which she should've let Natalie handle. While she thought keeping busy would help, it had the opposite effect, tearing a new strip off her heart.

She took a deep breath. Jack was her brother. Her responsibility to tie up loose ends and find closure.

Sunlight sparkled on an immaculate glass door. No fingerprints. The cleaning crew must be conscientious. As she entered the large, well-lit lobby, her low-heeled sandals clicked on the marble tile floor. A young, blonde receptionist sat behind a horseshoe-shaped desk. At Maggie's approach, she smiled.

"May I help you?"

"I'm here to see Greg Vander Haar. He's expecting me. Maggie Sinclair?"

"Oh, my. I am so sorry about your brother. Mr. Vander Haar told everyone. Mr. Sinclair was a very nice man. Always friendly."

Clenching her teeth, Maggie nodded. She had to toughen up. Remembering her parents' funerals, she knew she would hear similar expressions of sympathy often. A moment of silence passed before the receptionist glanced down at her desk.

"I'll, uh, just call Mr. Vander Haar."

Minutes later, the president strode into the lobby. "Ms. Sinclair? Greg Vander Haar."

He extended his hand and offered perfunctory condolences. Another Dutchman, she surmised from his name and blond hair. Although she did wonder about the salon-styling. The Dutchmen she knew prided themselves on their thriftiness. Okay, they were cheap and proud of it.

Vander Haar was younger than she expected for a president, not much older than she. He couldn't be the founder. Too young. More than his age, though, convinced her. He gave the impression that he never ventured out into the plant. Too clean. Too much of a *suit*, as her dad used to say. A hands-on manager, Dad had little use for execs who only sat behind a desk.

Vander Haar led her down a short hall then stopped in front of an open door. "This is the office your brother used."

She glanced around the small room—which she expected

to be locked since an audit was in progress. It was equipped with a desk, a short bookcase, and a computer. But, no files or papers stacked or spread out. She knew her brother was a neat-freak, but surely he didn't put everything away each night. Or maybe he did, in the desk.

"After Ben Voorheis explained the situation," Greg Vander Haar said, "I went through this office and found nothing of a personal nature. Quite frankly, I could have saved you the trip and what must be a painful—yet, unnecessary—task."

Though his words were logical, his tone wasn't solicitous, more aggravated.

"If by chance you do find something of your brother's here," he continued, "I'm sure you will understand that I have to examine it before you remove anything from the premises."

"I understand." She figured he had to protect his company's property, but he didn't need to stand over her like a vulture ready to pounce on an unsuspecting mouse. Rather than think of herself as prey, she tried the drawers in the desk. Not locked. She found a handheld calculator she recognized. When she turned it over, a label indicated it was Jack's. In another drawer, she found a pen engraved with Sinclair & Voorheis Accounting and a straight-edge. Since that's what Jack called a ruler, so did she. The ruler, too, had the company name stamped on it.

"Voorheis assured me the audit would be completed. This . . . incident will delay its completion."

Her brother's death was an *incident*? She wanted to smack the smarmy son-of-a-bitch. Damn inconvenient of Jack to get himself killed before he finished that audit.

Fuming, she checked the bookcase and overhead storage unit. Nothing. Vander Haar didn't say I told you so, but she'd be willing to bet her season tickets to the West Michigan Whitecaps that he forced himself not to smirk.

She held up the items from the desk. "I believe these belonged to my brother. Would you like to check?"

At the shake of his head, she tucked them into her purse. She started toward the door then turned around, as if she'd just remembered something. "Is there a coat closet he would have used?"

"In this weather? I hardly think so. Why do you ask?"

"I can't find his briefcase and laptop."

"I would assume it was in his vehicle. He always took it with him when he left."

"I've already checked."

At that, his eyes narrowed. "Proprietary information about this company is on that computer," he said stiffly. "So, it had better turn up quickly, or I will hold your brother's company liable."

What a jerk.

Certain that something wasn't right about the accident, Maggie drove to the sheriff's office. She had to convince the deputy to reexamine the case. Mentally, she lined up her reasons to present them in an orderly—not emotional—fashion.

The deputy she'd talked to the day before wasn't there. *Crap.* She couldn't demand that he come in on his day off, so she talked to a different deputy. The older man mimicked her father with a "now don't worry your pretty, little head" comment. Her emotions almost did her in.

Gritting her teeth, she laid out her reasons for wanting the case reopened.

"Too many discrepancies," she said. "His briefcase and cell phone are missing, possibly stolen. His—"

"Whoa, there." The deputy tapped his desk. "Because something is missing, it doesn't follow that it was stolen. It's probably at your brother's home."

"I checked there. His office, too." Before the deputy could interrupt, she said, "And where he had been working. The briefcase and computer are missing. So is his cell phone."

She had to give the deputy points—he took notes.

"And I think someone searched his condo."

That snapped the deputy's head up. "Something was missing from there, too?"

"Nooo," she drew out. "Well, not exactly."

He put down his pen. So much for note taking.

"Ma'am." He folded his hands on top of his notepad. "You're grasping at straws."

"Do not dismiss me."

When she glanced around, others were staring at her. She must have raised her voice.

A younger man, dressed in plain clothes and maybe in his early forties, came out of an office and strode over to them. "Is there a problem?"

The deputy jumped to his feet. "No, sir. I'm trying to convince—"

"He's blowing me off."

"Investigator Tom Watson." He held out his hand.

She rose and shook hands with him. He had dark hair and kind eyes.

"Come into my office, ma'am. Deputy, the file?" The case file in his hand, he led Maggie into an office similar to the one she'd been in the afternoon before.

Without opening the file, he asked her to tell him about the accident. He sat back in a casual but alert manner, ready to listen

Encouraged by him, she told him what she knew. "The deputy I talked to yesterday said because of the fog and, possibly excess speed, my brother broke through the end of an already damaged guardrail and down the embarkment. His vehicle—a 2005 Blazer rolled over and into the river."

Proud that she'd gotten through the description without breaking down, she leaned forward. "The deputy said he wasn't wearing his seatbelt. My brother always wore his seatbelt. Always. The deputy also said the airbags must have been stolen before the accident and hadn't been replaced. He rationalized that the seatbelt and airbag could possibly have saved my brother's life."

With a grimace, Watson nodded but didn't respond.

"You have to understand. My brother wouldn't have let that happen. He's, I mean, he was a fanatic about keeping his vehicle in perfect order. We—his friends and I—used to tease him about being OCD. I don't believe he forgot to put on his seatbelt, or that he didn't have time to get his airbags replaced. He would've made time."

She stared pointedly at the investigator. He didn't blink.

Finally, he nodded. "What do you think happened?"

"I think there was foul play."

Watson blew out a breath. "I understand your concerns. It's natural that you'd want to make sense of a tragic situation." He opened the file. "Give me a couple of minutes to read the report."

He was placating her. She needed to tell him more, about the briefcase and the phone, about Jack's condo. But she held onto her impatience, giving him time to read.

When he finished, he gave her a small smile. "You described the incident well. Do you have more information that makes you think this wasn't an accident?"

"Yes." Finally, someone was willing to listen to her. "He always carried his cell phone. It wasn't in the vehicle. The deputy gave me his wallet but not the phone. Same with his briefcase and computer. Before you ask, I checked his condo, his place of business, and the company he was auditing. None of those items was there."

"So you've concluded that they were stolen?"

"Yes. One more thing. His condo was searched. And don't ask what was missing because I don't know. At least, I don't think so."

"Then why—"

"My brother was a neat freak. Everything had to be in order. A few things were out of place." She blew out a breath. "I know this isn't much, but I know my brother."

"Again, what is your conclusion?"

"That someone wanted something my brother had and made it look like an accident to cover up something."

Watson raised his left eyebrow. "That's some conclusion."

"And I think Jack might have been knocked out or given a drug to make him sleepy." She hadn't even told Drew that. It had come to her on the drive to Vander Haar Manufacturing. Jack wouldn't just drive off a bridge. Damn, she should've looked for skid marks on the bridge yesterday.

The man sat back, elbows on the chair arms, his fingers steepled. He appeared thoughtful. At least, he wasn't dismissing her. She waited. And waited while he reread the report.

"Ms. Sinclair, I'm sure our deputy did a good job examining the crash site. However," he added. He must have sensed her disagreement. "I will check this out. We have to wait for the results of the tox screen to come back to see if he was intoxicated."

"He wouldn't drink and—"

Watson held up his hand. "—or if he ingested anything. The coroner is very thorough. I'm certain she would notice an injection site, if there was one. In the meantime, if you discover anything else that's out of the ordinary, contact me." He gave her his card. Then he stood, indicating their meeting was over.

She rose. "Thank you for listening to me."

His firm handshake conveyed reassurance. "Ms. Sinclair, I am very sorry for your loss. I understand what a difficult time this is for you. I promise to be thorough. I will share whatever I can with you."

"That's all I ask. Thank you." She started to leave then turned back. "When will the coroner release my brother's body?"

"According to the notes here—" He tapped the file. "—it's already been released. The funeral home you chose has already been notified. The toxicology report will take three to four weeks."

"Weeks?"

"Depends on the backlog. I'll do what I can to speed up the process." His mouth twisted in a wry grin. "It's not like TV, where they have the report back within an hour or so. I will contact you if the coroner found anything out of the ordinary." He glanced at the file and recited her cell phone number. "Is that correct?"

"Yes, thank you."

Maggie felt better leaving the station than when she'd entered.

CHAPTER SIX

Ellen Campbell pitched a fit, right in the middle of the sidewalk. Beth's mother had called Drew at eleven to say the girls had finally gotten up and were eating breakfast. He walked over to the Oostveen's. He figured the ten-minute walk home with Ellen would help him ease into the bad news.

"You didn't even tell me Uncle Jack is dead!" Ellen cried. "How could you do that to me? While I was playing at Beth's, Uncle Jack was lying dead." Her voice rose until the birds in the park a half mile away heard.

Drew didn't point out Jack had been *lying dead* while they camped in the woods. "You couldn't have done anything, sweetheart. Whether you were playing or mourning, he would still be gone."

"You should have told me. I hate you!" Sobbing, she ran down the street in the older, established neighborhood of modest ranches and two-story houses.

Drew shoved his hand through his hair. Why did he always seem to do and say the wrong thing to her? Considering it was Monday, he hoped his neighbors were hard at work somewhere and not witnessing his daughter's temper tantrum.

Though Lillian had often insisted they could afford a bigger house with a more prestigious address, he'd held his ground. He liked the abundance of mature trees—something newer subdivisions were devoid of. The schools were good, shopping convenient. He had fond memories of growing up in the quiet neighborhood. Plus, the convenience of living a couple of blocks from his parents' house meant he could make sure they were okay, and they could fill in as a babysitter in an emergency.

One more factor made him glad he stayed. With leaving the firm, his income would be greatly reduced. He would've had to sell an expensive house and uproot Ellen a second time.

At the corner, instead of turning right toward their house, she went left. Toward Maggie Sinclair's. *Damn it*. He hated that Ellen turned away from him. Just like Lillian who always turned to her mother whenever she and Drew had problems.

He hadn't been able to stop his wife from shutting him out. He'd be damned if he let Ellen continue in her mother's footsteps. Maggie had railed at him endlessly over the weekend about not listening to his daughter. It was a little hard to listen when she wouldn't talk. Or ran away from him.

No more. He strode after Ellen then loped to catch up. He wasn't going to allow her to shut him out.

He knocked twice on the front screen door then let himself in the same way Ellen had, jerking extra hard on the sticky handle. Still sobbing, she stood wrapped in Maggie's arms. The woman glanced over the top of Ellen's head as if to say 'why aren't *you* comforting her?'

Gently clasping his daughter's shoulders, he turned her around and held her, surprised and grateful that Maggie let go. Lillian wouldn't have. "It's okay, sweetheart. Go ahead and cry."

While he rubbed her back and murmured what he hoped were soothing words, he noticed Maggie leave the room. He heard the screen to the slider close and realized she'd gone outside, giving him and Ellen time alone. A thoughtful and unexpected gesture.

Eventually, Ellen stopped crying and let him lead her to the couch. She snuggled up next to him. Neither said anything for a few minutes. Only a few hiccupping sighs broke the silence.

"Once upon a time," Drew began, "in a neighborhood far, far away . . ."

"Oh, Daddy. It was this neighborhood."

"Who's telling the story?" He squeezed her shoulder. "Anyway, two new kids moved in. Jack Sinclair, who was eight like me, and—"

"—his bratty little sister, Maggie." Ellen giggled as she looked toward the slider through which they could see Maggie sitting at a table on the deck. She had her feet up on another chair and a book in front of her face. A minute or two later, Drew realized she hadn't turned a page.

He went on with his story. "Jack thought he was hot stuff. Of course, I had to show him who was king of the hill in *my* neighborhood."

When he paused, Ellen asked, on cue, "What did you do?"

"I rammed him into a tree."

Again, on cue, she asked, "And what did Gramma do?"

"What Gramma always did. She stayed inside so no one would know her kid was the neighborhood bully." His mother, the queen of denial.

Ellen snorted. "That's Gramma."

"Now," Drew continued. "Once Jack learned that I was King Arthur . . ."

". . . he played Lancelot."

"I was the Lone Ranger . . ."

". . . and he was Tonto."

He tried a new one. "Don Quixote?"

"Sancho Panza."

Surprised she knew that one, he said, "Heard this story before, have you?"

"About a hundred times." She stayed glued to his side. "Only the way Unc—" She faltered. "—Uncle Jack told it, he *let* you win."

Drew rubbed his knuckles on the top of her head. "Wishful thinking, on his part."

They talked about his and Jack's childhood, the terrors of the neighborhood. Then, before it got mawkish, he levered himself off the couch. "Why don't you ask Maggie if she wants to go to Mickie D's for lunch?"

Ellen bounced to her feet, all trace of tears gone— probably wiped on his golf shirt. "Gee, Dad. Last of the big spenders."

"Just keeping up the Dutch tradition."

Her mouth turned down. "Sometimes, I wish we were Dutch. 'Cause *if you aren't Dutch—*"

"—*you aren't much*," he finished a saying popular among the natives of West Michigan, especially from Grand Rapids to Holland. "But, we Scots are as good or . . ."

"... better." She laughed.

When she dashed out to the deck, Drew strolled around the living room. How different it was from when he and Jack were growing up, when he raced in and out of this house the same way Jack had raced in and out of his. The living room, decorated in bold colors, reflected Maggie's personality. Blues, reds, greens. No wimpy pastels, like her mother's decor. A wicker basket on the coffee table held a collection of artificial apples—wood, ceramic, even marble apples. He smiled. Apples for the teacher.

Oak bookcases were crammed full, a wide variety of books from reference books to history to classics plus several popular fiction novels. A massive entertainment center, also oak, held an assortment of sophisticated electronics—flatscreen television, CD changer, DVD player, and a receiver connecting them all. Yet, dainty knickknacks and small needlework pictures added softening touches. Whimsical wallpaper—dancing teapots—decorated the area above white wainscoting in the eating area and continued on the soffits above the kitchen cabinets. That he remembered from his youth. Lillian abhorred wallpaper. Yet, the whimsy also reflected the Maggie he remembered from childhood.

On top of the spinet piano near the front door stood picture frames—Maggie, her parents, and Jack—unusual since he was the self-appointed photographer. Several pictures were of Trish Morrow and what he recognized as the camping group. In the more recent pictures, Ellen seemed happier than he'd seen her since her mother died. Toward the back, he saw a picture of himself at eighteen, standing with Jack in front of the Blazer. That was the day they'd left for college. How young they were back then.

Young and stupid. At least, he was. He remembered their first visit home. The day he'd hurt Maggie.

She and Ellen came in through the slider, interrupting that painful memory of his clumsiness. He caught sight of Ellen's eyes swimming with tears as she brushed past him and beat it into the half bath next to the garage door.

Maggie put her hand in the middle of Drew's chest, forcing him backwards into the living room. *Aw, shit.* She was going to read him the riot act again. *What did I do now?*

"Nicely done, Drew," she said softly. "You didn't dismiss her grief. You handled her well."

Her praise came as a pleasant surprise. He scrubbed a hand down his face. "I appreciated the privacy."

She shrugged. "You needed it. It's about time—"

"You two aren't arguing again, are you?" Ellen came around the corner, her hair damp around the edges. She must have splashed cold water on her face. "It was so embarrassing on the camping trip this weekend, I wanted to die."

"Eighth graders can be quite melodramatic," Maggie drawled.

"Hey, I finished eighth grade, so, technically, I'm a freshman," Ellen retorted.

"Even worse." Maggie winked at Drew. "I'm just glad I have enough seniority I don't have to teach ninth graders anymore."

"I can't believe I'm old enough to have a kid starting high school." Drew groaned.

"Poor Daddy. Want me to get your cane?"

"All the better to beat you with, my dear." He glared at her with mock menace.

"Child abuse. Child abuse," Ellen chanted, dancing around him and Maggie.

Her abrupt mood swing disconcerted Drew. Yet, he was glad to see her teasing instead of crying.

"Child abuse isn't something to joke about." Maggie's comment sobered them all. Then, her expression quickly changed. "About lunch—"

"I'm not really hungry," Ellen cut in. "Beth's mom made pancakes and sausage. You *old* people can go." She ignored the lethal glares both he and Maggie shot at her. "I'll stay here and listen to music, if that's okay. Dad, Maggie has the sweetest sound system. Oh, and can I borrow some more CDs?"

"That's not necessary," Drew interjected.

"It's all right," Maggie said. "She's careful and always returns them."

"I didn't know—"

Ellen cut off his rebuke. "Thanks, Maggie. You're the

greatest." She opened the side cabinet of the entertainment center and began rifling through racks of CDs. Like Jack, Maggie enjoyed music. Even though she'd been a rough-and-tumble tomboy, she took piano lessons and, if he remembered from the recitals Jack had dragged him to, could play well.

"I'll take a raincheck on lunch," she said to Drew then motioned him to follow her out to the kitchen. "I need to talk to you."

"You'd better not fight," Ellen warned right before hard metal rock music blared from the surround sound speakers. A far cry from "Fur Elyse."

"Whoa." Ellen appeared in the archway. She had to shout above the music. "I didn't know you liked Metallica." Her voice held a mixture of surprise and awe.

"Jack must have left his CD here." An anguished look crossed Maggie's face, then disappeared just as quickly. "Turn it down a bit. The hearing you save may be my own."

"Mine, too," Drew added.

"Old people." Ellen flounced back to the living room. She lowered the volume . . . about half a decibel.

Maggie filled a tall glass with ice then grabbed a pitcher of tea from the refrigerator. "Let's go out on the deck so we don't have to shout to make ourselves heard."

Drew held the slider open for her. A half-finished glass of tea sweated on the round glass-top table. The tents and sleeping bag were gone, apparently packed away until the next time. This weekend, he remembered with dismay. He hoped she canceled. Because of her grief, of course. Then, he wondered when he started lying to himself. Walking over to first the Oostveen's then to Maggie's made him stretch still-hurting muscles.

Unlike the hot, sticky weekend, it had turned into a beautiful late June day. Clear skies, low eighties, little humidity. Maggie wore khaki shorts and a red scoop-neck sleeveless shirt that showed off light tan lines midway down her arms from the T-shirts she'd worn over the weekend. Not like the sunburn on his arms and neck. Wearing a tie tomorrow would be a bitch. He hadn't even thought about sunblock for the weekend. His bottle had a permanent place in his golf bag. Who thought about sunblock while walking through a forest, for God's sake? Apparently, Maggie did because she reminded the girls to slather up often. Like a lot of preparations for the weekend, he'd learned too late the value of that missed planning meeting. But after the scoldings he'd received, he'd be damned if he showed his regret over missing it.

Standing next to the railing on Maggie's deck, shaded by a large maple, he gazed at the spacious backyard where he and Jack played endless games of tag and wrestled on the ground. It was under that maple he'd tromped on Maggie's ego more than once.

God, he'd been such an ass.

When he turned around, Maggie gave him a questioning look. The last thing he wanted to do was tell her what he was thinking.

"You have a beautiful garden," he said over his shoulder. "Must take a lot of work."

She smiled. "It's worth it. Since Mom started all the perennials, it feels like she left a part of herself behind."

As he thought about how different their mothers were, he concentrated on the flowerbeds bursting with pink, red, and white peonies and the toppled irises that had finished blooming for the year. He worked hard not to think about what an ass he'd been at eighteen and paid particular attention to the fanciful ceramic figures that always graced her mother's garden. He even noticed the hard-packed earth around the plants from the dry spell.

Her swinging foot caught his eye. Despite his efforts to look everywhere except at her long, bare legs—bare feet, too—he fixed his gaze on the hanging baskets of red and white trailing geraniums. But not before catching sight of red nail polish on her toes. He never thought about tomboy Maggie Sinclair doing something so feminine as painting her toenails.

Maybe she wasn't a tomboy anymore.

Ellen slid open the screen door. "Dad, I just remembered. Beth asked if I could go to the pool with her this afternoon."

"I took the day off to be with you." At her pained

expression, he said, "But, if you really want to . . ."

"Da-ad." She huffed while tapping her foot.

He made a shooing motion. "Go. Have fun."

Ellen couldn't leave fast enough.

So much for helping Ellen with her grief and working on the dad-daughter relationship today. He'd known she would be upset about Jack. Since he'd been the closest thing to a brother, Drew encouraged her to call him Uncle. Lillian hadn't approved. According to her, only *true* relatives should be given the title of aunt and uncle.

One of the few times Drew had contradicted her, besides the house.

He flung himself into a deck chair across from Maggie. "So much for our dad-and-daughter bonding. Just like the weekend."

"Is that why you volunteered?" Her gaze held no recrimination. Only interest.

He nodded. "I assumed she and I would walk side-by-side, even hand-in-hand. Like we used to when she was little."

Maggie chuckled. "She's fourteen."

"And . . ."

"Peers are more important than parents."

"I miss the closeness we used to have. Since Lillian died . . ."

"Give her time. She's still working through her grief. During breaks in our meetings and sometimes afterwards, she talks about her mother."

That got to him. "Damn it. Why won't she talk to me?"

Maggie hesitated. "Because she's afraid you'll be sad. And . . . lately she's been mad at Lillian and doesn't want you to know."

"Mad?"

"One of the stages of grief. I'm surprised you didn't know."

With a grimace, he said, "I do know. I didn't realize Ellen was mad at her mother. Is she mad because Lillian died?"

"That and other things. She's taken Lillian off the pedestal she put her on after she died and talking about her in, uh, an unflattering way."

"What do you mean by *unflattering*?"

Maggie leaned forward on the edge of her seat. "When a person close to you dies, at first, you only remember the good things, the fun times. Gradually, you become more realistic. Ellen's in that realistic stage. When the other girls complain about their moms not letting them go to concerts or some such thing, Ellen complains, too. That's only recently. My opinion is that she's coming to terms with her mother's passing."

"You sound so objective about grief and the stages. How are you—"

"—dealing with my own grief?" She leaned back in her chair, her shoulders slumped. "I'm dealing."

He took a long gulp of the watered-down tea and waited. She remained silent, lost in her thoughts.

"What are you reading?" He pointed to the book on the table, hoping to distract them both from thinking about Jack. "A science fiction romance. Very interesting. You might like it."

He chuckled. "I don't think so."

"Why? You always liked sci-fi. Is it because I mentioned the word romance?"

"The kiss of death for a good science fiction novel?"

"Not for some of us. We like relationship stories along with the adventure."

He'd better get off that topic. "Would you like me to go with you to Jack's office? To check there for his briefcase?"

She straightened in her seat. "I cleaned out his office this morning."

"God, Maggie. First the Blazer and now his office? Are you a glutton for punishment? Where's your sack cloth and ashes?"

"I'm saving them for the funeral." Her glare could've cut diamonds.

He held up his hand. "Okay, okay. What about the funeral arrangements? Would you like me to go with you to the funeral home or have you done that, too?"

"Cut the sarcasm, Campbell. I'm having a tough time here."

Instantly regretting his attitude, he reached across the

table and clasped her hand. "I'm sorry, Maggie. This is a tough time for me, too."

The twisted sheets and blanket on the floor of his bedroom gave evidence to how he'd spent most of the night. His best friend gone. Forever. And the one chance he'd had to connect, he'd been too busy to call him back.

"I made the funeral arrangements this morning," she said in a matter-of-fact voice. "Visitation Wednesday, private burial on Thursday. You and Ellen are . . . were about the closest to him, I thought . . ." Her voice trailed off.

So, the matter-of-fact tone was just a façade. He should have known. "We'll be there."

Maggie gave him a small smile of appreciation. "You said you'd call his friends."

"I have and will call the ones nearby again now that I know the arrangements." He finished his diluted tea. "You've done quite a bit this morning. Anything else I should know about?"

She shrugged.

Something in the way she averted his gaze made him push for details. "You're not telling me everything."

Her mouth twisted in chagrin. "I might have stopped at the sheriff's office."

"Might have?" This was worse than getting Ellen to talk.

"The new investigator said he'd looked into the accident."

"What new investigator?"

She squirmed, took a long swallow of tea, then sat up straight. "The investigator at the sheriff's office." She looked like she was about to say more then clamped her mouth shut.

Leaning forward, forearms on the glass-top table, he eyed her with a stare that litigants paid attention to. "Go on."

She let her head flop back and closed her eyes. "Are you badgering me?"

"If you have to ask, I'm not doing a good enough job."

"You aren't going to like this."

"I'll be the judge of that. Tell me."

Shifting in her seat, she stared off to the left then the right. Just not at him. "I stopped at the sheriff's office *after* I went to Vander Haar Manufacturing."

94

"You what?"

Maggie gulped. "I said I—"

"I heard what you said. I can't believe you went up there." He rubbed the back of his neck. "We'll talk about Vander Haar later. First, I want to hear about your visit to the sheriff."

As she wondered about her self-destructive tendencies, Maggie knew she shouldn't have brought up her trip that morning. Drew's demand that she tell him everything got her dander up. She should throw him out of her house. Tell him never to return. Instead, she groused, "When did you get so bossy?"

"Maggie?" Again, a demand.

"All right, already." She told him about the uncooperative deputy and then about Tom Watson. "He paid attention to me, Drew. He took notes and promised to look into the case. I believe he will."

Drew covered her hand. The warmth of his hand conveyed strength and gentleness, something she'd been in short supply of even from Jack. Again, she pulled away. He was too darn bossy.

"I hope he wasn't placating you. That he will reexamine the case. If only to reassure you that nothing nefarious is going on." He seemed sincere enough, until he said, "Tell me about your visit to Vander Haar Manufacturing."

She wasn't fooled by his low, controlled tone. Ignoring his question didn't seem like a good option. Who was she kidding? She always had options. Instead of being intimidated by his bossiness, she could *choose* what to tell him.

"I wanted to check the office he was using there to search for his briefcase and computer." She stuck out her chin. "I'm taking care of my brother's business."

He stared at her with narrowed eyes. "You should have told me before you went."

After getting out of the chair, he walked around the table and stood in front of her. His intimidation tactics might work on prosecuting attorneys and battling plaintiffs, but nobody could out-intimidate a high school English teacher. At least, not *this* high school English teacher.

She jumped to her feet. "Well, golly, gee whiz. I didn't know I had to get your permission."

"Quit being such a smart-ass." He rubbed the back of his neck again. "Jesus Christ, I can't believe you went up there alone."

"And you criticize me for swearing?"

His mouth opened as if he wanted to say more but changed his mind. For a second. "Who did you talk to up there?" He leaned toward her—another intimidation tactic.

Without backing up, she assumed a nonchalant pose, even though she felt far from nonchalant. "Am I being interrogated?"

"Just tell me who you talked to." His tone wasn't the least bit approachable. *Damn.*

She folded her arms and cocked her head to the side. "Have I ever mentioned how much I detest being told what to do?"

"You might have mentioned it a few times when Jack and I tried to save your ass when you were a snot-nose kid."

"For your information, Mr. Hot-Shot Attorney, I'm not a kid anymore."

He stepped back and gave her a long look, all the way down her bare legs to her bare feet. She forced herself not to curl her toes.

"Yeah, I noticed," he mumbled, before quickly returning to his chair.

"What's that supposed to mean?"

"Exactly what I said. I noticed you aren't a kid anymore." He gave her an even longer look.

This one was so hot, it fried several brain cells. Maggie gripped the back of her chair so she wouldn't wave her hand in front of her face like a fan. Her toes curled without permission, and all she could say was, "Oh."

"Even as a kid, you weren't this stubborn," he went on, totally unaware that she was having flashes so hot she could scorch the deck. "And you never had such a mouth on you."

"Back to trading insults?"

Now that he was sitting, she strolled over to the corner of

the deck. She deadheaded the ivy geraniums in the hanging basket, tossing the dead leaves and buds into the grass below. Putting some distance between them wasn't much better. Even though she stood with her back to him, she knew he still stared at her. From any other man, that type of scrutiny meant lust. Not from Drew Campbell, though. He still treated her like a kid sister.

"Why are you so concerned that I went to the plant alone?" she asked lightly as she turned to face him. Placing her hands behind her on the rail, she leaned back.

"Did you meet Greg Vander Haar?"

Just like a lawyer—answer a question with a question.

She considered a different approach—since demanding hadn't worked. Maybe if she gave a little, he would give a little. And maybe she would discover more about what set him off. "Yes. He showed me where Jack was working. I didn't find anything. I'm sure he emptied the office before I came. Ben told him I was coming."

"How is Ben?"

Thank goodness, he changed the subject. "Very upset about Jack. He cried."

"They were that close?"

"Not as close as you and Jack, and you didn't cry."

He cast her a glance that made her mentally squirm. "How do you know?"

Clamping her mouth shut, she lowered her eyes. "I'm sorry."

The man hurt, almost as much as she did. They each tamped down their grief and discussed other topics. Anything to keep their sorrow at bay. Instead of carping at each other, or in his case, bossing her, they should unite and share their heartache.

"My case—one of my last ones—involves that company." He held up his hand when she started to ask for more details. "I can't tell you. Client confidentiality. Tell me what you thought of Junior Vander Haar."

"Junior?" She smiled, thinking about Mr. Yuppy President. "I can talk to you about him, but you can't talk to me?"

He gave her a smug smile. "Different circumstances."

Even though she hated smugness, she caved. "He seemed more perturbed that the audit wouldn't be done quickly than the fact that his auditor died after working late at his plant."

Drew nodded pensively. "I'm not surprised."

Okay, he knew something. "Is it because he's an asshole or is there another reason you're pissed off that I went up there and talked to him?"

He clucked worse than a prissy spinster. "Language, Ms. Sinclair. For a teacher, you certainly have a potty mouth. What kind of an example is that for your students."

"My students aren't here right now," she snapped before she realized his intent. He deflected her question by making her mad. "Nice try. Tell me what you know about Vander Haar or . . ." She paused to think up a good punishment.

A grin creased his face. "Or, what? You'll have the girls take me on a snipe hunt next time and lose me in the woods?"

"You know about snipe hunts?" In her surprise, she didn't keep the disappointment out of her voice.

His eyes turned murderously dark. "On my first—and only—camping trip when I was nine years old, the older boys introduced me to that particular *game.* They let me sit in the dark for hours waiting for a fictitious animal. And your rotten brother was in on it."

She let his teasing comment about Jack slide because she knew how much her brother loved a good prank.

"Darn." She snapped her fingers. "A snipe hunt had possibilities. Let's see. What would be a fitting punishment if you don't talk to me about Vander Haar?" She pretended to muse.

"How about making me walk twice as far as last weekend? Never mind. You're going to do that anyway." He snapped his fingers in mocking imitation of her gesture. "I've got it. You'll tie me naked over an ant hill."

"If I was going to tie you naked anywhere, Campbell, it wouldn't be on an ant hill." *Oh, God, did she just say that?*

"Ah." He grinned. "A little BDSM?"

"Would you like some more tea?"

"I can't wait to hear this. Tell me, Maggie May, where

would you tie me naked?"

"Are you calling me Maggie May just to irritate me? You know how much I hate that name."

"Every time I hear that song I think of you." A whimsical expression crossed his features. Then it was gone. "Where were we? Oh, yes. Tying me naked somewhere. Care to elaborate?"

Maggie stayed outside after Drew left. His teasing at the end discombobulated her. From his expression, it had also discombobulated him. Whatever possessed him to talk about her tying him to an anthill? Naked. Their joking had taken a weird turn, into flirting.

Maggie Sinclair never flirted. Flirting got her into trouble. That's how things started with Roger. They went downhill from there.

Instead of thinking about flirting and Drew, she remembered how he'd dealt with his daughter. He might be a slow learner, but he was teachable. She propped her feet up on the vacated chair. As she told him, he handled the situation with Ellen just right. With the slider to the eating area open and across from the living room, she'd heard most of the story he told Ellen—and smiled again at the *bratty, little sister* comment.

As Drew told the stories about him and Jack, a wave of grief had washed over her. She would never joke with her brother again. Never rag on him about his OCD ways. Then, nostalgia hit, and she thought about the fights she used to have with her brother when he wouldn't let her play with the boys. She'd been a wiry little kid, not gaining her height of five-nine until she was Ellen's age.

Even though Maggie was three years younger than the boys, by the time she was nine, she could pin Jack to the ground. She would sit on his chest and beat on her laughing brother with her small fists until Drew dragged her off. Then, the boys would race off on their bikes thinking they could escape. Since she could pedal faster, she caught up with them anyway. When Jack tattled at suppertime that she was always hanging around, Dad would ground her for risking her neck .

. . and then ground Jack for letting her. After the second time, Jack learned not to tattle.

Mom mitigated Dad's old-fashioned protectiveness of his *baby* girl by encouraging Maggie to spread her wings. Mom didn't actually defy Dad. She had a way of working around his dictates.

Despite her dad's efforts, Maggie was determined to show everyone she could take care of herself, that she was as good as the boys. On the empty lot where they played baseball, she could outthrow, outrun, and outhit most of the boys, including Jack and Drew. They only let her join them because the other team wanted her on their side.

High school had been torture. Senior Jack decided to emulate Dad. He made sure all the boys knew that if they messed with his freshman sister, they'd answer to him. And, that rat Drew Campbell backed him up. They might just as well have locked her in a nunnery for all the dates she had. The following year, the guys left for Northern Michigan University in the Upper Peninsula, and she thought things would ease up. They were nearly five hundred miles away, for heaven's sake. But, the boys she went to school with were always leery that Jack would come back and clean their clocks, and that Drew would help him. She had the most chaste dates in the history of her high school.

Maggie dropped her feet. No more traipsing down memory lane. She had too much to do.

But, her initial rush to deal with everything last night and this morning left her at a loss as to what to do next. She walked through the house to her old bedroom that she'd turned into an office. Last week, she'd dumped the crates she brought home from school there. She knew she'd have to empty out and sell Jack's condo, deal with his finances, find out the provisions for his business.

How was that for a switch? Maggie taking care of details. But, after packing up his office, Maggie wasn't sure she wanted to deal with her brother's home. Yet.

She sat on the floor and pulled one of the crates closer. Sorting handouts and making tentative lesson plans for the fall seemed like a good idea right now. Better than thinking about Jack's death and/or resurrecting thoughts of the past .

.. as she'd done out on the deck.

Because if she did, she was going to remember the summer she turned fifteen. *Oh, damn it.* She *was* going to remember what she'd thought of at the time as the worst moment of her life. Little did she know that worse moments were yet to come.

Like an idiot, she recalled the day she flirted with Drew and tried to convince him to teach her how to kiss. She'd even thought her ploy was working. Despite her inexperience, she was sure he responded. Until he disengaged her hands from around his neck, patted her on the head, and cautioned her to practice on boys her own age before trying out for the major leagues. He was a college man now and didn't waste time on naïve little innocents. Then, he hit her with the most devastating critique—she kissed like a guppy.

As the memory of humiliation rushed over her, she pulled out a folder and glanced at its contents. Memories were a bitch.

"Do you always leave your front door open?"

CHAPTER SEVEN

"Jesus Jenny!" Maggie scrambled to her knees. When she realized it was Drew Campbell standing in the doorway, her heart settled down to three hundred beats per minute. "You scared the shit out of me."

"Tsk, tsk, tsk. Swearing again?"

"Stick a sock in it, Campbell. You already got on my case for swearing. And don't ever sneak up on me like that again." She would be mortified if he knew the direction of her thoughts before he walked in.

"I know this is a safe neighborhood, but you should keep your doors locked even when you're home."

"You are absolutely right." She settled back down on the floor. "*Anybody* could just walk in."

Ignoring her jibe, he looked around the room. "Are you sure you weren't switched at birth? Jack Sinclair couldn't have a messy sister. And, by the way, I knocked on the screendoor since your doorbell apparently isn't working. I even called out."

"I thought I locked the screen." How far down memory lane had she gone not to hear him call to her? "I meant to replace the doorbell, and I will. Next week."

"I could do that for you."

"No need. Besides, I guess my mind wasn't in this room. It sort of took a hike all by itself." Right. A not-so-thrilling hike into memories.

He sagged dramatically against the doorjamb. For a moment, he looked boyish, playful almost. Like the Drew Campbell she used to know, not the buttoned-down professional Lillian had turned him into.

"Do not mention the word *hike*," he groaned. "Every muscle I own aches from the weekend."

"Like I said, you have to get into shape." Not that his shape wasn't darn good already. She glanced up at his long legs encased in summer-weight wool trousers. A narrow black belt provided a sharp delineation between his crisp white shirt and subtle gray trousers. He was even wearing a tie, for heaven's sake.

Wait a minute. He wore khakis and a green golf shirt earlier. Good grief, how long had she been daydreaming?

"Geez, Campbell, you didn't need to get all dressed up for me." Because she hated looking up at him, she rose with what she hoped was a modicum of grace. She flicked the end of the dark gray tie with flecks of red. "Whoa, that tie must have set you back a few buckaroos. Hermes?" She deliberately mispronounced the name so that it sounded like the Greek god.

Red tinged his ears. *Oh, goody.* Payback time.

"And your shirt? French linen?" She was mocking him and, from his expression, he knew it. Just like when they were kids.

"Oh, it's French, all right." He loosened the tie and unbuttoned the collar. "JC Penné." He unbuttoned the cuffs then turned back the sleeves.

She snorted. "Ri-ight. As if Lillian would let you wear anything so plebeian." She clapped her hand over her mouth. Criticizing his dead spouse was too much. "I am so sorry. Maybe you can find another shoe for me to put in my mouth."

He shook his head. "You're doing fine all by yourself. And you're right. No JC Penney's for Lillian."

An awkward silence ensued that she broke. "So . . . why are you back here? Forget something?"

He stuck his hand in his right trouser pocket and began to jingle his keys or coins. "I, uh, wanted to see if you were okay. You seemed rather . . . lost before I took off."

Lost? He had no right to be so perceptive.

"Thanks for your concern, but, as you can see, I have things to do." She waved to the crates and papers scattered across the floor. "Weren't the girls going to the pool? I figured since you enjoy 'better living through chemistry' that you'd join them and swim, too."

He didn't rise to her bait. Instead, he stepped over a crate, avoided the papers, and sat in her desk chair. "I stopped by. The girls are having a great time." He hunched over and rested his forearms on his thighs. "They think I went to the office."

"What did Ellen say when you told her you were going to work?"

"She pitched a fit worthy of a two-year-old," he said in disgust. "Almost as good as the one earlier when she ran sobbing through the neighborhood. She said I never have time for her."

"And you said . . ." she prompted.

"That she had a lot of nerve complaining when she'd made plans to go to the pool."

"Aannk. Wrong answer, Campbell." *Wasn't he ever going to understand?* "You were supposed to seize that opportunity and explain to her why you're working so hard."

"She's a kid."

"Actually, she's not. She's a young woman, and you'd do well to remember that."

"Lecture over?"

Maggie clamped her mouth shut. She had to quit yammering about parental responsibilities. "Yes, the lecture is over. Why did you really come here?"

"I told you I was concerned about you."

"No need." She studied the shine on his black dress shoes and wondered if he used a brush or a buffing cloth. She tried to think of something other than his long legs stretched out near her and how his suit pants showed off his strong thighs and—

"Why do you think I came back?" Drew needled.

When heat rose in her face, she rifled through the crate, pulled out a folder, and started to count the hand-outs . . . all the while keeping her head down.

"Are you hoping if you ignore me, I'll go away?" He sounded so damn smug.

Hoping the red had left her cheeks, she lifted her head. "Would it help?"

"No." He grinned. "What's with all the papers and folders? I thought school was out for the summer."

"It is."

He shot her a deliberately mocking expression. "You

teachers have it so easy. Six-hour work days. Three months off in the summer."

"That's so original." She wouldn't give him the satisfaction of a retort. But, she had to recount the papers.

"I was just ragging on you. About the short days and the vacations. Jack told me about the long hours you put in before classes start and long after school's out. And how much work you bring home to do at night."

"Was that revenge for me ragging on you about how ill-prepared you were for the camping trip?" She gave him a quick smile.

"Something like that." He shifted in the chair. "What *are* you doing?"

"I'm getting ready for the fall. I need to figure out what I have and what new pieces I need to make." She wrote sixteen on a sticky note and pasted it on the front of the folder. She definitely needed to copy more of that quiz.

"I'm surprised you're even thinking about school at a time like this," he snapped.

She couldn't believe he'd criticized her. As she glared at him, red crept up his neck.

"I'm sorry. I shouldn't have said that. Whatever helps put aside your grief." When she returned to counting, he said, "I did the same when Lilian died, resorted to bringing work home to do after Ellen went to bed. I couldn't stand the long hours alone. It became a habit, and I continued as I cleaned up my case load."

"That's why Ellen thinks you don't care about her."

He winced. "Tell me what you're doing. I promise not to make fun."

Since he appeared sincere, and embarrassed about criticizing her, she told him. "I'm working up plans for next year. For instance, I think I'm going to have the kids do a comparison of women's roles in Shakespeare's plays. I haven't done that since my first or second year teaching." She made a note on the legal pad on the floor next to her.

"Why don't you use what you used before?" His sarcasm was gone. "You've taught the same classes for . . . how many years now? Eleven?" He seemed genuinely interested.

"Twelve. If I did the same thing over and over again,

taught the same way, used the same lesson plans and hand-outs, it would be stale. I'd lose the kids' interest. I don't reinvent the wheel each year, but I make sure my work is fresh—that I'm fresh."

"I never considered that." He watched her work for a few minutes.

"Tell me about *Junior* Vander Haar." She wasn't going to let him distract her this time.

"You aren't going to give up, are you?"

"Nope."

"You're almost as tenacious as Jack."

"Terriers run in the family. You should see my aunts."

"How are they? Still treating you like you're ten?"

"Of course." Maggie gave a moment's thought to her mother's sisters. They meant well. The fact that they didn't have children never deterred them from giving her mother advice on childrearing. After Maggie's mother died, they doubled their efforts to *parent* her. Especially last night when she called about—

"Damn it," she said. "You are doing it again."

"What?"

"Trying to distract me. What about Greg Vander Haar? Your secretiveness makes me imagine the worst. Is he a criminal? Does he have mob ties?"

"Good grief, no." Drew blew out a breath. "I've been Vander Haar Senior's attorney since I began working at the firm. He started the company thirty years ago, built it up from scratch. Three years ago, his doctor told him to take it easy. His wife wanted to travel. Consequently, he turned the business over to Junior."

"And?" she prompted.

"I wondered about your perception of Junior." He gave her an innocent look that didn't fool her for a moment.

"Right, and if I believe you're just *wondering*, you have a bridge to sell—" She broke off. The picture of the Mackinac Bridge from Jack's office. "Wait here."

She jumped up, no grace this time, hopped over a crate, and rushed into her bedroom. She'd stacked most of the boxes from Jack's office in his old bedroom. They didn't all fit since he'd never emptied out that room. The box with the pictures had to go in her bedroom.

"Oh, my God. Now, I'm convinced you can't be Jack's sister." He'd followed her to what used to be her parents' bedroom. It had taken her over a year after her dad died to move in, despite Jack's encouragement. And another year before she began to make changes.

Drew Campbell stood in the doorway, surveying her bedroom.

Where was a convenient hole to crawl into? Her camping clothes lay in a heap where she'd dropped them last night. Used tissues from her crying jag decorated her nightstand along with her iPad and the two novels she was in the process of reading—somewhat simultaneously—a young adult fiction and a biography. The bookmarks showed her progress in each, with the YA winning the race.

Her bed—rumpled yellow flowered sheets, pale yellow blanket hanging half on the floor—and squashed pillows gave evidence to her sleepless night.

Maybe Campbell was right. Maybe she had been switched at birth and her brother's perfect sister had grown up in a house of messies wondering how she'd gotten there.

The silence stretched between them, making her even more aware that they were in her bedroom. The unmade bed, instead of being just messy, made the room more intimate. She kicked her purple panties under the bed and hoped he didn't notice.

She hastily knelt on the floor next to the boxes and pawed through the pictures she'd taken off Jack's wall. Finally, she found the right one and gave it to Drew. "I thought you'd like to have this."

"The Mackinac Bridge." He stared at the picture Jack had taken of the five-mile suspension bridge that linked Michigan's Lower and Upper Peninsulas. Creamy white towers and green steelwork below the roadway provided a sharp contrast to the blue sky and the blue of the straits where Lakes Michigan and Huron merged.

"How many times did we drive over this going back and forth to college?" he mused. "In the rain when we couldn't even see the towers. When it was so snow-covered we had to drive on the damn grating in the middle that drove me crazy from the noise. When it wasn't windy enough for them to close the bridge, yet we thought for sure we'd get swept over the side in his Blazer."

Maggie began to think it wasn't such a good idea to give him the picture.

"All those times we drove over this." Drew rapped the glass with his knuckle. "And he drives off a piddly-shit bridge in the fog."

Drew took the picture out to the living room and propped it against the back of the sofa. For several moments, he stared at it while memories rushed through his mind. They'd been so innocent on that first trip to college. They'd packed Jack's new Blazer with their gear and set off on what they thought would be a big adventure in the Upper Peninsula. The U.P. was nothing like he'd imagined. Jack knew because of all the camping trips his family had gone on up there.

Not Drew.

His mother wanted him to attend U of M. His dad, Michigan State. He stayed out of the rivalry and followed Jack to Northern Michigan University, disappointing both his parents. Northern was the farthest place away from home to go to college and stay in state, except for Michigan Tech in Hancock. Drew wasn't cut out for engineering, neither was Jack. He recalled the fun they'd had skiing and snowboarding in the winter. In the summer, they dived off the cliffs into the icy waters of Lake Superior. His mother would've freaked if she's known.

Being an only child meant his mother didn't just dote on him, she smothered. Or tried to. She was the original Helicopter Mom. Thanks to Jack, he had a fairly normal childhood. The kind he wanted for Ellen. But where his mother left off, Lillian had begun. Only her concerns were more about image than overprotection. Drew had stood up to his wife when Ellen wanted to join the camping group. Seeing her closeness to the other girls over the past weekend convinced him he'd done the right thing.

If only his dad had stood up to Mom after the Cub Scout

camping trip.

Water under the bridge. Long under the bridge.

"Thinking about Jack?"

Maggie must have come up behind him. He nodded before turning around.

"We had some good times up there, in Marquette." He cleared his suddenly clogged throat. "What can I do to help you?"

She hesitated.

"Maggie, you don't have to handle everything. It's okay to lean on someone on occasion."

She patted his hand then slipped to the side, away from his clasp. "I know."

"How about that lunch?"

"I don't . . ."

"Get dressed." He glanced at her shorts and tank top. "Or not. You haven't eaten lunch. You need to keep your strength up." He slapped his forehead with the heel of his palm. "I just sounded like my mother."

She laughed. "Yeah, you did. All right. Give me a few minutes."

While waiting for her, Drew paced her living room then to the front door. He made a note in his phone to get a new doorbell for her then checked the screendoor latch. Using a tool on his pocketknife, he straightened a piece then tried the latch. It worked. To make sure it locked and stayed locked, he tried it several times.

"Having fun, Campbell?"

Heat crept up his neck to his ears. "Your latch works fine now. No strange people walking in on you, just be sure to lock it." He folded his knife and stuffed it into his pocket.

"What's that? Wait a minute. Was that a Swiss Army knife?"

"Yes."

"It looks like the one Dad gave Jack."

"Your dad gave me one, too. I guess he thought I should *be prepared.*"

She grinned at his double entendre. When she smiled, her blue eyes glinted in amusement. "I know you weren't a Boy Scout."

"I can still be prepared. In fact, that little knife has come in handy many times." He noticed she'd changed—white slacks and sandals, a navy top with white trim. "You clean up well."

"It's been known to happen. Are we going, or are you planning to fix anything else?"

"Depends on what needs fixing." He stared at her for several seconds. "Any more loose latches or faulty locks?"

"I take care of my house." She gave him an affronted look.

"Sorry. No aspersions cast on your homeowner maintenance. I just meant if you have any other fix-it projects, I'd be happy to help." He rolled down the sleeves of his shirt and rebuttoned the collar, winced when it rubbed his sunburned neck. He unbuttoned it again. "I'll drive."

"Why don't we take both cars? I have errands to run afterwards." She edged him aside then locked the front door before striding toward the garage.

"I can help with your errands." On the way, he checked the slider to the deck. "A dowel in the track will keep intruders from lifting out the door, lock or no lock."

She stopped and turned around, her mouth pinched and a dangerous light flashed in her eyes. "Thank you for your security advice."

Damn it, why was she so touchy? "Just trying to be helpful." He locked the door between the house and the garage behind him.

"You don't need to go with me to run errands."

"I don't remember you being this argumentative. The past three days have been a real eye-opener." As he slid into the passenger seat of her Suburban—he didn't need to fight her on who drove, he could pick his battles—she glanced over at him.

"Thank you for being concerned." She sighed. "Jack told me about a rod in the track when he was here on Friday. Do you two know something I don't? Have there been break-ins in the neighborhood?"

He knew the moment she realized what she said, as if Jack were still alive. Her mouth turned down and she hastily donned sunglasses.

"Not that I've heard. Still, it's good to be proactive," he said.

"What about Ellen?" Maggie backed out of her garage then hit the remote to close the door.

"She thinks I went to work, and before you ask, my housekeeper is at home and will take care of her until I return."

"And what about the rest of the summer?"

"Mrs. Boersma waits until I come home. Now, are you going to continue lecturing me?"

"Sorry."

Several minutes later, she pulled into the funeral home. "This is where the visitation will be. I need to run in for a minute. They called right before you and Ellen arrived and said they had his effects. I can leave the car running so you have some air."

"No. Just roll down your window." He recognized the place. There were plenty of funeral homes in the area. Why had she chosen the one he'd used for Lillian? "I hope you don't mind if I stay out here. I'd rather not go in."

"This is where your wife was buried from, isn't it?" Without waiting for his answer, she said, "Is that going to be a problem? For you and Ellen? It's where my folks were buried from and I . . ."

"No problem. It makes sense to use someone you know."

"I don't want to cause difficulties for you and Ellen."

"Told you it's no problem. Can we drop the subject?"

"Okay. I'll be right back."

Drew hadn't meant to snap at her. It wasn't her fault. He thought he'd gotten through his grief over Lillian's death. Yet, times like this, it snuck up on him and whapped him in the head. *Why did car accidents claim the people he loved?*

Less than five minutes later, she jumped back into her Suburban.

"That was quick," he said.

She shot him a cheeky grin. "Told you."

"What did they give you?"

Her face tightened as she opened the bag. "His university class ring, change from his pockets, his belt, and his cell phone holder."

"No cell phone?"

"Nope. No clothes, either. Dennis said they usually throw them away. I don't think I could handle seeing them." She put the bag in the center console then started the engine.

"Dennis?"

"Do you remember him from high school? He's a year younger than me, so maybe not. His dad owns the business. When he retired, Dennis took over."

"You got all that in five minutes?"

"No, silly. This morning. Now, let's get lunch. I'm starving."

Lunch started out awkward, for him. He needed to apologize for snapping at her over the funeral home. After he did, he lightened up and put thoughts of his dead wife aside. When he asked about the scheduled camping trip, she became animated.

"You really enjoy camping." Leaning back in the booth, he gave her a broad smile.

"Of course. I wouldn't go if I didn't like it. And the girls. They want so badly for Trish to come back and go with them to Isle Royale."

"That's the plan? Isle Royale? I hear it's quite primitive."

"It is. But the girls will manage."

"You've taught them well. And it's obvious they love you."

She tried to brush that aside.

"They do. They respect you and admire you. You're a great role model."

Before she ducked her head, he caught a glimpse of a blush staining her cheeks. She took a quick sip of water then stood. "We can leave now."

He couldn't win. Give the girl a compliment, and she wants to run away.

CHAPTER EIGHT

As soon as they got in her Suburban, she said, "I'm going over to Jack's place. Do you want me to drop you off at my house first? Then you can get your car and go to work."

"Why do you need to go to Jack's?"

"I just do." She'd set her mouth in that mutinous expression he'd come to recognize.

"I'll come with you." He waited a moment. "You're going to search his place again, aren't you?"

A tell-tale blush decorated her cheeks. "What makes you say that? Maybe I want to get a different tie."

He snorted. "Jack hated ties. The one I picked out yesterday is fine."

"Just shut up, or I'm going to drop you off right here."

Since *right here* was along the side of the expressway, he knew she was bluffing. He kept his mouth shut anyway. Their needling each other reminded him of their youth, especially in high school. She never let him or Jack get the best of her. Once she realized she'd never be more than one of the gang, she treated him like a buddy, even though it had been obvious she wanted to be more.

He knew about her crush on him from the time she was twelve. At first, he was flattered, and he became more aware of her as a girl, instead of a tomboy. But, Jack had a heart-to-heart where he told Drew his sister was hands-off, and he realized his friendship with his best buddy wasn't worth dallying with Maggie. They'd grown up together, for God's sake. She was more like the sister he never had.

Telling himself that every night through high school hadn't work.

"We're here."

How deep into his thoughts had he been not to realize the car had stopped?

He made a noise in his throat, hoping she'd take it for

assent. They walked up to the front door. When the lock released easier this time than before, he held the door for her. As she sailed past, he caught a whiff of her perfume—the floral fragrance had nearly driven him to distraction in the close confines of her car.

"I won't be long, just—" She sniffed. "Do you smell something?"

He wasn't going to tell her the only scent he noticed was her perfume. "Not anything different. Why are we here?"

She hesitated then took the cushions off the sofa.

"What are you doing?"

"Searching." After replacing the cushions, she got down on her knees and looked under the sofa. Within moments, she got up then checked behind the sofa.

"Are you looking for Jack's laptop? Do you think he hid it?"

She snapped her finders. "Bingo. You'd make a great detective."

Then, she proceeded to look behind and under the rest of the furniture. Without moving bookcases, she squinted behind and under them—not that there was much room under the heavy walnut bookcases. Apparently satisfied, she went to the kitchen and searched under the sink and inside the pantry. She opened cupboards above and below the counters. Finally, she explored the small laundry room.

A woman on a mission.

"Tell me where you want to search. I can help." He didn't believe Jack's accident was anything but. Still, he could humor her.

"I'd rather do it myself."

When she headed down the hall to the bedrooms, he stopped her. "You check his office, I'll search his bedroom. There may be things he wouldn't want his sister to see." He gave her a quirky grin.

She raised her eyebrow. "Like what? *Playboy* under the bed?"

"You guessed it."

"I'm going to recheck his bedroom, so don't waste your time. Go sit in the living room and read a magazine."

"You are a stubborn woman."

Maggie knew it had been a mistake to let Drew accompany her. Still, she searched all the possible places where Jack could've hidden his computer. She never figured out why he would hide it. Nor why someone searched his condo. If they were looking for the computer, what was on it?

Searching Jack's office took little time—behind the desk and file cabinet, in the closet. She found Drew on his knees looking under Jack's bed.

"Anything?" she asked.

"Dust bunnies." He rose, holding a black sock. "And this."

"I didn't think dust bunnies would stand a chance here." For the first time since she came into the condo, she let a little smile escape.

"I checked behind the dresser," Drew said. "And the linen closet in the bathroom. You take the clothes closet. I'll go downstairs."

"The basement." She smacked her forehead. "I didn't even think to look down there when we were here before."

He gave her a smug grin. "I know."

After making a thorough search of Jack's closet—moving clothes and shoes—she was satisfied that he hadn't hidden the laptop there. Before going down to the finished basement, she checked the slider (the only other entrance to the condo). Locked, with a broom handle-size rod in the track. Apparently, Jack practiced what he preached when he told her to do the same.

As she went down the steps, it hit her that whoever searched the condo had gotten in using Jack's keys. But, she had his keys. Had they made a duplicate? How? When?

Drew came out of the furnace room. "You're welcome to recheck, but I searched his workshop—nice setup, by the way. I noticed many of your dad's tools and machines."

"Jack had more interest in woodworking than I did. Dad taught him a lot."

"You probably don't remember, but your dad taught me, too."

She smiled. "I remember. I tried to get interested so I

could hang out with you guys, but I couldn't. I didn't have the patience, either. Did you check the utility/furnace room?"

"Yep. There aren't that many places that are out of sight for hiding something in there. You can look if you want to."

"Thanks. I trust you."

Drew slapped his chest. "Be still, my heart. She trusts me."

"Quit being a wise-ass."

She crawled around the finished family room, looking under furniture, while Drew searched on top of the tall bookcases.

"Do you think there's space under the pool table?" she asked. "Like between the table and the base?"

"We can check, but I don't think so."

A few minutes later, he asked, "Are you ready to give up?"

She glared at him. "I still think his accident wasn't an accident, that someone was here and searched for something. I thought he might have hidden his laptop here. It's the only logical place. I might be wrong about that."

"She admits she could be wrong." He pumped his fist.

"Piss off, Campbell." She stalked up the stairs, leaving his chuckling behind her.

At the front door, she paused. "I could swear I smelled an odd scent when we walked in. Not unpleasant. But something that wasn't here last night."

"Maggie? Find it. I hid it in plain sight."

Maggie jerked awake, certain she'd heard Jack's voice. She yanked off the covers and got out of bed on shaky legs. That had been downright creepy. She stumbled to the doorway but had to clutch the frame for balance. For several seconds, she stood there waiting for her heart rate to slow down and for her spaghetti legs to stiffen.

Without turning on lights, she walked out to the kitchen. Enough illumination from the streetlight next door plus a full moon helped her avoid stubbing toes on furniture legs. She got a glass of water and, standing at the sink, she downed the water in four swallows. Then she stared out the window at her backyard. Long shadows stretched across the grass.

Wait. Did a shadow just move?

Holding still, she peered intently. She must have been mistaken. Nerves. She never let nerves dictate her behavior. Setting the glass on the counter, she waited another moment before turning away from the sink. Out of the corner of her eye, she saw movement. Whipping her head around gained nothing. Nobody jumped out of the bushes or from behind the thirty-foot tall blue spruce on the left side of the yard. Then, the neighbor's tabby strolled out from under the spruce and across her yard.

The dream had left her jumpy. Other than the cat, nothing else moved.

On the way back to bed, she glanced at her clock. Three-seventeen. Another night of little sleep. Ignoring what she'd thought were moving shadows in her backyard, she crawled under the covers. The weather had changed with a cool breeze coming from the front of the house. She'd left her window open from the top. Normally, she would have enjoyed sleeping with just a sheet to cover her.

Drawing up the lightweight blanket and quilt, she snuggled down. Nothing/nobody was outside. Her overactive imagination, fueled by Jack's death, made her dream of him. That was logical. Someone had searched Jack's condo. No wonder she thought she'd heard him say he left something in plain sight.

Now, she was wide awake.

She could get up, do a load of laundry, clean the oven. Instead, she turned on the bedside lamp and picked up the young adult novel she'd been reading. The story didn't hold her attention the way it did before. Cars out on the main street. Music blaring from sub-woofers kept up a thumping rhythm. Squealing brakes. All far away yet grabbing her attention.

A lone car, or SUV, slowly drove down her street. She held her breath until it passed.

The next morning, Ellen came over to help Maggie find pictures for a display board. "Grandma Nora and I made one when Mom died. Grandmother Helene said it was tacky." She made a face. "But Grandma Nora told me we did a good job."

The difference between Drew's mother (Nora) and Lillian's (Helene) went way beyond disagreeing over a display board at a funeral. Maggie agreed with Nora. "I remember seeing that. Great pictures."

Rapid knocking on the screendoor sent Maggie running from the dining room to see who was there.

"You should have a doorbell that works." Sarah Jane DeHoesen, Jack's girlfriend, stood impatiently on the porch.

As Maggie opened the door, Sarah Jane breezed through, a computer bag slung over her shoulder. "I made a video for the visitation, but I don't have very many pictures. I assume you have some."

Maggie all but let her mouth gape over the woman's abrupt entry. "Of course. Sarah Jane, this is Ellen, Drew's daughter. Ellen, Sarah was Jack's friend."

Ellen had followed Maggie. From her expression, she, too, was overwhelmed by Jack's girlfriend.

"Ellen and I were choosing pictures for a display board." At the sudden downturn of Sarah Jane's mouth, she added, "A video is a great idea. Thank you so much for thinking of it."

"I told you I would help. Where can I set up?"

Maggie led her to the dining room where the table was covered with albums, loose pictures, and supplies. "I have some videos, but I didn't know what to do with them."

Sarah Jane stacked the albums then set up her laptop. "I can handle that." She made a shooing motion. "Go back to what you were doing."

Ellen glanced at Maggie, questions in her eyes. She knew exactly how Ellen felt. The whirlwind named Sarah Jane left them both stunned.

"Okay, then. I'll get my laptop with the videos for you, Sarah Jane. Ellen, will you go through that box of pictures and see if there are any you want to use?"

As they worked side-by-side, Maggie understood why Sarah Jane appealed to Jack. Her no-nonsense attitude, no need for chit-chat, and get-to-work attitude matched his. But whereas Jack loosened up, Sarah Jane didn't seem to. At least, Maggie had never seen a playful side of her.

"You knew my Uncle Jack?" Ellen ventured.

Blinking, as if coming out of a trance, Sarah Jane nodded. "We went to high school together. We worked at the same accounting firm before he started his own business."

That was maybe the most Maggie had ever heard from her.

"Was he your boyfriend?"

"Yes." She didn't look up from her laptop. "I need to concentrate."

Maggie crooked her finger at Ellen to follow her to the kitchen. There, she whispered, "Don't let her brusqueness bother you. That's the way she is."

Ellen grimaced. "I get it. I thought she was rude, but she's probably sad because Uncle Jack is . . . well, you know."

"He's dead." Sarah Jane stood in the doorway, looking stiff and uncaring. "I wish he weren't." She cleared her throat. "Is that all the videos you have?"

Hoping Sarah Jane hadn't heard their whispering—but almost sure she had—Maggie pulled out her phone. "I might have more. Here, you can look."

After giving her phone to Sarah Jane, she patted Ellen's shoulder. "I think we're almost done. Let's set up the display board and see."

Ellen helped set the board on the peninsula counter. As Maggie examined their work, tears filled her eyes. Ellen had chosen excellent photos that showed Jack's many sides, playful, serious, fun-loving, hard at work. She'd chosen the picture from Jack's desk—the one of the fearless three-some—as the center. Maggie's throat choked up. Tears filled her eyes.

A soft sob made her turned to Ellen, who promptly threw herself into Maggie's arms. She held the girl and let her cry, wanting desperately for someone to hold her while she did the same. For a moment, she regretted their work since it made them sad.

Ellen snuffled then grabbed a tissue from her shorts' pocket. "We did good, didn't we?"

"You did." Again, Sarah Jane had come up behind them so quietly Maggie hadn't heard. "Good job. I finished. Do you want to see the video?"

Even though she knew that watching Jack in a video would undo both her and Ellen, she said, "Of course."

They pulled the dining room chairs around so they could see the screen. Ellen and Maggie waited for Sarah Jane to start the video. That close to Sarah Jane, Maggie sniffed.

"Were you in Jack's condo recently?"

Sarah Jane looked over her shoulder. "I took some of my things."

"When?"

"Yesterday, after I talked to you on the phone."

"So you have a key?"

"Of course. Jack was never sure when he could get away. He said he didn't want me to sit out in my car waiting for him." She paused. "I never lived there."

Maggie nodded. That explained the odd scent she'd smelled the day before. One mystery solved. As they watched the video Sarah Jane put together, they laughed and wept. At the end, Maggie said, "Well done. You captured my brother in ways that I never could have."

"Putting together videos is easy."

Maggie chuckled. "Not for me. Thank you, Sarah Jane."

When she reached to hug her, Sarah Jane busied herself putting away her laptop. Abruptly, she turned to Maggie. "You saw Jack on Friday."

"Yes. He stopped here for lunch. Why?"

"Did he say anything to you?" She stared at Maggie.

"He was here almost an hour. So, yes, he spoke to me. What are you getting at?"

Sarah Jane stuffed her laptop into the bag before looking up. "I thought he might . . . Never mind." She held up a USB drive. "I'll give this to the funeral director."

"Thanks, Sarah Jane. I really appreciate that, but we can take it when we take the display board and some pictures."

"It's on my way home."

Without waiting for Maggie's reply, she left.

"Wow." Ellen breathed out. "She's not what I expected. What did Uncle Jack see in her?"

Maggie shook her head. "I think she's shy. Maybe she was different around him. They were together on and off for at least five years, that I know of. And they were friends in high school."

"She never cried."

"People show their grief in different ways. Look at all the work she did with that video."

Ellen piled the albums and picked up loose pictures. "Why did she ask what Uncle Jack said to you?"

"I don't know."

"Would you please hurry?" Maggie said.

"Daddy, the speed limit is forty, and you're not even going that fast."

Drew shot his daughter a look in the rearview mirror. "Just what I need . . . a front- and a back-seat driver."

Next to him, Maggie clenched and unclenched her fingers. He took one hand off the steering wheel and covered hers. They trembled, but at least they weren't still plucking at her dress. This was maybe the third time he'd seen her in a dress—at his wedding and then at her parents' funerals. No one knew what she wore to her own wedding. She'd eloped.

Jack had had serious misgivings about the man Maggie married. He'd even asked Drew to use whatever resources he had to check the man out. Roger Dixon appeared to be an upstanding citizen. Yet, Jack's concern had rubbed off on him. Something about the man seemed false. Other than doing a cursory check, Drew had let it go. He and Lillian were still in the honeymoon phase of their marriage. His concerns at that time had been about her and their surprise pregnancy. Jack never said what happened to Maggie's marriage, and she never talked about it.

"Dad-dy." Exasperation oozed from the backseat.

Ten minutes ago, he'd pulled into Maggie's driveway. At the same time, she'd bolted out of the house. Her skirt swirled around her kneecaps when she'd turned to lock the front door. The white lace collar relieved the severity of her navy dress, and the matching navy belt emphasized her trim waist. She wore nude hose with strappy navy high-heeled sandals. Damn, she looked good.

What surprised him the most was her hair. She'd pulled

her dark brown hair up from the sides, and curls cascaded down her back. As she got into his Town Car, he noticed she wore makeup. It wasn't obvious, a subtle transformation from outdoor girl to sophisticated woman.

Very good, indeed. But, just as anxious as she was now.

"We'll get there in plenty of time," he said. "Besides, people will wait if they get there before the family."

Now, it was her turn to shoot daggers at him.

Drew patted the dashboard then underneath the steering wheel. "Can't find it."

"What are you looking for?" Maggie roused from her silence.

"The button that will elevate the car, so we can fly over all the others in our way."

"Dad-dy."

He didn't have to look in the rearview mirror to see if she rolled her eyes. "Guess this model doesn't have one," he drawled. "And that would be the only way we could go faster."

At fifteen minutes to four, he pulled into the funeral home parking lot. As he eased the Lincoln Town Car into a parking slot, he pointed to the LED display. "We're early."

He discovered he'd talked to an empty car. Drew caught up with Maggie and Ellen in the lobby of the elegantly-appointed home, the same one from which he'd buried Lillian. A wave of remembrance washed over him. Remembrance and misery. He worried about how Ellen would fare. But, she appeared more interested in the older man and woman who'd walked out of the main viewing room and approached Maggie.

"You must be Mr. Sinclair's sister," the woman said. Her purple floral dress and black patent-leather shoes came from an older era. As with the man's suit, her clothes probably only saw service at funerals and weddings.

"He talked about you," the man said. "Proud as punch about what a great teacher you are."

"Those were real nice pictures in there. And that video, oh my. That was good." The woman nodded over her shoulder at the room they'd exited. "We recognized you from the ones with Mr. Sinclair."

Drew didn't know how Maggie and Ellen did it. He'd offered to help with the poster until he picked up a picture of Jack and him riding their bikes so hell bent for leather their images blurred. When he realized it wasn't the picture that was blurred, he left the two of them at Maggie's dining room table and got out of her house.

". . . don't mind us coming early," the man apologized. "We need to get to work soon. We're Max and Hazel Martin." He shook hands with Maggie first. "We work at Vander Haar. Mr. Sinclair was always real nice to us."

"Most people aren't, you know," his wife added. "They don't think the janitorial crew is worth speaking to. They just look through us—especially the higher ups."

"Now, Hazel," her husband warned.

"Not Mr. Sinclair," she went on, ignoring him. "He treated us real nice. Always polite. Couldn't believe when we heard about his accident. I told him to be careful because of the fog." Hazel dabbed her handkerchief to her eyes. "Sorry, ma'am."

Up to this point, Maggie had nodded politely as Max and Hazel carried the conversation by themselves. Now, she perked up. She straightened her shoulders and cocked her head to one side. "You saw Jack that night?"

"Oh, yes," Hazel nodded vigorously. "He was working late. Didn't leave until twelve twenty-five. I remember because I was dusting the receptionist station when he came by. There's a big clock on the wall across from it."

The man tapped his watch. "Hazel . . ."

"We're real sorry for your loss, ma'am." The older woman dabbed at her eyes again. She awkwardly accepted Maggie's hand.

Max cleared his throat. "Sorry. We have to get to work. Just wanted you to know we thought a lot of Mr. Sinclair, even though we only knew him for a week. And we wanted to give you this, too." He handed over a cell phone.

"It's Jack's," Maggie exclaimed.

Hazel smiled. "We know. We found it yesterday after the trash haulers emptied the dumpster. I knew it was his. Told him that our boy used to watch *Doctor Who* so I recognized the TARDIS on his cover."

"He must have dropped it Friday night," Max continued. "And it slid under the dumpster. It's a good thing when the trash hauler set down the dumpster, that phone wasn't underneath."

"Thank you so much," Maggie clutched the phone to her breast. "You can't imagine how much I appreciate your bringing it here."

"Wasn't nothing," Hazel said. "But I knew you'd want it."

One of Maggie's aunts appeared in the doorway. "Maggie May?"

Even though her aunt didn't raise her voice, Drew heard the rebuke. That plus the fact that her lips were pursed and she stared pointedly. He needed to head her off. Coming to the funeral home was hard enough for Maggie. She didn't need to be scolded.

While Maggie thanked the Martins for coming and for returning the cell phone, which she slipped into her pocket, Drew walked over to Maggie's relative. He thought this was Aunt Louise. She and Aunt Anne looked so much alike he never kept them straight. When he and Jack were kids, The Aunts—Jack always referred to them in capital letters— scared the bejeebers out of them. Neither had had children but still thought they could comment on their sister's child rearing techniques. He never did understand how Mrs. Sinclair stood the criticism. They might have considered it constructive criticism. Drew wasn't so sure Mrs. Sinclair did.

He put his hand on Aunt Louise's shoulder and led her back into the viewing room, doing his best to pacify her. "It was my fault Maggie wasn't here earlier . . ."

Two hours later, Drew marveled at how well Maggie was holding up. A steady stream of people had come ever since they arrived. She didn't sit down once. Instead, she stood and greeted the people who came to pay their respects for Jack Sinclair. Maggie appeared to do more comforting than was comforted herself. His friend had touched many people's lives.

"What are you doing here, Campbell?"

Greg Vander Haar. He seemed surprised to see Drew. Ever since he'd cautioned the senior Vander Haar about turning over the operations to his son, Junior had treated him with contempt. Greg used another attorney for routine company business and had replaced his father's auditor with Ben Voorheis. Like Ben, the new attorney was a college friend. By severing ties with his father's attorney and auditor, he seemed determined to show that he was in charge.

"Friend of the family," Drew responded.

Vander Haar went on a fishing expedition to discover more about Drew's connection with the family. Drew chose not to satisfy his curiosity.

Ben Voorheis hobbled in, a crutch beneath his good arm. Maggie mentioned he'd been injured in an accident, but Drew hadn't realized how badly. Ben hobbled up to Maggie, ignoring the line of people waiting to speak to her. She patted the arm of yet another of Jack's friends and pointed toward the back of the room, where Drew stood. Then, she steered Ben to the seat her aunts had reserved for her, the one she never used.

Ben was openly crying and for several seconds the room went still. Maggie stooped and patted his knee. She spoke a few words, patted his shoulder, and went back to the line.

Next to him, Drew felt Vander Haar stiffened. He drifted away when Jim Harper—the man to whom Maggie was speaking when Ben interrupted—approached.

"Bad thing," Jim said after shaking hands with Drew. "Could hardly believe it."

Drew nodded and let the man talk. Jim had been part of the neighborhood gang who tore through the quiet streets on their bikes and played baseball in the vacant lot. Jim was usually the captain of the other team that always wanted Maggie on their side.

". . . haven't seen little Maggie in years," Jim went on. "Whoa. What a babe."

Something that felt ridiculously like jealousy surged through Drew. "Better not let your wife hear you say that."

"Hell, a man can look, can't he?" Without waiting for an answer, Jim said, "Isn't that Rob Lloyd? Heard he and his wife split."

When Drew glanced toward another old-time friend, he noted that Vander Haar had button-holed Ben. The two were in an intense discussion in a corner. Junior probably wanted to know when his audit would be done, Drew thought with disgust.

A young woman in a black pant suit, relieved by a white blouse, charged up to the two men. Drew was too far away to hear what she said, but both men eyed her warily. She spoke again then abruptly turned away from them and headed to Maggie. Instead of speaking to her, the woman went up to the casket. She touched Jack's chest then spun on her heel and walked out. As she passed Ben and Greg, she glared at them. Once she left the room, Ben leaned toward Greg. Whatever he said had Junior Vander Haar looking worried.

Meanwhile, Jim carried on a conversation with Rob, and soon several of the old gang stood with Drew and reminisced about Jack. When one of the guys mentioned he needed a smoke, they all trooped outside. The evening was still warm with a gentle breeze that fortunately dissipated the cigarette smoke. Drew felt as if he stood apart—in the middle, yet apart—from them. He remembered that feeling at his wife's funeral. Part of him listened to the men talk about the good times they'd had with Jack as kids, and another part of him wondered if Maggie felt the same.

". . . Maggie. Who'd have thought that tomboy would look so good in a dress?"

Drew's ears perked up at Rob's comment. She did look good in a dress, and he realized he would rather be inside watching her then out here with old friends. Other comments about her in the same vein as Rob's made Drew want to plant his fist in a few mouths—and then was appalled at his violent reaction.

"Hey, Campbell," Rob said. "You and Jack did a good job of putting up the 'no trespassing' signs in high school. I'm surprised you never went after her yourself."

The others nodded.

Drew shrugged. "She was like a sister. Jack and I knew we had to protect her from you vultures." His grin made the others chuckle.

"Are you still?" Rob persisted with a speculative expression.

Drew remembered Jim saying Rob was single again. "Yeah. Still protecting."

Even as he said it, Drew realized it was true. He also knew Maggie would have his head on a post if she knew. But, he wasn't thinking of her as a sister. Just as those hadn't been sisterly feelings coursing through him when she practiced her kissing technique on him at fifteen. God, he was a bastard. He'd been so flustered when she Frenched him, he said the first thing that popped into his adolescent brain to get her to stop. It was a wonder she hadn't decked him because of his ham-handed rejection.

He'd seen a different side of her on the camping trip. Her ease with the girls, her knowledge of the outdoors, her strength and determination dealing with her brother's accident. It didn't hurt that she was easy on the eyes. She'd grown into a striking woman. Still athletic, with a trim, muscular body that caused a certain part of his body sit up and take notice.

Silence brought him out of his thoughts. The guys were staring at him.

"What?"

Jim chuckled. "You've got it bad, son. Just like in high school."

Drew eyed him, certain he'd heard wrong.

The rest of the guys laughed. Ron said, "Your face is red, Campbell? So, what's she like now that she's all grown up? Have you had a piece of her yet?"

His leer was just as obnoxious now as it had been in high school.

"Piss off." The words flew out of Drew's mouth before his mind said to ignore the jerk.

While the guys nervously laughed, he saw his dad searching for him. Drew approached him, grateful for any excuse to leave his old high school friends behind.

"Is it okay if we take Ellen home with us?" Dad asked.

"Is Ellen all right?"

"Your mother thinks she's bored. I promised her we'd make popcorn and watch a movie, if it was okay with you."

"Bribing my daughter?" Drew grinned. Good old dad. The family rescuer.

Peering closer at his father, Drew noticed the brackets around his mouth appeared deeper, and his eyes showed the depth of his grief over Jack. This had to be hard on him. Dad had always liked Jack, thought he was a good influence on Drew despite, or because of, Mom's objections.

"Sure. It will take her mind off losing Jack."

They found Ellen and Drew's mother just inside. After hugs and kisses, the trio left. Ellen seemed relieved to be leaving. He'd debated whether it would be good for her to come to the visitation. In the end, he didn't have a choice. Since when did fourteen-year-olds inform their parent they would do what they wanted?

He had so much to learn about parenting.

Junior Vander Haar had left. Ben Voorheis approached and started bending Drew's ear. Ben and Jack had been friends before they went into business together, when they worked together at a big accounting firm. The depth of Ben's mourning surprised him. He chalked it up to a surfeit of emotions from Ben's own accident—there but for the grace of God . . .

At ten to nine, Drew clapped Ben on the shoulder and thanked him for coming. "You need to get home and rest."

Maggie's aunts were ushering stragglers toward the door. Maggie's mother's sisters were a formidable duo. Drew wasn't easily intimidated, but even he stood in awe of their efficiency. Finally, only Maggie and The Aunts remained. Drew assured the older women he would take her home and, yes, he would be sure she was on time for the funeral service in the morning.

When they left, Maggie gave him an apologetic smile. "They mean well."

"I know. Are you ready?"

She hesitated. "I, uh, I need a few minutes, okay?"

He nodded and waited at the door. She sat on a chair close to the casket. For several moments, she just sat there and then, in the stillness of the room heavily scented with flowers, he heard a soft sob. She hunched over, and her shoulders shook.

Skirting the chairs, he must have made a noise. Before he reached her, she stood and went up to the coffin. She straightened the Boy Scout Eagle pin on the lapel of her brother's dark gray suit, took a deep breath and turned away.

She collided with Drew, and he steadied her, his hands on her shoulders. For a moment, he was tempted to draw her into his arms, the way he did Sunday in the lot of wrecked cars. He checked her expression for a sign that she wanted comfort.

Her blue eyes shimmered, but her mouth was set. "Don't say a word."

Her fierce tone made him take a step back and release her shoulders. Bad timing. He pulled his handkerchief out of his pocket and handed it to her. On the way out, she unfolded the handkerchief and blotted her eyes. As she pulled herself together, Drew marveled at her control. Hell, he knew what this took out of a person. Dealing with the mourners and well-wishers when Lillian died had left him more devastated than the initial shock of her accident. According to those wiser than him, wakes and funerals were supposed to give the family closure.

Closure, hell. They wrung a person out, squeezed their hearts until nothing was left.

Outside, the sun was low on the horizon, a round red ball. "It's hard to believe it's still light out," he said. An inane but neutral comment.

She nodded. "Summer solstice was last week. Longest day of the year."

He put his hand in the middle of her back to walk to the car. "We'll stop and get some dinner."

He was still kicking himself for not insisting that she take a break for something to eat. The funeral home provided a light buffet for the family, as well as a lounge where they could rest. Maggie used neither.

"I'd rather go home and ordered a pizza," she said. "I want to get out of these shoes, this dress, and my pantyhose." She waited while he opened the Town Car's passenger door.

He thought about the discussion with the guys on the porch and waggled his eyebrows. "I'll be happy to assist."

She appeared flummoxed. At least, the tears were gone with only red-rimmed eyes as evidence of her grief. When he started the engine, she said, "You meant the shoes, right?"

"If you want to think that . . ."

"Are you flirting with me, Campbell?"

"Guess I'm doing a lousy job, *Sinclair*, if you have to ask."

"Why?"

"Maybe I like to. Ever think of that?"

"No. You never did when we were teens." Despite her buckled seatbelt, she turned to watch him.

He could imagine where her mind was going. Still, he had enjoyed teasing her. "It wouldn't have been right for me to flirt after Jack warned off the other guys in high school."

"You, too, don't forget." She pouted. "Nobody wanted to date me because of you two. Geez. I couldn't even get a good-night kiss."

"Kept you safe, though."

She snorted. "Oh, yeah. I had to wait until college before getting Frenched. Shame you didn't teach me the right way."

Drew sucked in a breath. "Do you want to go there?"

After a pause, she said, "Not really. Why did you start flirting tonight?"

"Took your mind off Jack, didn't it?" *Okay, Ace, that was dumb.* Where was a convenient wall on which to smack his head?

She took a shuddering breath. "I was surprised at the turn-out."

"Jack was well liked."

"I saw you talking to Greg Vander Haar. Smarmy guy. I wonder why he came?"

"To offer his condolences? Jack was working at his company."

She made a rude noise. "I'll bet he only came to see Ben."

"He did rather corner the poor guy."

"He probably wanted to know how soon his audit would be done."

Since she voiced his own suspicions, he kept silent.

"His father was very nice."

The senior Vander Haar made a brief appearance. He'd nodded to Drew, gave his son—still in deep conversation with Ben—a sharp look then left after speaking to Maggie.

"He's your client, right?"

Drew nodded. "He can be very polite. But, I wouldn't apply the word *nice* to a man who single-handedly built up a business from a one-man machine shop to a one hundred plus employee operation and fended off an attempted union takeover. He's a shrewd businessman who has one weakness—his son."

When Drew pulled into her drive, she said, "I think I'll take a raincheck on that pizza. I don't feel like eating."

"It's going to be some rainy day when you collect on those checks." He shut off the engine. "I'll be a good lad and walk you to your door."

"No need. I'm just going to run over to Jack's and get a different tie."

"What?" He stopped her from exiting the car by clasping her wrist. "You're going to eat and go to bed. You're exhausted."

"No," she said with exaggerated patience. "I'm going to Jack's for a new tie."

Why did she have to be so stubborn?

"The tie he has is fine," he said. "Besides, the tie he's buried in hardly matters."

"It matters to me." She pulled her wrist out of his grasp. "I don't like the one he's wearing. You go on now. Ellen's probably waiting up for you." Though she made her dismissal definite, he wasn't having any of it.

"My folks took her home with them. She and Dad are watching old movies on Netflix." With resignation, he restarted the engine. "Buckle up. I'll take you to Jack's."

She folded her arms, a mutinous look in her eyes. "Maybe I want to be alone in my brother's condo."

"And commune with his spirit?" He scoffed. "I know you better than that, Sinclair. You're going to search his place again."

The setting sun and rising street lights revealed a rosy flush to her face. *Bingo.*

"Has anyone ever mentioned how pushy you are?" The mutinous look vanished as she rebuckled her seatbelt.

"Nah. Everybody says what a nice guy I am. Even-tempered, considerate—"

"Loyal? Trustworthy? A regular Boy Scout?"

He grimaced. "Unfortunately, no. I flunked out of Cub Scouts after my first camping trip." He steered the car out of the subdivision.

"Jack mentioned something about that. He laughed his head off, when I told him you were going camping with the girls and me."

"It was all his fault," Drew said self-righteously. "That's how I know about snipe hunts. You wouldn't believe what other tortures the older boys tried."

"I'm surprised you gave up. That wasn't like you."

He blew out a breath. "I have never told anyone this, not even Jack, and if you ever repeat it . . ."

"Okay, okay. My lips are sealed."

An absurd desire to seal her lips with his own shot through him. What was the matter with him? All the talk with the guys ogling her had jolted him. He didn't want anyone gawking at her, lusting after her.

"About that camping trip?"

Drew remembered the topic at hand. "My mother heard about the snipe hunt. Jack was yakking away to my dad about all the pranks the big boys played on us. She sent Jack home right after hearing that they'd left me in the woods for several hours and made me quit."

"Jack never knew."

"I made sure he didn't. When Mom found out your dad didn't punish the others, she yanked me out of Cub Scouts and forbade me to ever go back. She even reported your dad to the Council office—what a bad leader he was, endangering the lives of the boys, yada, yada, yada. My dad was no match for her when she took a stand. I begged her to let me go back. She wouldn't budge. And if you ever tell anyone that my *mommy* made me quit Cub Scouts, I'll have to hurt you." He gave her a mocking grin.

"So that's what happened between our folks. They were always friendly before. Not *friends* but friendly neighbors. Then, all of a sudden, they weren't."

"Yeah, well, your dad tried, but he ended up blaming my dad for not standing up for me against my mother. Said she was turning me into a Momma's Boy. My dad never got angry. I think that was the only time I saw him lose his temper. He told your dad to mind his own business. But, you know, your dad never let his feelings toward my parents affect how he treated me. He always made me feel welcome in your house. So did your mother. There were times when I envied you and Jack."

"I'm sorry things turned out that way. And I'm sorry you never got to enjoy the outdoors the way Jack and I did."

When she pressed her head against the side window, Drew let her have a few minutes of peace. At Jack's, she leaped out of the car, not waiting for him to open her door. In fact, not even waiting for him to turn off the engine. A determined woman. He let her go. The sun had set, spreading a rosy light across the sky. The streetlamps glowed, illuminating driveways and the front of the condos.

As she walked up to the door, Drew followed, watching her skirt swish across her hips and how her calves tightened with each step. In those high heels, her legs went on forever. He didn't say a word. He couldn't, not with his tongue lolling out of his mouth, like a panting dog.

"Are you breathing heavy back there, Campbell?"

He wasn't saying a word.

"Man, you really need to get into shape," she said over her shoulder. "Our next hike is going to be twice as long as the one last Saturday."

He wasn't saying a word.

"Was that a groan?" At Jack's door, she turned around to face him. "Geez, Campbell, your face is red."

"Give me the damn key," he growled. She was entirely too perceptive.

"First thing tomorrow morning, before the funeral, we're walking. Gotta get you in shape."

"You are canceling the trip this weekend, aren't you?" He pushed the door open for her. As before, a lamp on a timer softly illuminated the room.

Maggie gasped. "Oh, my God."

CHAPTER NINE

Slashed couch cushions. Yanked out stuffing. Overturned coffee table. Scattered magazines. DVDs smashed against the wall.

Someone had trashed Jack's condo.

Fear and horror warred. Maggie's stomach lurched. Anger shot to the fore. How dare he—she was sure it was a he—violate her brother's home.

"Out." Drew clasped her shoulders to pull her out of the condo.

Needing to see the rest, she dug in her heels. "No."

Ignoring her protest, he propelled her outside to the porch. Maggie blistered his ears with every choice word she knew.

He held her around the waist, refusing to let her back into the condo. "I never realized the extent of your vocabulary."

"I took lessons on the docks." She blasted him with a few more epithets, guaranteed to make a trucker blush. "Release me. I need to—"

"You don't. They might still be inside." He let go of her waist then clasped her face between his large hands. "Please, Maggie. I'm trying to protect you."

When she nodded, he let go. She sagged against the porch rail. Defeated. Anger only carried her so far.

Drew pulled his cell phone off the clip on his belt and dialed 911. "There's been a break in. And vandalism."

Since she stood next to him, she heard the operator take the information then said to get out, in the event the perpetrator was still there. Drew arched his eyebrow at her. She ducked her head, not willing to acknowledge that he was right. He told the dispatcher they were outside. She said to stay there and to remain on the line until an officer arrived.

He stared at Maggie. "I'm not going to say I told you so. About getting out." He paused. "For what it's worth, I believe you. About someone searching this place on Sunday. I should've listened to you. Unless he has nerves of steel listening to us talk, the person is probably gone. Hold my phone and don't tell the operator. I'm going back inside to check."

"But she said—"

He yanked open the door. "If someone runs out, don't let him get past you."

"What? How?"

"I don't know. Hit him with your purse."

"Funny, Campbell. Real funny. *I* want to check to see if anything is missing."

"Wait for the police."

Realizing the danger if the vandal was still inside, she clung to his arm. "Don't go in. Please. You could be hurt."

A patrol car pulled up in front of the condo, and she breathed out a sigh of relief. "Aren't you glad you didn't go back inside?"

Drew explained the situation to Officer Grace Neill who told them to wait on the porch.

"This might be the second time the condo has been searched," he added.

Her left hand on the door handle, her right on her weapon, Officer Neill stopped. "Explain."

Maggie charged into the conversation, explaining in detail the other time. "Obviously, someone is looking for something, and they haven't found it."

"Wait here," Neill ordered.

After she searched the condo, she told them they could come in. "A lot of anger here. This is more than routine vandalism." She pointed out the kitchen where cereal boxes had been dumped on the counter, scattered along with the contents of other boxes. She waved her hand to the contents of the freezer on the floor. "Definitely searching for something."

"I know they searched over the weekend," Maggie protested. "Why would they think they'd find something this time?"

"You said the funeral visitation was tonight. It's possible this B&E isn't related to the other time. I don't see signs of a break-in. Who else has a key?"

Maggie glanced at Drew before saying, "Jack's ex-girlfriend, I mean girlfriend. Sarah Jane DeHoesen." She turned to Drew. "You know how I told you I smelled an odd scent on Monday. When Sarah Jane came over to help with the—never mind. Not important. I recognized her perfume and asked her if she'd been here. She said she came over to get her personal items."

Officer Neill wrote down Sarah Jane's name. "You said *ex*-girlfriend then switched to girlfriend. Why?"

"She said they had an on-again, off-again relationship. Friends with benefits."

"Could she have done this?"

"I don't think so. As you said, a lot of anger. She's quiet and little strange in a geeky sort of way. Like my brother." Maggie grimaced.

"But she did have a key." The officer persisted.

"Yes. I'm sure her address is in my brother's cell phone." She pulled it out of her pocket. "Damn. I haven't even looked at it since the Martins gave it to me tonight."

"Okay. Let's sit at the table while you explain." Neill pointed to the table in the small nook. "Someone gave you your brother's phone tonight?"

Maggie told her about the missing phone and the janitor who found it. Then, she scrolled through the contacts and gave her Sarah Jane's phone number and address. "I'd hate to think she had anything to do with this—this destruction."

"But she did have a key."

Drew added, "Maggie seems to think her brother's car crash wasn't an accident. Her theory is he knew something, and someone killed him over it." He rubbed the back of his neck. "I'm ashamed to say I didn't believe her until now. If she's right, it's possible whoever killed him made a copy of his condo key to search."

Officer Neill nodded. "That's a possibility, but highly doubtful. This is vandalism."

Maggie drew herself up. "More like search and destroy."

She dug in her purse and came up with a card. "Please report this to Sheriff Tom Watson. He knows about the other break-in, as well as the so-called accident that killed my brother." She whirled on Drew. "I *knew* it was no accident. Somebody killed Jack because of what he knows—knew."

All the way home, she blistered Drew's ears about his earlier non-belief. She had no hesitation about reminding him she told him so. "I can't believe that officer fixated on Sarah Jane."

"It was logical. She had a key."

"Neill should have given your theory that the killer copied Jack's key more credence."

When they returned to her house, Drew mentioned Jack's phone. After inviting him in and kicking off her heels, she took the phone out of her purse.

"Here. Look through it while I get out of these clothes."

"Need some help?" He raised his eyebrow.

From his expression, she wasn't sure if he meant it or was teasing, like before. She guessed the latter, an effort to distract her from the destruction they'd seen. She played along.

"Golly gee, Mr. Campbell. Little ole me is so helpless. A big, strong man like you would sure come in handy." Then she quickly changed her innocent expression to the one she used on high school boys. "Forget about it."

His chuckle followed her down the hall to her bedroom, where she shed her dress, slip, and pantyhose. For a moment, she wished more than his laughter had followed her. Heat washed over her. If he did, what would she do? Throw herself into his arms? She glanced at the closed door. Would he come? Did she really want him to?

Their flirting raised her awareness of him to another level. Heat rushed through her, singeing every nerve ending. Did he feel it, too? Or was he trying to distract her from her grief? From the break-in at Jack's?

She grabbed a T-shirt and a pair of shorts out of her dresser and quickly changed. She came out and found Drew leaning against the kitchen counter, still examining Jack's phone. His suit jacket and tie hung on the back of a chair, and he'd rolled up the sleeves of his white dress shirt.

"Did you find anything?"

"In the Notes section, he wrote 'EV to M. Call D. Legal stuff. My resp.' Can you interpret his shorthand?"

Maggie peered. "I think I'm 'M' and you're 'D', but I'm not sure about 'EV'."

"Evidence, maybe?"

"Evidence of what? It looks like he wanted to talk to you about legal stuff." She grinned at him. "But why his responsibility? At least, I think 'resp' means responsibility."

"Go back to his first note, 'EV to M.' If it does mean EVidence to Maggie, did he bring you something when he stopped by on Friday?"

She leaned her back against the counter. "A Detroit Tigers hat. And a CD he wanted to listen to." As a thought hit her, she raced into the living room then stooped next to the shelf with CDs. She flipped through the jewel cases until she came to one without a label on the spine.

"Did you find something?" Drew squatted down beside her.

With a disgusted sigh, she said, "'Maggie's Party Mix.' He's always making CDs for me to play when I grade papers."

She continued to search the CDs. "Nothing."

"What about the ones you took from the Blazer? Where are they?"

"Laundry room." She leaned on the shelf to lever herself up. Drew helped her, instead. His large, strong hand encompassed hers. A warm sensation passed between them. That awareness grew from warm to hot, traveling from his hand to her breast. Then, lower. Dear God, what was happening to her?

"Are you okay?" He eyed her with uncertainty.

She pasted on a broad smile. "Old bones. Damn high heels. My legs are still cramping from them."

He laughed. "Don't forget my bones are three years older."

"Yeah, yeah."

He followed her to the laundry room, where she opened the cupboard above the dryer.

"I forgot all about these. So much has happened. I didn't even clean them." With chagrin, she handed him the dried mud-smeared CD cases. "I'm not sure we could even play them after being in the mud."

"We can try." Drew took them out to the kitchen. When he opened the first case, mud coated the disk. "Okay. Plan B, let them dry." He put the disk in the dish drainer to the right of the sink."

As he did the same for the other cases, she edged around him to get two glasses from the cupboard. "Want something to drink?"

"Yeah. Got any Scotch?"

"I do. I keep it for Jack." A lump appeared in her throat. "I mean . . ."

"I know what you mean." Drew came up behind her.

She reached over the refrigerator to open the cabinet. With her hands over her head, she felt a breeze against her waist where her shirt had risen up.

Then a warm hand replaced the breeze. That same hand slid around her waist and flattened on her stomach.

"Maggie?" He drew her back against him.

The heat she felt previously was nothing compared to what streaked through her. She let her head fall back against his shoulder. When his fingers splayed across her abdomen, she sighed. *Touch me. Higher.*

Then, he did. One hand covered her breast while the other edged inside her shorts. Pressed back against him, she felt his erection. Oh dear Lord. He nuzzled her behind her ear. Tingles raced from there to her breast to between her legs. She wanted his fingers just inside her waistband to go lower. *Kiss me.*

"Drew?" She slowly writhed against him. Not waiting for him, she turned in his arms and looped hers around his neck.

When his mouth slammed down on hers, she knew he must have heard her thoughts, her desires. Clasping her bottom, he pressed her closer. Slipping his hands inside her shorts and panties, he kneaded her bottom while he kissed her.

No tender kiss. Their teeth clashed, their tongues warred, each seeking dominance, neither giving way. She'd never been kissed like that. He devoured her. She wanted that and more. She slid her hand down between them and stroked the front of his dress slacks. His hardness thrilled and excited her, while his tongue did imaginative things to her mouth.

Suddenly, his hands came out of her shorts and up to her shoulders. Gently, he pushed her away. "Dear God, Maggie. What are we doing?"

She leaned against the refrigerator, wishing for the cold air to cool her down. Her lungs struggled for breath, and her heart raced faster than if she'd run a marathon. Drew, leaning back against the counter, seemed to be having the same lung and heart problems.

"Still think I kiss like a guppy?"

"Oh, God, Mags." He reached for her and, idiot that she was, she let him. He held her close, cupping the back of her head. "Can you ever forgive me?"

"For the guppy remark or for kissing me just now?"

"How can you be so flippant?" His growl rumbled under her ear.

"It's either that or cry."

"Okay. I'll take flippant over tears. I am so sorry for the guppy remark. I regretted it as soon as I said it. Chalk it up to teenage hormones run amuck."

"I was so embarrassed." Her face hidden in his pristine shirt, she was glad she couldn't see him.

"I know." He caressed her neck. "For the record, I didn't think you kissed like a guppy then, and I sure don't now. I wanted you."

"When? Then or now?"

"Both."

"Then why did you stop now?" She wasn't going to let him off the hook. "You had to know I wanted you, too."

Stepping back, he slid his hands down her arms then clasped her hands. "Are we ready for what would've happened next? I don't do casual sex."

"I don't, either."

"I haven't been with anyone since Lillian died. And never after we started dating."

His confession should've surprised her. A faithful man. She'd known he was honorable. But his wife had been gone for a year. Surely, he hadn't been celibate all that time? Staring at his sincere expression, she deduced he told the truth.

"I haven't been with anyone for a while. My, uh, ex put me off men for several years."

"I had a feeling something wasn't right, especially last Saturday night when you flinched from me." He paused. "Did he abuse you?"

Oh, God. She didn't want to talk about that. About his fists. The scathing words. The guilt. The fear.

"Mags?" His thumbs rubbed her knuckles, his gentleness a contrast to what Roger had done. "Did he hit you?"

She took a deep breath, recalling her therapist's advice. It wasn't her fault. "Twice. The second time I left. The emotional abuse was worse." *Enough.* She couldn't expose her humiliation at the hands of an abuser. She hadn't even told Jack. "That's all I'm going to say about that subject."

She pulled her hands away from his. Using the dispenser in the refrigerator door, she filled the glasses with ice.

"Would you get the Macallan?" She wasn't going to reach up again. It would be like waving a red flag. Tempting.

"Single malt. Jack always liked the good stuff." He held the bottle. "I didn't think you liked Scotch whisky."

"I don't. Jameson for me."

He poured the Irish whiskey over the ice then did the same for the Scotch. After handing over her drink, he clinked glasses. "To better times."

"Better times." She took a sip of the smooth Irish whiskey and let the warmth flow through her.

Drew knocked back a good slug. For several moments, they stood in her kitchen quietly drinking. Was he thinking about Jack's condo, their kiss, or her confession? No way was she talking about her short-lived marriage. Better that she chose the topic.

"Do you think the officer was right about Sarah Jane?"

Drew set his glass on the counter on which he leaned. "You know her better than I did. Jack never talked about her that much. Scratch that. He yakked about her all the time when we were in college." He snorted. "I had to physically hold him back once when he wanted to drive all the way down to Ann Arbor to see her. A nine hundred mile round trip just to see her?" His mouth curved in a wry smile.

"Our folks would've had a stroke if they'd known."

"I know. Anyway, that was in college. Since then . . ." He shrugged. "He never said much about dating when he and I got together. Not that we got together that often."

"I thought they'd split up. Shows how much I know."

After reaching around her for the bottle, he refilled his glass. He took a slow sip of Scotch. "Ellen mentioned Sarah Jane put together that video."

"She did, yet she didn't stay long at the visitation. She went up to the casket, laid her hand on Jack's chest, then took off." Maggie had wondered about that at the time, but then someone had been talking to her, and she had to focus on him. "She didn't even stop to say anything to me."

"That was Sarah Jane?" He finished off his second drink. "She stopped and said something to Ben and Vander Haar. They weren't very happy. In fact, Junior glared at her as she left."

"I assumed she knew Ben. Besides being Jack's girlfriend, they all worked together before Ben and Jack went off on their own. Why would Greg be upset with her? Would he even know her?"

"I hate to say it—and don't you dare say I told you so—but something bizarre is going on."

"Moi?" She raised her glass. "Would I say I told you so?"

"Point taken."

"Are you going to call that guy at the sheriff's office? Watson?"

"I'll wait until tomorrow, after he gets the report from the police. If she sends it."

After Drew set his empty glass on the counter, he looped his arms loosely around her waist. "Maggie? I want you to be careful."

"What? Why?"

"I think you stirred up a hornet's nest by insisting the crash was no accident. The anger behind the destruction at Jack's worries me. What if that person comes after you?"

Fear zinged through her. She shook it off. "Why? I don't know anything."

"Just be careful." He kissed her lightly on the lips. She tasted Scotch and knew he must taste hers.

He pulled back. "I'm going to walk home. I'm not drunk, but I'd rather not get pulled over. I'll be back in the morning for my car."

As he turned to leave, she grabbed hold of his shirt and pulled him close. "If we aren't going to do anything more tonight, I want a better kiss than that."

She planted her mouth on his and made sure he wouldn't sleep any better than she would.

Kissing Maggie May was just about the dumbest thing he'd done in years. Leaving her was harder. That last kiss nearly destroyed his resolve not to stay the night. She had to be in no doubt as to his desire. He hadn't hidden it. With a stupid grin, he strolled down her driveway, feeling as giddy as a teen and twice as horny.

As he turned toward his house, he caught movement out of the corner of his eye. A curtain twitched in Mrs. O'Malley's living room window. A wicked urge to wave at her surged through him. Being a sensible adult, he refrained. He glanced at Maggie's house and noticed the lights in the kitchen still blazed. For a moment, he watched her gather their glasses and take them to the sink.

If he could see all that from the street, he cringed at what the eagle-eyed neighbor must have observed. He hoped she wouldn't tell Maggie. Knowing Mrs. O'Malley from his youth, he doubted the old woman would keep it to herself. Maybe he should give Mags a heads-up.

As he strolled down the quiet suburban street, he pulled out his phone.

"Forget something?" she answered.

"Uh, maybe you should close the drapes in the living room. Your friendly Neighborhood Watch is hard at work."

"Dear Lord. Thanks."

He glanced back at her house in time to see the curtains close. He chuckled softly to himself. Oh, she was going to hear about it.

Dogs barked as he passed, and owners tried to shush them.

Who knew Maggie had learned to kiss so well? Without

him to teach her. What an idiot he'd been all those years ago. No, not an idiot. Smart. Neither of them was ready for a sexual adventure back then. At fifteen, she'd been jailbait, while he had his eighteen-year-old life planned out and ahead of him.

Just like they weren't ready for sex tonight. It wouldn't have been casual. If they'd kissed any longer in her kitchen, he would've picked her up, set her on the counter, and taken her. Right there. In the kitchen. Lights blazing. Wouldn't that have given Mrs. O'Malley an education? Or not. Entertainment?

He could've attributed his overwhelming desire to abstinence. He'd told her the truth about his non-existent love life. Even though he and Lillian had been drifting apart for years—she with her activities and he with his work—his marriage vows meant he stayed faithful to his wife. He'd wondered about her, though. Her accident cut off his suspicions that she might have had a lover. After she was gone, he didn't want to know. What did it matter at that point?

Abstinence alone hadn't dictated his actions with Maggie. She wasn't just an available female. The talk out on the funeral home porch with the guys hadn't provided an impetus. Thoughts of making love with her had haunted his dreams since the camping trip last weekend, similar to his adolescent dreams but with more of an impact. He'd have to be careful not to give away his feelings around Ellen. According to Maggie, his daughter was still dealing with her mother's death.

He let himself into his house. It felt empty, lonely with Ellen at his folks'. In the light over the stove, he poured himself another Scotch. He didn't need any more lights. In fact, since Lilian died, he often sat in the dark, nursing a drink and pondering his life's direction. Nights when he felt loss and hope for a better life.

As he settled in his recliner, thoughts about Maggie May Sinclair drifted into his mind. Once the whole affair with Jack was resolved, they were taking their mutual attraction to a higher level. He was ready. From her response in her kitchen, she was, too.

Drifting off to sleep, he heard dogs barking and a truck slowly driving down the street.

Jack's funeral was a somber affair attended by Ben and a few other of Jack's close friends, Maggie's friends, and Drew's family. She was surprised that Sarah Jane hadn't come. Neither had Greg Vander Haar, not that she expected him to. She'd seen enough of him the night before at the funeral home.

The priest called it a celebration of life. It didn't feel that way to Maggie. Visitations and funeral services were supposed to be for the living, to give them closure. She didn't want closure. She wanted answers. Just like at her parents' funerals, the songs she'd chosen, though beautiful and uplifting, made her cry. And would bring tears every time she heard them in the future.

Drew gave a eulogy that made the congregation laugh and many, including herself, cry. Maggie heard Ben sobbing behind her. Drew started the eulogy the same way he told the story to Ellen on Monday morning. The girl clung to Maggie's arm and laughed between tears. Maggie patted her elbow while wanting to be somewhere else. A happier place. While Jack wasn't big on religion, their upbringing was such that a service seemed appropriate.

She was going to leave instructions for whoever had to deal with her death that she didn't want any of this. No visitation. Nobody looking at her and saying, "Doesn't she look natural?" There wasn't anything natural looking about a dead body. She wanted to be cremated and her ashes scattered out on Lake Michigan. They could have a memorial service. She didn't care about that. Nothing would really matter to her then. She'd be dead.

Drew's squeezing her hand brought her back to the present. Apparently, he'd finished, slid into the pew next to her, and the priest was winding up the service. Thank you, God.

Now, she just had to get through leaving the casket at the cemetery—no way was she watching it lowered into the ground—and a luncheon where she'd have to listen to stories and receive more condolences. Who was the sadist who thought this was a good idea? She wanted to smack them.

Maggie pulled packages of dried fruits, nuts, sunflower seeds, and M & Ms out of the cupboard and set them on the counter. Even though Drew suggested they cancel Saturday's camping trip, she needed the normalcy of it. She thought Ellen might need it, too.

When she talked to Tom Watson at the sheriff's office about the vandalism at Jack's, he reassured her he was investigating. He also said he'd had Jack's Blazer towed to the State Police lab. Guilty panic swamped her. She told him how she'd emptied the vehicle. Had she destroyed evidence? Despite his assurances, guilt continued to plague her the rest of the afternoon.

Now, if she didn't get her rear in gear, she'd be late for the meeting with the girls. As she grabbed a box of plastic sandwich bags out of the cupboard, she heard a soft sound in the living room. She froze. There it was again.

She walked around the corner to check. She had no idea who was more startled. She or the man standing in her living room.

"Maggie!"

"Ben!" she said at the same time. "What . . ."

"I rang the bell," he said in a rush. "I was worried when you didn't answer. Your garage door is open, and your SUV is inside. I thought . . . maybe . . . you needed help."

"Maybe CPR after the fright you just gave me." She forced a wry smile. "My doorbell doesn't work. Why are you here?"

Ben had dark shadows under his eyes and white pain creases along his mouth. He leaned heavily on his crutch as he limped farther into the room. Suddenly he stumbled, and she reached out to help. His crutch caught the leg of the square coffee table, causing the basket of apples to wobble. He grabbed her around the waist then fell into an easy chair. She tried to regain her balance and failed.

"Oh, my goodness," she cried out as she fell on top of him. "Did I hurt you?"

"You could never hurt me, Maggie." He held her closer. "This feels right, doesn't it?"

She didn't think sitting on his lap felt right, at all. In fact, she felt awkward and then uncomfortable. She tried to get up, but he tightened his arm.

"We could be good together, Maggie. Jack would've wanted me to take care of you."

As if she needed anyone to take care of her. She'd done a fine job for the past thirteen years. With as much grace as possible, she tried to extricate herself from his embrace. Even with one arm disabled, he had a strong grasp. Panic raced through her at being trapped by his muscular arm. Remembering her therapist's advice chased away the panic. *Be firm. No wimpy request. Demand.*

"Good God, Ben. What are you thinking? Let me up this minute."

"I'm sorry, Maggie. So sorry." His contrition made her feel guilty.

But he did release her. She quickly backed out of his reach. He looked so pathetic, she tried to soften her rejection. "You should be home resting. You're trying to do too much, too soon after your accident."

"There's so much to do." He wearily shook his head. "So many loose ends to tie up."

What was that all about? She didn't have time to ask. "Ben, you have to leave."

Tears welled up in his light blue eyes. "I'm sorry. I didn't mean to grab you. I lost my head when I fell. It's just . . . I've always wanted us to be together. I promise not to grab you again. Please let me stay." His voice cracked with emotion.

Now, she felt worse. "I'm not throwing you out because of that. It was an accident." *Good grief. I'm apologizing for his bad behavior.* "I have a meeting with the girls. I need to leave."

Guilt easily erased, his eyes cleared, and he levered himself off the chair. "A meeting?"

She picked up his crutch. "The girls and I are camping this weekend. We always have a meeting to finalize our plans. The meeting starts shortly. I have to go."

"Camping? You're going camping?" He latched onto that

instead of the fact that she needed to leave. "Jack said you didn't do that anymore."

"The girls wanted to start going again. That's where I was when Jack—" She cleared her throat and blinked rapidly to hold the tears at bay. Wouldn't that be a sight? Two blubbering fools. She looked at her watch. "I really need to get to that meeting."

"Where is it? I could drive you."

She waved aside his offer. "I'm fine." With her hand on his back, she ushered him toward the front door. The open front door.

Hadn't she closed it earlier and locked it? When she was getting ready for the meeting? Jack's funeral must have discombobulated her more than she thought.

Ben stopped at the door. "I could help you. I've always liked to camp out." He looked as eager as a puppy waiting for a treat. She stared pointedly at his crutch and sling, and he grimaced. "Not this time, I guess. But, you shouldn't go alone. It's not safe to go by yourself."

She walked past him and out to the porch where she held the screendoor for him, hoping he'd take the hint. "I don't go alone."

"But, your friend—the one you camped with—didn't she move?" He walked out onto the porch.

"Yes. One of the dads is going with me to chaperone. Drew Campbell." *Okay, Ben, one more step and then down to the sidewalk.*

He stopped. He still had one foot—the uninjured one—on the porch. "Campbell?" His eyes narrowed, and his blond eyebrows came to a point above his nose. "You're letting Campbell go with you?"

Oh, brother. She should've kept her mouth shut about Drew. "Ben, I really need to leave."

She couldn't take his arm and *encourage* him to start walking. Not with one arm in a sling and the other holding the crutch for balance. So, with her hand in the middle of his back, she started walking toward the vehicle in her driveway, a big, black 4 x 4 that could probably climb mountains.

Ben hobbled alongside her. At least, he was getting with the program. "Be careful around Campbell, Maggie. His reputation is . . . well . . . he's a shark."

"A shark? That's rather harsh." She reached around and opened the driver door for him, wondering how he was going to climb inside. Even with her long legs, she'd have trouble, and he wasn't much taller. He'd obviously figured out a way since he threw the crutch across the seat and effortlessly hauled himself up into the vehicle.

Ben's eyes narrowed. "Are you sleeping with him?"

Maggie didn't bother to hide her shock. "What! That is none of your business."

"But his car—"

"What about his car?"

"It was in your driveway last night."

A chill ran through her. "How do you know that?"

"I, uh, drove past. To make sure you got home safely from the funeral home." He added the last in a hurry. "Jack would've wanted me to watch out for you. To take care of you."

If she were a cartoon character, steam would be coming out of her ears. She took several deep breaths to quell her anger. "The person you need to take care of is yourself. Go home and get some sleep. The world won't come to an end if everything doesn't get down instantly. Your clients will understand." She closed his door.

He leaned through the open window. "I meant what I said about Campbell. I know he was Jack's—" His voice cracked. "Jack's friend. But the man will stop at nothing to get his way. Be very careful around him, Maggie."

"Go home, Ben. I won't listen to another word about Drew." She stalked back to the house then turned around when he started the engine. Above the rumble, she said, "Do not enter my house unless I invite you."

She didn't wait for his response or watch him back down the drive. Fury over what he said about Drew spurred her into the house. How dare he ask if she was sleeping with Drew! The thought of him driving by her house at night gave her more chills. How many times had he done that?

He mentioned Drew's car. How did he know what Drew drove? Had he followed them from the funeral home? Did he sit outside and wait to see if Drew left? Remembering Drew mentioned Mrs. O'Malley and the open drapes, she groaned. Oh, God. Who else had seen her and Drew kissing?

As she burst into her kitchen, she told herself to calm down. To think about the girls and the meeting. Ben's actions and words raced through her as she loaded everything for the meeting in her wagon, a red Radio Flyer from her childhood. With Ellen's house only a few blocks away, she'd planned to walk. What little time she would save by driving would be eaten up with reloading her supplies into the Suburban. Now, she would have to run, dragging the little wagon behind her.

She quickly locked the house, especially the front door. Darn, she needed to replace the doorbell. Why hadn't he knocked? He said he'd called out. In her concentration with the meeting, she must have missed that. For Ben to walk in made her feel . . . vulnerable. At first. Anger quickly overcame vulnerability. She was not vulnerable. She was strong, capable.

She recalled how Drew had walked in on her. Although startled by him, it wasn't the same as when Ben did.

What had gotten into him? The wheels of the wagon rattled behind her. He sounded so lonely, forlorn, devastated by Jack's passing. And what was all that about Drew? A shark? She didn't think so. But, maybe Ben knew something she didn't. No. She knew Drew. Ben's comments smacked of jealousy.

By the time she reached Ellen's drive, she was winded and sweaty. Maggie waited at the curb until a van pulled away.

"Hi, Ms. Sinclair, can I help you with the wagon?" Gretchen said.

"Thanks, I—"

"Where have you been?" Ellen raced down the front steps.

"I'm not late," Gretchen protested.

"Not you." Ellen fisted her hands on her hips and glared at Maggie.

"I'll, uh, just go inside," Gretchen said. "And get some of the girls to help bring in the supplies." She ran into the house.

Ellen continued to glare at Maggie. "You are late."

150

Maggie was still irritated at Ben for delaying her as well as his unexpected embrace. During the brief time she sat on his lap, she was certain he'd been aroused. That perturbed her more than him not releasing her immediately. What had gotten into him?

But, she couldn't take her frustrations out on Ellen. "I'm sorry. I got held up by an unexpected visitor. Is everyone here already?"

"Except you and my father." She spit out the last word. "He went to work after Uncle Jack's funeral, and he's still there. He does this all the time. He's always late for stuff that's important to me. He never—"

Maggie held up her hand. "Could you save this until after the meeting?"

Just then Mrs. Boersma, Drew's part-time housekeeper, came out of the house. "I'll be leaving now. Tell Mr. Campbell his dinner is in the refrigerator and only needs warming up in the microwave."

Head erect, she strode down the street toward her own house a few blocks away. For a woman in her early seventies, she could really book. Head high, back erect, a lengthy stride. Maggie hoped when she was that age she had that kind of energy.

The rest of the girls came out. At Gretchen's directions, they hauled the supplies into Ellen's house. After giving Maggie a mutinous look, Ellen picked up the last box. Maggie left the wagon on the wide front porch next to a large planter with colorful geraniums.

Once in the Campbell's spacious family room, Maggie apologized to the girls for being late. Ellen started in again about her father then burst into tears. The other girls huddled around her, as supportive as they'd been since Ellen's mother died. Except for Susan who sat a little apart, close to tears herself. Her parents were divorcing, and her father had moved out two months ago. The last time Ellen complained about Drew, Susan snapped that at least she was still living with her dad. To head off another confrontation, Maggie caught Gretchen's eye and nodded. Gretchen called the meeting to order.

Three months ago, when the girls started discussing the

Isle Royale trip again, they unanimously elected Gretchen their leader. She had been quite shy when she first joined the troop. The girls soon recognized that they could depend on her to do what she promised. She'd blossomed with the responsibility of leadership.

At ten after seven, the rumble of the garage door stopped all discussion. The girls turned toward the doorway to the hall leading to the garage. The garage door was still rumbling for a second time when Drew rushed into the family room. His collar open and his tie loosened, he appeared harried.

Ellen shot to her feet. Once again, she planted her fists on her hips and glared. "You are late."

Before Maggie or Drew could speak, Gretchen said, "Ellen, you are out of order. Beth, continue with your report on the food."

Torn between wanting to ream out her father and obeying the elected leader, Ellen finally chose the latter, and she sat down.

After Beth wrapped up her report—a total of two more sentences—Gretchen looked at Drew who still hesitantly stood between the kitchen and the family room. "Mr. Campbell, we're very glad you came. We just started reports on the last camping trip. Please join us. When we break for snack, we will give you the highlights of what you missed. Okay, Susan, you're next. How was the equipment?"

Drew caught Maggie's eye. An amused twinkle glinted from his eyes. Had he been summarily dismissed or what? Maggie marveled at how effortlessly Gretchen smoothed over the awkward situation. Trish had set the precedent during their first year together. The meeting started on time. Latecomers were welcomed, and the meeting continued. No reviewing what had been said so far. Knowing they wouldn't miss anything only encouraged people to be tardy, Trish claimed. The girls learned well.

During the break, while munching on Beth's no-bake cookies, the girls clustered around Drew, several talking at once.

"You're coming with us again, aren't you?"

"It's going to be so much fun!"

"We got you a new tent!"

"We'll show you how to put it up!"

Ellen stood off to the side. Her face expressed several emotions. Anger, jealousy, envy, longing. Maggie could see how much she wanted to join the other girls, yet pride kept her from doing so. Pride could ruin relationships faster than a raccoon tearing through nylon to get to food. As Maggie well knew. Her own pride had gotten in the way of friendships too many times.

"One minute," Beth, this meeting's time-keeper, announced.

Promptly, the girls went into action cleaning up and then returning to the family room for the remainder of the meeting. Drew glanced over at Maggie in a state of shock. Because Maggie and Trish had worked hard in the early years—and those early years had been very difficult—Maggie was used to the girls' efficiency and the way they ran the group.

During their youth, she and Trish had been in a troop where the leader did everything, made all the decisions. They were planning to quit when the leader moved, and a student from near-by Hope College volunteered to lead their troop. She encouraged them to take on responsibility. And although they'd grumbled at first, the troop soon discovered the joy and pride of doing it themselves. That Girl Scout Leader was so exceptional Trish and Maggie patterned themselves after her.

". . . Ms. Sinclair?" Gretchen's voice penetrated Maggie's reminiscence of her youth.

With a look of chagrin, Maggie said, "Sorry?"

"You were going to demonstrate the most efficient way to pack our backpacks? Because some of us have forgotten." Gretchen stared pointedly to Maggie's left at Janie and Susan who ducked their heads.

As soon as the girls left, Ellen stomped up to her bedroom. She didn't even stop to say anything to Drew. He'd have to talk to her after she calmed down.

"Gretchen could give George McCrucheon, our senior partner, lessons on how to run a meeting," he mused. "I can't get over how they jumped to without you nagging or even telling them what to do."

Maggie smiled. "You think this happened all by itself? It was like pulling teeth at the beginning. But, Trish wouldn't give up. She started out small and gradually turned over running the meetings to the girls. They took turns but soon discovered they liked how Gretchen kept things running smoothly. Oh, they complain sometimes that she's too bossy, but she laughs and doesn't let power go to her head."

"You know, at first, I thought the girls were too serious." He poured them both a glass of the sun tea Mrs. Boersma made each day. "I mean, isn't this group supposed to have fun?" She started to protest, but he hurried on, "They changed my mind during the break when they were all giggly."

"You mean when they talked about their summer vacation?"

"Don't forget the *cute* lifeguard at the pool." He made a face. "My God, I didn't think girls thought about a guy's, uh, *attributes*, let alone talked about them."

"You're joking, right?"

"Hell, no. They're only fourteen, for God's sake."

She just laughed. "Come to enough meetings, and you'll get a real education."

"Speaking of meetings." Drew shoved his hand through his hair. He'd procrastinated long enough. He deserved a good dressing down from Maggie. Better he brought it up first, though. "Listen, I'm sorry I was late."

"You weren't the only one. I had an unexpected visitor. Ben." She shook her head. "Never mind. Listen, Ellen's mad at both of us."

"I'll talk to her."

"You should. Help her understand that it won't always be like this." Maggie glanced at him. "It won't, will it? You will cut back on your hours?"

"Yes," he sighed. "One more week, and I'm through."

"Through?"

Surprised that she didn't remember, he said, "With the firm. I'm leaving. I'm wrapping up the last of my cases." He yanked off his already loosened tie. In his new office, he wasn't going to wear a tie. Only to court.

"That soon? I didn't realize. You really need to talk to Ellen. You're making a major change in both your lives."

Expecting another lecture, he was surprised that she just walked to the front door. "I need to get home."

He had mixed feelings about her leaving. He wanted her to stay, to talk to her about his plans. Yet he had to talk to his angry daughter. "Even though I hate to admit it, you've been right all along. About Ellen, about the job." He started up the stairs. On the fifth step, he turned around. "I didn't see your Suburban out front. How did you get here?"

She gave him a saucy grin. "Bipedal power. You should try it some time. Oops. I forgot you walked home last night. You still need to walk more."

"Nobody likes a smart-ass, Maggie May."

Her face crumpled. She blinked several times. "Jack said that the last time—" She opened the door. "I gotta go."

"Maggie?" He took one step down the stairs.

"No. Your daughter needs you. I'm fine. See you Saturday at seven."

For a moment, Drew was torn. He wanted to comfort Maggie for inadvertently bringing her to tears. Yet, his daughter needed him. Family won.

Ellen was lying on her bed, iPod on her stomach, earbuds in place, eyes closed, lost in music so loud he could hear it. Drew flipped the light switch, which controlled the overhead light and ceiling fan, up and down to get her attention. It didn't.

He called her name. She didn't respond, except for a tightening of her mouth.

Okay, she knew he was there and was being stubborn. He walked into the room, avoiding the clothes, shoes, books, and *girl* paraphernalia strewn across the floor. He'd told Mrs. Boersma not to clean Ellen's room, that it was her own responsibility. Looked like he needed to take a shovel to it. If he said something about it now, it would only distract them both from his real purpose.

He called her again, this time tweaking her big toe.

"Go away," she said over the music, without opening her eyes.

"No." He sat on the edge of her double bed, switched off the iPod, and removed the earbuds. "We need to talk."

"I don't want to talk to you." She rolled on her side away from him.

"Then, listen while I talk. I know you're upset because I was late."

"A-gain."

He put his hand on her shoulder and rolled her over. She glared up at him. A minor improvement. At least, she was looking at him.

He smoothed her hair away from her forehead. She'd inherited a combination of features from him and Lillian. As a baby, Ellen's hair had been nearly blonde, much to Lillian's delight who kept her own hair blonde, with help from Mr. J. As Ellen grew older, her hair darkened until it was nearly as dark as Drew's. She had his eyes and forehead. Thank God, she got Lillian's small nose and not his honker. Unfortunately, she also had Lillian's stubborn chin.

"Baby, I want you to know that the long hours I've been putting in are going to end next week."

"Promises, promises." Good Lord, she sounded like her mother. She even crossed her arms and set her jaw in perfect imitation of Lillian.

"I'm serious. Next week is my last at the firm."

Ellen sat up, her eyes wide. "Oh, Daddy. Did you get fired?"

"No, nothing like that. I'm going to set up my own practice. I have to finish—"

"But, Daddy, we'll be destitute."

"What?"

"If you leave the firm, we won't have any money. We'll be poor," she wailed.

"Where did you ever get such an idea?"

"That's what Mom said. I heard you guys arguing once, and I asked her if you were getting a divorce, and she told me you wanted to leave the firm, and she said we wouldn't have any money, and we'd be really poor and—"

Stunned, Drew held up his hand. "Whoa."

He'd talked about going out on his own two years ago. He knew he was missing too much. Ellen was growing up too fast without him. Lillian seemed to have her own life. He wanted—needed—his family back. Yet, when he mentioned either cutting back on his hours or starting his own practice, she'd gone nearly ballistic. He remembered that argument but wished Ellen hadn't overheard.

"Oh, baby." He pulled her into his arms. "We have enough savings to carry us until my practice grows. We won't be poor. Or destitute. God, I can't believe you thought that. We might have to cut back on a few luxuries, but you won't have to sell all this stuff—" He waved to indicate the over-abundance of possessions strewn around the room. "—for our next vacation."

"Dad-dy."

"If things get bad, I can always stand at the exit ramp of 131 and Pearl with a sign that says 'will work for country club dues'."

She batted his arm.

"Or, you could turn over your babysitting money for the house payment, though." He snapped his fingers. "That might not be enough. You'll have to raise your rates. Or, better yet, you'll have to quit school and get a real job. Let's see now. Are there any sweatshops nearby? Since you can't drive yet, you'll have to walk."

"You are being silly." Ellen almost smiled. "When I wanted to get a job at McDonald's, like Beth's sister, you told me there are laws about kids working."

"You got me there." He hugged her. "Don't worry about money. You should worry that I'll be home more and have to crack the whip so you clean your room."

She pulled away and gave him a fake look of astonishment. "You would beat your child? You could be arrested."

He waggled his eyebrows. "But, I know a good lawyer." He pointed his thumb to his chest.

"Didn't you say that a person who defends himself has a fool for a client?"

Drew stood. "Do you have a photographic memory or what? I can't say anything without my words coming back to haunt me."

"You're really leaving the firm? Will they let you?"

"They're not very happy, especially George, but they can't force me to stay. I've leased a small office about two blocks from the high school." Drew was flying by the seat of his pants now. "Maybe you'd like to help me get the place set up?"

"Really? I could help?" She bounced up on her knees, looking surprised. And eager. God, what a fool he'd been not to talk to her before.

"After school starts you could walk over to the office and—"

The ringing of his cell phone cut him off.

"Don't answer that," Ellen said.

Drew was tempted to listen to her. If he did answer, it could destroy the tentative peace between them. "It could be Grandpa," he said lamely, then pulled his cell off his belt. "Not Grandpa," he said. "Maggie."

He raised his eyebrow in question. "If you say so, I'll ignore the call."

"No. You should answer it. At least, it's not work."

"Drew?" Maggie sounded shaky. *"Sarah Jane is dead."*

CHAPTER TEN

When Drew ran up Maggie's driveway, she was talking to Grace Neill, the officer who'd responded to the vandalism at Jack's condo. She was from the police department of the suburb where Jack had lived, not here. Standing nearby was Mrs. O'Malley, official Neighborhood Watch.

"Drew, thank goodness you came." Maggie gave him a grateful smile. "Ellen? I don't think—"

Drew spun around. "What are you doing here? I told you to wait at home."

She set her mouth in a mutinous line. "I heard what Maggie said on your phone. I know Sarah Jane." Eyes filling with tears, she looked at Maggie. "What happened?"

"That's what I'd like to know," Mrs. O'Malley drew herself up. "As soon as I saw the Walker PD car here in Jennison, I knew something bad had happened."

Seeing Maggie's exasperation with her busybody neighbor, Drew said, "Maybe we should go inside."

Maggie mouthed 'Thank you' then said aloud, "Thanks for your concern, Mrs. O'Malley. We won't keep you."

The older woman didn't take the hint. She started to follow Maggie and Officer Neill inside. Drew stopped her. "You can go home now, Mrs. O'Malley."

"Well, I never," she huffed then shuffled back across the street. If Drew wasn't mistaken about her muttering, she was heaping all kinds of dire threats on his head.

Officer Neill, Ellen, and Maggie sat at the dining room table, in silence.

"Thank you for waiting for me." He pulled out a chair.

"As I told Ms. Sinclair, I went to Ms. DeHoesen's apartment to question her about the vandalism in Mr. Sinclair's condo."

"Vandalism?" Ellen exclaimed. "At Uncle Jack's?"

Drew patted her hand. "I'll tell you later. Go on, Officer."

"She did not appear to be at home. When I checked with the neighbors, they said they'd heard arguing earlier. One neighbor had a key. I found Ms. DeHoesen in the bathtub—" She glanced at Ellen and stopped.

Drew knew what came next. "You don't need to go any further, Officer."

"What?" Ellen demanded. "Why did you cut her off?"

"Officer Neill thinks Sarah Jane killed herself," Maggie said softly.

"No," Ellen wailed. "Not Sarah Jane. She wouldn't do that."

Maggie caught Drew's eye. She had the same suspicion he did.

"I'll be back. Don't wait for me." Drew stood. "Ellen?"

Ellen pouted before reluctantly shoving back her chair. "You just don't want me to hear the grisly details."

"That's right." He tried to take her elbow, but she yanked away. "I'm sorry, Maggie. You and Officer Neill carry on."

After dropping Ellen off at his parents' house—what he should've done in the first place—he made it back to Maggie's in twenty minutes.

The squad car was gone. The curtain in Mrs. O'Malley's front window twitched. He knocked on the front door. He had to replace her doorbell. Tomorrow.

As soon as the door opened, Maggie threw herself into his arms. "What is happening?"

He held her, cradling her head, rubbing her back. When he heard a 4 x 4 rumble down the street, Maggie yanked him inside and slammed the front door behind them.

"I think Ben is stalking me."

Not what he expected to hear. "What?"

"His 4 x 4 just went by. I've heard it several times since Jack died."

"I heard a rumble like that last night after I got home."

"I need a drink. And forget iced tea." She filled glasses with ice while he pulled down the liquor bottles.

"After the day you've had, I understand. Tell me what Officer Neill said. I assume Sarah Jane cut her wrists."

"That's what it was supposed to look like. Grace Neill is one smart cookie." Maggie took her drink out to the living room. After glancing at the picture window—the drapes were closed—she curled up in the corner of the sofa.

Drew took the chair across from her. "I thought the same last night, even if she fixated on Sarah Jane for the vandalism."

"She'd already done research on Sarah Jane before she went to her apartment. Neill said when a person cuts their wrists, they make a few tentative slices." Maggie shuddered. "I am so glad you took Ellen to your folks'. She didn't need to hear this."

"Let me guess. No tentative attempts. Just slashes."

Maggie nodded before taking a slow sip of her Irish whiskey. "What is going on, Drew? What can of worms did I open?"

"*We* opened it. I've been with you all along investigating Jack's death."

"Reluctantly." Her smile was supposed to reassure him.

In a salute, he raised his glass. "Reluctantly."

"Thank you for coming tonight. I'd stopped outside to pull some weeds in the front yard when Officer Neill drove up. She told me about Sarah Jane, and all I could think about was telling you."

Her face crumpled. He set his glass on a nearby table and sat next to her. He held her hand. "Any time you call, I'll be here."

"I know." She squeezed his fingers. "Neill said they have to wait for a tox screen, but she thinks Sarah Jane might have been doped. No bruises as if someone forced her into the tub. No fingerprints, either. Not even hers. Someone wiped down the whole apartment."

The next morning, Maggie strode into Ben's office. She didn't even pause at Natalie's desk, leaving the receptionist's mouth gaping.

"Did you drive by my house last night?"

Ben jumped. He'd been staring off to the left when she stormed in. "Wh-What?"

"You heard me." She stood with her hands on her hips. "A black 4 x 4 with tinted windows, like yours, drove down my street around nine last night. Was that you?"

"Uh." He reached in his drawer then popped something in his mouth.

"Was that you?"

"You're upset. What is this all about?"

"Sarah Jane DeHoesen was killed yesterday." She ignored his gasp and plunged on. "What did she say to you and Greg Vander Haar at the funeral home?"

His eyes widened. Despite his initial pale, a flush started at his neck and swiftly rose. "I-I don't know what you're talking about?"

"Do not lie to me, Ben Voorheis. I teach high school. I know when boys are lying to me. Drew saw Sarah Jane stop and say something to you two before she left the funeral home. What did she say?"

He perked up. "Campbell? You can't believe anything he says." When she glared at him, he cleared his throat. "She offered her condolences. She knew Jack and I were friends. I told her the same thing."

While that sounded reasonable, she remembered what Drew said about their expressions. Offering condolences would not cause anger or fear.

Ben seized on her hesitation. "Campbell misconstrued what he saw. I told you he has his own agenda."

While what Ben said sounded logical, her instinct said he wasn't being totally honest with her. She realized he'd evaded her question about him driving past her house.

"You said Sarah Jane was killed?" he asked. "How?"

Maggie decided not to tell him what Officer Neill said. Not everything, anyway. "Suicide."

"Oh, God." He walked around his desk and hitched his hip on the corner. He scrubbed his good hand down his face. "I'd never guess Jack's death would hit her so hard."

"You think that's why she did it?"

"Of course. She left a note, right?"

"No." Officer Neill would have told her.

Ben tapped his knee. "How did you find out?"

"Jack's condo was vandalized while we were at the visitation."

"What? Why didn't you tell me?"

162

She ignored that. "The officer who responded thought Sarah Jane had done it, since she had a key. She went to talk to Sarah Jane and found her in the tub, her wrists slit."

He blanched. "Oh, God. I can't believe . . . ."

"Neither can I."

"You said she *was* killed." He hesitated. "Why didn't you say she killed herself?"

Amazed at his perception, she realized he was right. Because she wasn't sure if she should share her misgivings about how Sarah Jane had died, she shrugged. "I don't know. I can't believe such a strong woman like Sarah would do such a thing."

"Nobody is strong all the time." He came toward her. "You don't have to be strong all the time, Maggie. I'm here for you."

Realizing his intentions, she evaded his hug by folding her arms and taking a step back. "Ben, what is going on? First Jack's accident and now Sarah Jane's suicide? Has the world gone crazy?"

He rubbed the back of his neck. "I don't know. I just don't know."

"Mr. Campbell, that's a sassafras tree," Beth, the self-appointed tree identifier, informed him. "People used to make tea from the bark."

"Wait," Susan pointed to a fallen tree about two feet from the trail. "Come and look. But be careful not to disturb the area too much. This is a habitat for insects."

What Drew had thought of as just so much dead wood, best used for a nice fire on a winter evening, was crawling with bugs. He shuddered. But, Susan, who said she wanted to be an entomologist, proceeded to identify the different insects.

They walked on through the woods until Gretchen held up her hand then pointed to her ear. They all stopped and listened. They'd done this several times the previous Saturday, but Drew had been so absorbed in his own discomfort he hadn't paid much attention. This time, he heard a bird's song and chirping of some sort. A soft rustle over on the left. Leaves flapping in the slight breeze.

One by one, in a soft whisper, the girls identified the sounds, even the type of bird. He was amazed by their knowledge and intrigued. Even more so, he was fascinated by their desire to share their knowledge with him. Last weekend, they didn't seem to know how to treat him, as uncomfortable with him as he was with them. He thought it might be the change in Ellen's attitude.

As they walked together, she didn't say much, just walked beside him in comfortable silence. That was what he'd expected last week. Since he told her about leaving the firm and starting his own office, she'd changed toward him. Maggie was right. He should have told Ellen months ago.

When Ellen pointed out a nest high in a tree, he said, "Must be home to Big Bird."

"Squirrel's nest, Dad," she said patiently without the disgusted sigh at his ignorance. Then, she trotted ahead to catch up with Beth.

"How are you holding up?" Maggie asked.

He hadn't realized he'd lagged behind, intent on another squirrel's nest and pleased with himself that he recognized it. "Very well, Ms. Tour Director."

The path was wide enough for them to walk side by side.

"Better than last week, Tenderfoot?" Her grin dispelled the irritation he would've felt last Saturday. The difference in volunteering and feeling conned.

"Those kids sure know a lot. I'm embarrassed at my ignorance."

"Don't be," she said. "They love showing off, especially since you treat them with respect."

"Really? I didn't think . . ." He shrugged. "I try to treat them the way I treat Ellen."

"Good job."

When they came around another bend in the trail and he saw no clearing, no place where they could rest, he asked, "Are we stopping soon?"

"Tired?"

"Hungry. Isn't it time for lunch yet?" His watch, like his cell phone, was locked in the glove box of the Navigator. He felt naked without either of them.

When Maggie reminded the girls that they were on Nature's Time, the few who wore watches had removed them and left them in a covered box in her Suburban. Not that she ordered him to, but Drew complied. Then, she reminded them about no cell phones. As he'd learned before, she only carried hers for emergency purposes. Again, he complied. What kind of example would he set if he protested?

"Eat some trail mix," she suggested.

No way was he telling her he'd already eaten all of it. "I'm saving some for mid-afternoon."

Her smile at his lie made him wish he'd told her the truth. The girls had stopped again, another listening exercise. He and Maggie waited until the troop moved on again.

"In another mile, we'll come to a nice spot for lunch. It's a pretty, little glen."

"How do you know? Have you been here before?" They'd returned to Manistee National Forest but in a completely different area.

She gave him a disbelieving look. "Of course. You don't think I'd take the girls anywhere I hadn't scouted out first?"

"I hadn't thought about it." He also hadn't realized all the preparation she put into the trips. "You and Trish came here?"

"No. When the girls started talking about the Isle Royale trip and I knew how much practice they needed, I came up here a couple of weekends ago and checked out the area."

"With Jack?"

She went still for a moment. "He was too busy. I came by myself."

He stopped. "You hiked and camped by yourself? Are nuts? What if—"

"Stop," she said softly. "We have an audience."

Drew turned around. Sure enough, the eight girls who had been about fifty yards up the trail ahead of them were now about ten feet in front of them. Bad time for the girls to stop.

"Lead on, Ms. Sinclair," he said quickly. "I'll bring up the rear this time and make sure no one dawdles." He winked at the girls. Those who remembered Maggie's directive last weekend giggled. The others looked perplexed.

They finally reached the primitive campsite, their stop for the night. Maggie was grateful for the rest. She'd pushed it a little too much this time. The girls began to get cranky about an hour ago. The pace had slowed, but they'd all trudged on. At least, the humidity wasn't as bad as last weekend's, and a nice breeze ruffled hair and dried sweat.

The girls dropped their packs and sprawled on the ground, moaning in agony. Maggie wished she could. Drew appeared dead on his feet, about the way she felt.

He gave her a little smile, then announced, "Five minutes, girls. Then, we set up camp." He looked so pleased with himself for parroting her words, Maggie just smiled.

When he set his own backpack down and slumped on a log at the fire circle, she joined him. "We'll make a camper out of you yet, Campbell."

"Don't push it, Sinclair," he said softly. "I'm not sure if my feet are still attached."

He wasn't as disheveled as last week. Tousled, casual, but not bedraggled. His soft yellow golf shirt had stayed tucked into jeans that must have been washed several times. In fact, he looked better than she did.

"No goofing off, Ms. Camp Director." He stood and held out a hand. "Need help getting up?"

"Of course not." She promptly rose.

"You never could resist a challenge." He gave her a knowing smile before walking over to where the girls lay. "Okay, troop. Up and at 'em."

Groans and protests met his announcement.

"Are you girls too tired?" he said sympathetically. "I guess Ms. Sinclair will have to show me how to put up my tent."

They scrambled to their feet, each yelling, "No, I will."

Maggie chuckled. They were as unable to resist a challenge as she. God, he was good with them.

Drew must have dropped off to sleep before his head hit his make-shift pillow—the carry bag for his tent stuffed with his change of clothes. In fact, he hadn't moved all night, still lying on his right side.

The calls of morning birds—he'd have to ask Madison, the bird expert, what they were—were more effective than an alarm clock. He rolled on his back to listen and realized his arm was numb. *Oh, God, I'm too young for a heart attack.*

The pins and needles sensation quickly disabused him of that morbid thought.

The camp was quiet. On his way to the pit toilet, he watched where he stepped to avoid snapping twigs or clumping like an elephant. If the girls chattered and giggled long into the night the way they did last weekend, they probably wouldn't hear a bear charging through the forest.

The early morning sun cast a pinkish gold glow across the still lake surface. Maggie sat at the water's edge, her knees drawn up to her chin, staring out at the water.

She must have been up for a while, since the pan of water on the campstove was lukewarm. While he waited for the water to boil, he rubbed his arms. It wasn't exactly chilly, just a good deal cooler than he expected for almost the end of June. That was Michigan weather for you—beastly hot and humid one day, cool enough to need a sweatshirt the next.

One week until he left the firm. One week until he was on his own.

A trickle of fear crept down his spine. Trepidation had been doing that more often lately. In the beginning, he'd been filled with excitement and hope. But, as the time grew closer, he worried whether this was the right decision. Only yesterday, George McCrucheon, the senior partner, begged him to reconsider.

Not that George would admit to begging. He couched his words so that they sounded like concern. Did Drew know that over fifty percent of new businesses went under in the first year? Had he considered all the changes in lifestyle his reduced income would produce? What about health insurance? What George really meant was how would the firm adapt to reduction of a quarter or more of its income. Not to be immodest, Drew knew the loss of his rainmaker ability would greatly affect the firm. Despite his concern for his colleagues, Ellen came first.

The water wasn't boiling, yet hot enough to dissolve the instant coffee crystals. Careful to turn off the little stove, he took his coffee down to the water's edge. Maggie hadn't moved from where she huddled into herself, her arms around her knees. He didn't want to startle her, so he wasn't as careful about the noise he made.

He stopped beside her. "Mind if I join you?" he whispered.

"Go away, Campbell." Her voice was muffled against her knees.

She wanted time alone. He could understand that. He walked about ten feet down the narrow beach and took his first sip of coffee. The bitter taste made him realize he'd misjudged the amount of crystals again. Over and between the birds' singing, he heard another sound. A sob.

Maggie's shoulders were shaking. He rushed over and stooped next to her. She lifted her tear-stained face to him. "I miss him so much. He loved mornings like this."

She swiped at her eyes, which didn't do much good, and pressed her forehead to her knees. Her quiet sobs wrenched his heart. She was talking about her brother.

"Go away," she said again. "Just go away."

This time, he didn't. He could no more walk away and leave her in misery than he could tie a clove-hitch knot. He sat next to her, but when he put his hand on her shoulder, she flinched. Okay, easy does it, Ace. She'd kept so much bottled up inside. At Jack's funeral Thursday morning, she'd been dry-eyed and stoic, even when Ellen broke down. Maggie had held his daughter, offering comfort yet receiving none in return. He'd tried, but she stiffened her back, as well as her resolve, and said she was fine. She wasn't. He knew it and couldn't do a damn thing about it.

He surmised she continued with the camping trip as a way to keep busy, to hold grief at bay. It's what he did when Lillian died. As he discovered, grief got you sooner or later. It snuck up on you and when you least expected it, wham, grief slapped you upside the head.

When Drew couldn't stand the sound of Maggie's sobs, he put his arm around her shoulders and drew her close. She resisted for a moment before relaxing against him. Her sobbing tore at his heart. His own grief over the loss of his best friend sucked at his resolve. He had to be strong for her. Forcing down his emotions came easily. Almost easily. He'd done it before for Ellen. He could be strong for Maggie.

They sat like that, her head tucked into his shoulder, his cheek resting on her head. Even after her crying ceased, she didn't pull away. She'd been right. Jack would've enjoyed the beauty of the sunrise.

Susan and Janie were pains in the butt, Ellen thought. She'd tried to be understanding because Susan's parents were getting a divorce, and Janie's mom had lost her job. But, when they came back from the pit toilet, whispering and snickering, it was annoying. Ellen never liked sharing a tent with them. They acted so superior, like they were better than anyone else. And they stuck together like glue, excluding Ellen, Gretchen, and Beth. And that was just wrong. Not only for herself but for Gretchen, especially. Ellen really liked Gretch. She was fun, even if she was bossy at times.

But, Mrs. Morrow, and now Maggie, said they had to learn to get along with each other. So, each camp-out, they drew lots for tent assignments. At least, Beth was Ellen's other tentmate. But, she was still asleep.

Ellen rolled over trying to ignore the whispering. Until she heard her father's name. Then Maggie's. And then the words "making out."

She bolted upright. "What are you talking about?"

Susan gave her a smug smile. "Why don't you go out and see?"

"See what?"

Janie pointed to the tent opening.

Ellen scrambled out of her sleeping bag. In her haste to open the tent, she jammed the zipper. She had to listen to more snickers while she worked to release the fabric caught in the teeth of the zipper.

Finally, she opened the flap. Her dad and Maggie sat on the beach about a foot apart. Ellen whirled around on her knees. "They are *not* making out. You made that up."

"Did not."

"Did, too."

"Hey." Beth yawned. "Izzit time to get up?"

"We know what we saw," Susan said in a sing-song voice.

Beth rolled out of her sleeping bag. "Gotta go to the john. Come with me," she said to Ellen.

They had to use the buddy system, even though it was a pain in the butt when you were asleep and your buddy had to go. This time, Ellen was glad to leave the tent.

Halfway down the path, Beth said, "She just said that to make you mad."

"Huh?" Ellen watched her dad. He wasn't moving. And it didn't look like he and Maggie were talking, either.

"About your dad and Maggie."

"You heard?"

"A little hard not to. That elephant Janie stepped on my foot when they came back."

"They made it up," Ellen said defiantly.

"Why do you let her get to you?" Beth opened the door to the pit toilet. The smell was disgusting. But, better than trying to find a spot in the woods where there wasn't any poison ivy, especially at night.

After Ellen took her turn, Beth said, "Would it be so bad? Your dad and Maggie?"

Ellen didn't want to think about her dad dating . . . or, yuck, making out. She still felt guilty that she used to wish Maggie was her mother, instead of Lillian.

Drew kept an eye on Maggie during the long walk back. She showed no more signs of breaking down again than she did two minutes after he held her at the water's edge. Though he admired her control, her letting him hold her while she sobbed made him feel useful, like he really helped her.

More than once on the hike, he heard hushed giggles. Girls and their secrets, he mused.

They were a bedraggled bunch when they reached the parking lot where they'd left their vehicles. Instead of walking back the way they'd come, Maggie had led them along another path, one shorter than yesterday's. They had stored all the gear when Gretchen said, "Excuse me, Ms.

Sinclair and Mr. Campbell. Would you please stay here?"

Then, she called the rest of the girls together in a tight group at the opposite end of the deserted parking lot.

Drew sauntered over to Maggie. "Do you know what's going on?"

Maggie shook her head. "But, something is. They've been acting weird ever since we broke camp."

Several minutes later, the girls approached, Gretchen in the lead. The little girl shoved her glasses higher on her nose. She looked determined while the others appeared subdued. Ellen wouldn't look at him. Whatever lay on the pavement next to her foot held her undivided attention.

"We want to apologize," Gretchen said. "Someone was spreading rumors which stop here and now." She looked back at the girls behind her. Drew couldn't see who was the recipient of the stare. Gretchen must have learned from the expert, Maggie.

What was that all about?

"We know how much it hurts when people make up stories and spread lies," Gretchen went on. "Ms. Sinclair, we want you to know that we don't believe that you and Mr. Campbell were on the beach this morning . . . naked—" Gretchen blushed but went on. "—and having . . . um . . . sex."

Drew felt like he'd been hit in the face with a 5-iron. Maggie must have felt worse as her face flushed as red as the berries along the trail that she said were poison.

"And we also don't believe you slept in the same tent last night," Beth piped up.

While Drew reeled from what apparently had gone through the group, Maggie found her voice. "Thank you, Gretchen, for your faith in Mr. Campbell and me. You are absolutely right. We didn't. First, it was a little cold this morning to get naked." A few giggled, which didn't deter Maggie. "And did you see that beach? It wasn't even comfortable to sit on let alone—" She gave a droll smile. "Let's just say, rolling around on sharp grasses and rocks wouldn't be a lot fun."

Drew heard a few "I told you so's."

"Mr. Campbell is an honorable man. He joined us at great cost to himself. He doesn't even like being outdoors.

But, he sacrificed his weekends, so we could camp. As far as what apparently started this—"

Drew cut off Maggie by placing his hand on her shoulder. "As I'm sure you are all aware, last weekend, Maggie lost her brother. This morning she was crying, and I comforted her—much the way some of you, I'm sure, comforted Ellen after her mother died. Gretchen, I commend you for bringing this out in the open. You have a lot of courage."

"You really weren't kissing her?" Ellen asked softly. She sat up front with Drew, a change from her usual scramble into the back seat to sit with Beth and leaving the shotgun seat for one of the other girls.

"No," he said, just as softly. "I wasn't kissing Maggie."

"Oh." Ellen sank further into the seat.

Several miles passed, the girls in the backseat chattered away. While Drew wanted more kissing with Maggie, he wasn't doing it in front of eight little girls. After the two of them practically attacked each other in her kitchen, he'd taken his cues from her. She would tell him when she was ready. Only then would he take their relationship to the next level.

Kissing the all grown up Maggie was not the same as kissing the lanky teenager who wanted him to teach her how.

She'd been fifteen, and he'd been a dolt.

It was the first time he and Jack came back from college. They were so full of themselves. They were supposed to go out and cruise around the high school and their favorite hang-outs. Jack had been on the phone in the kitchen trying to convince his girlfriend to come with them.

Thoughts of Sarah Jane pierced his reminiscences. He'd talked to Maggie the day before and discovered how she'd confronted Ben Voorheis in his office. Drew's lecture on going alone to see Jack's partner who was possibly stalking her set back their relationship. His highhandedness, according to her, had to stop. She was a big girl and perfectly capable of taking care of herself. While he agreed with her being a big girl, he had problems with her thinking she could fend for herself.

Which brought him full circle around to that memory of his teenage blunder.

Rather than listen to Jack's abject pleading with his girlfriend, which made him want to barf, Drew had gone out to the Sinclair's backyard. He was throwing sticks for Maggie's dog, Whiskey, to fetch. The reddish-brown cockapoo-terrier mix thought he was a bird dog. He was good at retrieving but not releasing. Until Drew threw another stick. Then, Whiskey let go of the first one to run after the second.

When Maggie came out, she was dressed in a lime green halter top, that barely covered her budding breasts—breasts he'd had no business thinking about—and white shorts so tight he could see the lines of her bikini panties—panties he also shouldn't think about. She'd twisted her long hair into what he now realized was an artfully casual twist. Thinking about her breasts and panties drove his hormones into high gear.

But, Christ, she was his best friend's little sister. A kid he'd known since she was six. And he wanted her. Even more so, when she leaned against the tall maple and watched him for a few moments. That pose, vampish and coy in an older girl, made his jeans tighter than normal.

Then, she let out a little whimper. "I think my hair is caught in the bark."

Her helpless voice should have alerted him. Maggie May was never helpless.

But, He-Man that he was, Drew ran over to release her from the captivity of the big, bad maple tree. Almost free, she wiggled against him. He thought it was an accident. "Hold still," he'd said. "I've almost got your hair out of the tree."

She gave him a sultry smile. As soon as her hair was loose, she looped her arms around his neck. Her lips were moist, as if she'd just licked them. "Kiss me, Drew."

"What!" He tried to jerk away. But, not very hard.

"I want to know how to kiss."

Before he could protest, she pressed her soft mouth against his. She even Frenched him! What could he do? He had to respond. Had to. Ri-ight. Then, she gazed up at him, her blue eyes liquid and adoring. She sighed. "That was wonderful."

In the ensuing silence, he'd heard Jack calling him. Jack. Thank God, his best friend hadn't caught him. Guilt shot through Drew with the efficiency of a perfect flip at the end of a pool lane.

He disengaged her arms from around his neck. "I shouldn't have done that."

Her face fell, for a moment. "Sure. Well, now I'll know how to do it when someone special comes along."

Someone special? She was experimenting on him?

"Next time, little girl, practice on someone your own age. You kiss like a guppy."

God, she'd only been a year older than Ellen was now.

"I guess I wouldn't mind if you did kiss Maggie. Or someone." Ellen tentatively broke into his thoughts. "I mean, guys have to have . . . sex. Or they go crazy."

Drew almost drove off the highway. "Where did you hear that?"

"That's what Janie's sister's boyfriend told her when she wouldn't do it with him."

"El-len." Beth leaned forward. "*My* sister said guys just say that to get you to do it. They don't really go crazy. Do they, Mr. Campbell? I mean you're a guy, and you would know about stuff like that."

Oh, Christ. Sex Ed on the road?

"Uh, no," he said. "They don't." *They just think they will.* "And, yes, that is a line a guy who doesn't care about a girl will say to get her to say yes."

"What other things do they say?" asked Gretchen, who like Madison, was leaning forward as far as the seatbelts would allow. "We should know stuff like that so we're prepared."

"Right," said Beth.

Help.

A blue sign was his salvation. "Rest Area, one mile," he announced. "Ellen, let Maggie—I mean, Ms. Sinclair—know we're pulling off."

Ellen picked up the walkie-talkie and announced their intention.

"But, Mr. Campbell," Gretchen said in a bewildered voice. "We don't need to stop."

He came out of the men's room and saw the girls clustered around Maggie. She said something to them, and they all ran to the vehicles. Then she sauntered up to Drew. "I hear there was an interesting discussion in your car."

Heat crept up his neck.

She made chicken noises.

"Flap your arms and I'll have to hurt you," he said softly.

"So, what lines *do* guys use to get into a girl's pants?" She smirked.

He leaned down and whispered, "The day before we left for college, Jack told Jenny Simpson he had a terminal illness and wasn't going to live to see Halloween."

"What!" Maggie jerked away. "That is so lame."

"Yeah, that's what Jenny said. She didn't believe he had a miraculous recovery, either."

"Well, I got you off the hook this time. I told the girls that would be a good topic for our next meeting."

"That's one I'll be sure to miss," he said.

"You owe me, Campbell."

Drew slung his arm around her neck. "You're a good sport, Sinclair." And he gave her a noogie.

On the drive home, Maggie thought about the hornet's nest her sitting on the beach had stirred up. She would be forever grateful to Gretchen's putting the kabosh on the abounding rumors. Good grief, she could just hear the phone calls from parents who already thought primitive camping was, well, too primitive. Even though she knew Janie's mother often let *her* boyfriends spend the night, and Susan's father had cheated with his administrative assistant, Maggie also knew gossip could destroy her reputation faster than a line drive to the shortstop.

She'd always kept her personal life private—what little personal life she had. Her dates were few and far between. She found it took too much effort with too little reward. After

Roger-Dodger, she hesitated exposing herself to ridicule, or worse, again. Even counseling hadn't managed to totally restore her confidence in herself as a sexual woman.

Going out in groups with friends from school meant she could be social. And it thwarted attempts by single males— and some married ones, too—to get her to go out with them alone. She either ignored their non-verbal messages or pretended they were joking. She'd perfected her 'just one of the guys' persona and ignored the veiled references to her sexual orientation.

Yet the other night when she fairly attacked Drew in her kitchen, she discovered a different aspect of herself. She had wanted to do more than kiss him. If he hadn't stopped them, she would've dragged him into her bedroom.

Making love with Drew Campbell would have fulfilled her teenage dreams. Yet fraught with danger. Not the kind of danger her ex presented. Drew would never abuse a woman. She knew that as surely as—

"Ms. Sinclair, shouldn't we call Madison's mom to let our parents know we're almost home?" Susan's question brought Maggie back to the present.

She'd daydreamed for the past ten miles, driving on automatic pilot, and was at the light at the top of the exit ramp. She was never that inattentive while driving other people's children.

"Another successful camp-out?" Mike Randolph asked Drew. "Gretchen sure does like them. It's been good for her. She used to be such a bookworm."

"Da-ad," Gretchen protested.

Drew had seen Mike in the neighborhood—he was a runner—but hadn't connected him with Gretchen. "Yes," Drew said. "We had a great time."

"I was surprised to hear they roped you into helping," Mike went on. "Wouldn't catch me eating bugs and berries."

"But, Dad—" Gretchen began.

Drew cut her off. "You'd be surprised how tasty grasshoppers and slugs taste cooked over a campfire. Almost like chicken." Drew managed to keep a straight face especially when Gretchen dissolved into giggles.

"Well, um . . . if you say so. Guess we'd better get home, munchkin." Mike led his daughter down the drive. From the man's pained expression, Drew knew Mike wasn't sure whether to believe Drew or not.

Gretchen looked back at Drew and winked. "Yeah, Dad. Maggie has this great recipe for fried earwigs and . . ."

"That was cruel," Maggie said once Gretchen and her dad were in their car. "Scaring off potential help?"

"Nah. You wouldn't want a wuss like him along, would you?"

Maggie appeared to ponder that. "Gee, Campbell. If I could turn a wuss like you into a camper in two weekends, imagine—"

"A wuss like me?" Drew advanced on her in mock menace.

She ran behind Ellen and pretended to hide. She giggled, just like Gretchen. It was so refreshing, so like the young Maggie he'd grown up with.

"When you two stop acting like teens, I'll take my daughter home," Nora Oostveen interrupted with a wide grin. Beth stood beside her looking bewildered. "I gotta know one thing. How ever did you manage hot sex with eight chaperones?"

"Mo-om," Beth protested. "I told you Susan and Janie made it all up,"

Her mother snapped her fingers. "Darn. What juicy gossip for bunco night."

Drew knew the neighborhood women had organized several card groups as well as bunco and a book discussion group. There was even a group they called 'chix flix' for going to movies they couldn't drag their husbands to. Lillian only joined the bridge group. She thought bunco and canasta were just excuses for women to sit around and gossip, and the book group didn't require that a person actually read the designated book. Consequently, she deemed them a waste of time.

The women also organized a summer cook-out in July and a 'chase the winter blues away' chili bash in February at the nearby community center. Drew liked the camaraderie and the opportunity to visit with neighbors he rarely saw. Now, he had to wonder how the gossip factor would hurt Maggie.

"You know, Maggie," Nora said. "If you come to bunco, nobody will say a word."

Maggie laughed. "I supposed I'd have to go to canasta, pinochle, and bridge, too. Gee, that would sure fill up my nights. I wouldn't have time for a torrid affair."

The women laughed while Ellen and Beth shook their heads and looked helplessly at Drew. He shrugged his shoulders. "Women," he mouthed to the girls.

"Guess I'd better get home and do Beth's laundry," Nora said. "We need to finish packing for our vacation. Stu wants to leave at dawn tomorrow." She made a face.

"Like that's going to happen," Beth said then followed her mother down to their mini-van parked at the curb.

Drew scanned the area. He and Ellen were the last. "We should leave, too."

"Oh, Maggie?" Ellen stopped at Drew's Navigator. "You said I could check out that movie website on your computer. I know I'm right that Sean Astin who played Sam in *The Lord of the Rings* was the same actor who played the little kid in *Goonies*. I'm going to get Grandpa on this one."

"Maggie's probably tired and—" Drew broke off when he realized he was talking to Ellen's back. She ran through the garage and into Maggie's house.

"It's all right," Maggie said. "I told her she could—"

"Maggie!" Ellen ran back out, her face pale, her eyes wide. "Somebody broke into your house!"

CHAPTER ELEVEN

Drew beat her inside the house. And Maggie was not happy.

She had a glimpse of disarray in the laundry room, but the kitchen captured her attention. The cabinets and drawers were open, contents on the floor. The living room was worse.

She staggered at the sight.

Books littered the floor. Every CD and DVD she owned lay in heaps. The pictures and lacy scarf had been swept off the piano, the glass of the frames shattered.

"Oh, God."

The words had barely left her mouth when Drew propelled her and Ellen, who'd followed, out the way they'd come through the garage. By the time they made it to the driveway, he had his cell phone out. He only hit three numbers, and she knew he was calling the police.

She paced between him and the vehicles. "How soon?"

"Soon," he said curtly.

"Yoo-hoo," Mrs. O'Malley called as she shuffled in her house slippers down her own driveway.

Not now. Maggie groaned.

Her neighbor barreled across the street without a glance and was nearly hit by the patrol car that pulled up in front of Maggie's house. The officer slammed on his brakes just in time.

"Oh, my goodness." Mrs. O'Malley stopped wide-eyed. "Whatever is wrong?" she called across the hood of the patrol car.

"Wow, Dad, that was fast," Ellen said.

The tall, lanky officer who got out of the car admonished Mrs. O'Malley about looking both ways before crossing the street. Maggie thought he looked so young his mother had probably just given him that advice.

"Ms. Sinclair," he said. "Are you all right?"

She peered at him. He seemed familiar but . . .

"Joe Pfeifer. I was in your Humanities class." He held out his hand and she shook it.

"Oh, my. That was four years ago," she said.

"Five. But, who's counting." When he grinned, she remembered him.

"You got here quickly," Drew said, then introduced himself.

"I was two streets over when I got the call. As soon as I heard the address, I knew it was your house." She must have appeared bewildered because he said, "All the guys know your house. Mostly because we all had a crush on you." Then, the young man in blue, who wore all the trappings of a police officer—badge, utility belt, gun—blushed.

He cleared his throat. "You had a break-in, Ms. Sinclair?" He became Officer Joe Pfeifer again, taking down information about when they arrived and what they found.

"I doubt anyone is still in there," Maggie said. "We've made enough noise." She told him about the camping trip and how the girls ran in and out of her garage storing gear.

"Wait here," he ordered in such an authoritative voice that Maggie was hard pressed to remember the high school senior who thought he was the class clown.

He walked into the garage, his weapon drawn. *Oh, God.* Though she stood outside her garage, she could still see into the house.

"Police," he announced loudly then walked into the house and repeated the warning.

For several long agonizing minutes, Maggie waited for him to return. Drew put his hand on her shoulder. "It will be all right, Maggie."

"I can't believe anyone would break into your house and me not notice," Mrs. O'Malley said. "Of course, if it was last night, I wasn't home. It was Bingo Night at the Senior Center. Harriet drives because I don't see so well. The doctor wants me to have cataract surgery but I—"

Officer Joe Pfeifer came out. "Nobody's inside," he announced. "I found a broken window and a ripped screen in the back bedroom, the one you use as an office. That's probably how they got in. Doesn't look like burglars, though. Your television, laptop, and sound system are all still there.

Sweet sound system." He cleared his throat. "I mean, a fence would pay a lot of money for that. You'll need to check to be sure nothing's missing. What it really looks like is somebody was mad at you. Did you fail anybody? Keep them from graduating?"

She shook her head.

"Okay, then. I should get more information. When were you last in the house?"

Maggie dreaded going back inside. Her initial glimpse before Drew hustled her out was bad enough. That made her pathetically grateful to answer questions if it delayed viewing the damage.

"Mr. Campbell and I took a group of girls camping. We left yesterday morning at seven."

"Seven-oh-five," Mrs. O'Malley put in. "That's what that new girl on WOOD-TV said just as you were pulling out of your driveway."

Joe Pfeifer took her name and gave her an encouraging smile. "Did you notice anything else while Ms. Sinclair was gone?"

"Nope." The old woman shook her head so vigorously her tight gray curls bounced. "Just like Wednesday night. I didn't see anything." She smirked at Maggie.

"Wednesday night?" Joe glanced up from his notes.

"Uh . . . Wednesday?" Maggie peered at the old woman.

"When you came back after your brother's visitation." Mrs. O'Malley cleared her throat. "You and Andy here? Making out in your kitchen? That was some hot kiss you laid on her, Andy."

Oh, dear God. Could things get any worse?

When Maggie didn't reply, Mrs. O'Malley added, "And his car was parked in your driveway all night. But, like I said, I didn't see anything." Again, she smirked.

Ellen swiveled her head from her father to Maggie. "You slept at her house? You kissed her?"

"Hold it." Drew held up his hand. "Someone broke into Maggie's house. They trashed it. That's what we should be talking about."

"You are correct, sir." Joe sounded way too serious for a fresh-faced kid just out of police academy. A kid she taught five years ago.

five years ago. "We should go inside so you can see if anything is missing."

Even though that was the last thing she wanted to do, she squared her shoulders and followed the young police officer through the garage and inside. As he'd said, the flat screen television and sound system were still there. Same with the DVD and CD players. She gasped at the mess in her bedroom. The contents of her dresser drawers had been dumped on the floor, the drawers themselves tossed on top. Every box on the shelf in her closet suffered the same fate. Snapshots she'd never gotten around to putting in albums lay in heaps. Everything in the boxes from Jack's office was unwrapped and strewn about. More glass from the frames lay embedded in the carpet. No going barefoot for a long time.

The other bedrooms were the same. The crates from her classroom had been dumped upside down, the folders and papers scattered. Her files—paper and CDs—lay in disarray across her desk and on the floor. Though it didn't seem possible, Jack's old bedroom was even worse.

"Ms. Sinclair?" Officer Pfeifer asked. "Do you see anything missing?"

She shook her head. Afraid she was going to be sick to her stomach, she wrapped her arms around her waist. She prayed she wouldn't. Not out of embarrassment but because she'd have to step over the contents of her medicine cabinet and the vanity under the sink to get to the toilet. To have a former student see her tampons and maxi-pads strewn about was too much.

She took a shuddering breath and found herself propelled out to the kitchen table, into a chair, and her head shoved between her knees. It took her a few moments to realize that was Drew's hand on top of her head. As if from a distance, she heard him order Ellen to wet the hand towel hanging on the oven door handle. Then, she felt a sopping wet weight on the back of her neck.

Had she almost passed out? Did they think she was a wimp who fainted at the sight of—

Joe, Officer Pfeifer, stooped in front of her. She didn't want to talk to anyone, didn't even want to look up. "I know this has been a shock for you. I need to call this in. You're sure nothing's missing?"

"I don't think so. I don't know. It's such a . . ."

"I know." He patted her hand. "I'm sorry."

Drew handed her a cold can of Vernor's. "Drink. Ginger ale will help."

Joe walked into the kitchen and activated the two-way radio on his shoulder. After identifying himself, he said, "Reporting a B&E at 14587 West Elm. Perps have fled. The home owner isn't sure if anything's missing. I'm going to dust for prints."

After a pause, a female voice said, "Negative, Officer Pfeifer. The captain says no. You aren't qualified for that."

"But, I have the equipment and—"

"The captain says, and I quote, get the report then get your ass back into your car and continue your patrol."

At that, Maggie sat up and peered at him. The wet towel fell down her back.

Joe's ears reddened. "Roger, copy that." He deactivated the two-way and glanced at his watch. "I'm off duty in half an hour," he said to Maggie. "Do you think you could wait and not touch anything until I get back?"

"Maggie Sinclair, what kind of an example are you setting for—oh, my God!" Susan's mother's strident voice brought Maggie out of the fog. The woman had burst in from the garage. Intent on her own agenda, she was halfway to where Maggie sat in the dining room before the destruction registered.

"What do you mean barging in here like this?" Drew demanded.

Officer Pfeifer drew his weapon. "Who are you?"

Susan's mother gasped, her eyes widening.

Maggie almost felt sorry for the woman. "Joe, I mean, Officer Pfeiffer. This is the parent of one of the girls in my camping group."

Joe glared sharply at her then holstered his weapon. "What do you want?"

At his demand, she stuttered, "I, uh, my daughter, uh, what happened?"

Maggie started to get up, but Drew put his hand on her shoulder. His gentle touch kept her seated.

"There was a break-in while we were camping," he said.

"It's that camping trip I want to talk to you about." Apparently recovered from seeing the mess—and a policeman in the kitchen—Susan's mother stared pointedly at Maggie. "I won't have my daughter subjected to such immoral behavior. You two on the beach. My God. It's bad enough her father—"

"Susan is a big, fat liar," Ellen cried.

"How dare you call my daughter a liar."

Ellen didn't back down. "She and Janie started the rumors just because my dad let Maggie cry on his shoulder. Susan even admitted that's all they saw."

"I'm pulling my daughter out of your troop, Margaret Sinclair. And I'm reporting you to the council. You are an unfit leader."

Maggie thanked God the woman hadn't brought Susan. The poor child didn't need to see her mother losing it.

"You need to leave." Drew advanced on Susan's mother. "You are not welcome here. And her name isn't Margaret."

"That's hardly the big picture," Maggie said.

"What does your wife think about you carrying on with that slut." She pointed to Maggie who sat into stunned silence at the invective.

"Even if those rumors were true, which they're not, that's hardly an issue since my wife is dead."

Susan's mother gasped and started backing toward the garage door.

"You owe Ms. Sinclair an apology." Drew followed the woman. His low threatening voice made Maggie glad she wasn't the recipient. "If you continue along those lines, you will find yourself slapped with a defamation of character suit."

The woman had just opened the door to the garage when Joe Pfeifer said, "One moment, ma'am. I'd like to ask you a few questions. Where were you last night?"

With two large men advancing toward her, Susan's mother shot Maggie a panicked look. After her nastiness, Maggie didn't feel sorry for her.

"Ma'am." Officer Pfeiffer's tone made Maggie jump. "Last night. Where were you?"

"I, uh, I was home."

"Can anyone corroborate that?"

Maggie wanted everyone to leave. She had a headache, exacerbated by Susan's mother's accusations. While Officer Pfeifer interrogated the poor woman in the kitchen, Drew came back to stand by Maggie's chair.

It was too much of an effort to get up. "Guess I'd better go to bunco on Tuesday." Maggie tried to smile.

"Don't forget canasta, pinochle, book group, and bridge."

"I hate bridge." She could see Susan's mother standing at the counter with Joe Pfeifer towering over her. "Is he finger-printing her?"

"Looks like."

"I thought he couldn't do that," Maggie said.

"Serves her right," Mrs. O'Malley said. "What a bitch."

In all the confusion, Maggie didn't realize her neighbor was still there.

"I almost feel sorry for that woman," Maggie said.

"Don't," Drew snapped.

"I think I understand Susan a lot better now. Too bad it's too late." Maggie shrugged. "Her mother's in for a real surprise when she reports me to the council."

"Reminds me of my mother." Drew gave her a wry grin.

"Grandma?" Ellen said. "Grandma's not as bad as her."

Drew hugged her. "Never mind. What did you mean about her being in for a surprise?"

Maggie shook her head. "We've never been part of any organized group. She should know that."

"She's obviously not thinking straight," Drew said. "But, that doesn't give her the right to spread lies about you."

"Oh, Mrs. O'Malley, you don't need to do that." Maggie tried to stop her neighbor from putting the tablecloths and placemats back into the sideboard drawers.

She listened as well as Ellen did a few minutes later when Maggie saw her putting the CDs and DVDs into the specially-designed racks inside the entertainment center. Maggie thought Ellen might be eavesdropping on the interrogation out in the kitchen at the same time. Not that she blamed the girl.

"Dearie, it gives me something to do besides watching television. Nothing good on Sunday nights until ten. That's when Dateline comes on. I love that show. Have you ever seen it? Ooh, that Lester Holt. He's such a good-looking man."

Mrs. O'Malley could carry on a conversation all by herself—and frequently did.

"Wow, Ms. Sinclair." Officer Pfeifer came back into the dining room. "What did you do to piss—er, I mean, upset her?"

"Nothing. Ms. Sinclair did nothing," Drew said.

Joe continued to watch Maggie. She sighed. "I didn't. She and her husband are divorcing. And—"

"And you're catching the brunt of it," he added. "I reported this new development. Is there anything else we should know?"

Drew nudged her. "The break-ins at Jack's."

Maggie explained to Joe Pfeifer about Jack's accident—suffered through well-meaning condolences—and mentioned what they'd found at his apartment. "I'd appreciate it if you would send a copy of your report to Tom Watson at the Muskegon County Sheriff's Department. He's handling—"

"What's going on?" At the new voice, Maggie groaned. Ben Voorheis had walked in the front door. "Why is there a police car in front of your house? Oh, my God."

What was with these people who just let themselves into her home without a by-your-leave?

Joe pulled out his weapon again.

"Out." Maggie jumped up and pointed to the front door. "Please, everybody go home."

"But, darlin'," Ben protested. "I just got here."

"Darlin'?" Drew and Joe swiveled to look at her. "Darlin'?"

CHAPTER TWELVE

Maggie wanted to slap Ben. "What are you thinking?" She fisted her hands on her hips.

"Huh?" With an expression of total surprise, he hesitated. He must have seen the officer's weapon because his eyes widened, and he tripped over himself trying to back up.

Frustrated and angered by the break-in and Ben's acting like they had a special relationship, especially after what she'd told him Thursday evening, she poked him in the chest. "Have I ever given you reason to call me *darlin'*? I am not your *darlin'*. Never have been. Do not call me that again. And do not ever walk into my home again. Not like you did on Thursday, either. Knock."

"Thursday?" Drew stepped forward.

"Yes. Before the camping meeting. I did not invite him." She eyed Ben. "And I'm not likely to invite you here again if you even think about walking in."

"He's the one I saw." Mrs. O'Malley edged to the fore and pointed with an arthritic-knobbed finger. "I thought Maggie let him in. Shame on you, young man."

"You walked in uninvited?" Even though he'd holstered his gun, Officer Pfeifer drew himself up into full police mode. "That's invasion."

Flummoxed by the eyes trained on him as well as the disapproval, Ben stammered, "But, Maggie dar—Maggie. I didn't mean—I'm sorry. I—"

While Ben faltered, Maggie wanted everyone out so she could deal with the aftermath of the break-in. "Please. Everybody. Go home."

"B-But—" Ben stuttered.

"No buts. Out. Everybody." Then, she realized she was telling the police to get out. Joe might have been her student once, but she needed to treat him with more respect. "Officer

Pfeifer, do you need anything more from me?"

"I'll take this man's fingerprints." He nodded at Ben.

"What? I didn't do anything." A deep red crept up his neck.

"You were here Thursday," Joe said before looking at Maggie. "Where was he when he was here?"

"Just the living room."

"Did you come back after Ms. Sinclair left yesterday morning?" Joe eyed him.

"No. Of course not. You don't think . . . Maggie, I would never vandalize your place. You must believe me."

He looked so pathetic, she let go of her anger. "I do, Ben. It's been a bad day. With Jack's funeral and coming home to this—" She broke off on a sob.

Although Ben tried to reach for her, Drew wrapped his arm around her shoulders and pulled her against him. She reached up and squeezed his fingers. Ben's sharp glare gave her pause. More than sharp. Furious. Then it was gone so quickly she wasn't sure if she imagined it. Why couldn't he just leave her alone? She wasn't interested in him. She'd made herself clear. She thought. But she'd had to deal with him because of Jack.

Oh, dear God. Jack. He was truly gone. Grief slapped her so hard only Drew's arm around her kept her from falling. She had to get away from the people crowding her. Her throat clogged and tears threatened to fall. She had to put a stop to the noise and confusion.

"See yourselves out, folks. Drew, please lock up." She rushed to her bedroom before she broke down and cried in front of everyone. She couldn't deal with much more.

Before she closed her bedroom door, she heard Drew take over. "Officer Pfeifer, please take care of whatever business you have. Mrs. O'Malley, I'm sure Maggie appreciates all your efforts. Ellen, as soon as the others are gone, you and I will leave."

Maggie heard the murmur of voices. Drew's quiet but forceful. Ben's whining protests. Officer Joe's directions. She ignored them all as she sat on the edge of her bed and surveyed her room. What a mess.

Her dresser drawers had been pulled out, much the

same as Jack's. Clothes thrown on the floor. Oh my God, whoever had done this had touched her underwear. She shivered at the violation. The contents of her nightstand also lay on the floor. Even her box with change had been dumped.

What were they looking for?

What little jewelry she owned appeared to be all there, laying on top of her clothes. Was this theft or vandalism?

Unable to deal with the chaos, she bent over and laid her forehead on her knees. She wanted to crawl under the covers, pull them over her head, and go to sleep. With a groan, she realized she had to change the sheets first. Oh, God. How much more could she take?

A lot more. You're tough. You can handle it.

Jack would have chided her like that. She'd dealt with worse. A student pulling a knife on her after hours, a student's father's rage, Roger Dixon. She'd handled all that. Vandalism should be a walk in the park. Her pity party was officially over.

Opening her eyes, she stared at the floor, at the pile of coins and earrings she'd tossed into her little box rather than in her jewelry box. She could start there by picking them up. As she grabbed a handful of coins, she found an SD card underneath, a memory card like the ones in Jack's box. Where did that come from? Her cell phone backup or her camera?

She picked up the tiny card and shoved it into her pocket. She channeled Scarlett O'Hara and decided to think about it tomorrow. Hammering from the back of the house surprised her. She was about to get up to see what it was when she heard a knock on the bedroom door.

"Maggie?" Ellen. "Dad says we're going unless you want our help. We can stay if you need us."

Maggie wiped away her tears and let her mouth curve into a little smile. Drew knew she wouldn't yell at Ellen. Smart guy.

With the slowness of an old woman, she got up, stepped over her nightstand contents, and walked to the door. Ellen appeared so worried Maggie hugged her.

Over the girl's shoulder Maggie saw Drew coming out of her office. He raised his eyebrow. "Okay?"

"How can I be okay when someone broke into my house, rifled through my things, my clothes?"

"I understand." He even looked like he did. "I found a board in the basement and nailed it over the window. I also stacked all the papers in your office. I'm sure you had an order to it." He shrugged in a helpless expression.

"Mrs. O'Malley and I picked up all your CDs and DVDs." The worry on Ellen's face made Maggie want to comfort *her*. "She picked up the candles and threw the broken ones away."

"I appreciate all your help. I'm going to get a hotel room tonight. I can't stay here."

"You don't need to get a hotel room," Drew said quickly. "You can stay in our guest room."

"That's a good idea, Maggie." Ellen's face brightened. "I don't blame you for being scared to stay here. I'd be scared, too."

She hesitated. They meant well, and she appreciated their offer.

Drew must have seen her indecision. "Throw your things in a bag. You can ride home with us."

Her things? Some perv had touched all her clothes. Until she washed them, she wasn't wearing any of them.

"Thank you. Both of you. I'll take you up on your offer of a bed for the night." She sighed. "You two go on ahead. I need to run over to Target."

Drew peered at her like she had a screw loose. "You're going shopping?"

As much as she didn't want to explain, she said, "I'm not wearing underwear that some creep put his grubby hands on."

After running through the store like her pants were on fire, Maggie finally headed over to Drew's.

"What took you so long?" he demanded immediately on opening the door.

"Hello to you, too. I told you I was going to Target."

Ellen elbowed her father. "He was worried about you."

"Sorry. Is it okay if I come in now?"

Drew stepped back. "I'm sorry, too. I shouldn't have—

let's say I could've greeted you better."

"Oh, Daddy. Maggie understands. She yells at us, too, when she's scared for us. She always gives us a big hug as an apology." Ellen smirked. "Are you going to give her a hug?"

"Uh, that's okay." Maggie edged away from Drew, discombobulated by his daughter's words. "I don't need a hug."

Recovering quickly, Drew grinned. "I can give you a hug."

"No need." She turned to his daughter. "Ellen, do you want to show me where to go?"

When the girl's grin disappeared, it dawned on Maggie she was trying to play matchmaker. That was so sweet. If she'd seen them in Maggie's kitchen Wednesday night, Ellen wouldn't waste her efforts.

Ellen led her up the stairway to the second floor. She pointed out all the rooms. Two bedrooms faced the street, a bathroom between them. The master bedroom faced the backyard. The guest room, first room on the left, was decorated exquisitely in neutral colors with burgundy accents. Lillian's taste went far beyond Maggie's meager efforts. She placed her bag of purchases on a wingback chair near the window.

"This room is lovely," she said.

"We share the bathroom." Ellen opened a door that Maggie thought was a closet. "Mom said our rooms are called Jack-and-Jill because they connect with the bathroom in between."

"Hmm. I never heard that expression before."

"Mom was always looking online for a new house. She said that's what realtors call our bedrooms."

Maggie followed her down the stairs. "You were going to move?"

"Mom wanted to," Ellen said over her shoulder. "Dad didn't. I'm glad we didn't move. I like it here, especially with all my friends and you being so close."

They'd reached the bottom of the stairs. Maggie hugged her. "I'm glad you didn't move, too."

"What's this about moving?" Drew came out of the kitchen, wiping his hands on a towel.

"I told Maggie about Mom wanting to move to a bigger house."

He cleared his throat. "I'm happy right here. I made a snack if you guys are interested. And I put lasagna in the oven for dinner."

"He cooks?" Maggie grinned. "Always a good skill."

Ellen blew a raspberry. "Mrs. Boersma's. He knows how to turn on the oven and the timer and follow direction."

"Another good skill."

Their laughter eased the tension Maggie had been holding ever since she found her house vandalized.

After a delicious dinner that included a salad and garlic bread, Maggie sat back. "That was so good. I hope I don't pop the button on my jeans."

Ellen and Drew joined in with her laughter.

"That was a good meal the girls made last night," Drew said. "Foil dinners, huh?"

"The s'mores were better." Ellen grinned. "Too bad your marshmallows kept falling off the stick, Dad."

"Laughing at your father's ineptitude shouldn't be allowed." Drew chuckled. He'd taken the girls' teasing good-naturedly, as he did his daughter's now.

The laughing and teasing made Maggie relax. Almost too relaxed. Together, they cleared the table and put away the leftovers, despite their assurance that guests didn't need to clean up.

Working together, they finished quickly.

"I hope I'm not being an ungrateful guest, but I'm going to take a shower and go to bed. Thank you for taking me in."

"We're happy to have you, Maggie." Drew squeezed her shoulder. "I'm glad we could help."

Breaking camp, hiking all morning, and driving two hours home had sapped her strength. The damage to her home added to her fatigue. Emotionally, she was a wreck. Physically, her muscles ached, and tension tightened her shoulders. The hot shower helped ease some of the stiffness. The T-shirt and boxers she'd purchased as nightwear fit well. Not wanting to monopolize the shared bathroom, she sat on the edge of her bed to put moisturizer on her face and neck. Even with a cool breeze both days, the sun had been deceptive. Although she'd reminded the girls to use sunscreen, she could see added tan on her arms and slathered on lotion.

A knock on the adjoining door caught her rubbing lotion on her legs.

"Maggie?" Ellen's voice was soft, tentative.

"Come in."

Ellen stuck her head around the door. "I didn't want to disturb you."

"You're not. Come in."

Ellen glanced longingly at the bed. Maggie scooted over and patted the side. "What's up?"

Not waiting a second longer, the young girl parked herself at the bottom on the bed, crossing her legs Indian style. Like Maggie, she wore a T-shirt and boxers.

While Maggie propped herself up with her pillow against the headboard, Ellen picked at a loose thread on the cream and burgundy quilt. "What Susan said about you and Dad was mean."

Maggie thought so, too, but declined to respond. She wanted to see where the conversation would go.

"I think she's jealous that you and my dad are good friends." She glanced up quickly to see if that brought a response. "And she's being hateful to me because her dad is gone, and I still have mine."

"Hmm."

"She used to be nice. We all used to be friends. Why do things change?"

The way Ellen regarded her, inquisitive and sad at the same time, Maggie knew she had to respond. But what could she say to ease the hurt in the girl's eyes? "Good question. The easy answer is I don't know. I asked myself the same question when my parents died. And again this week when Jack did."

"It isn't fair."

Maggie patted Ellen's leg. "Got news for you, kiddo. Life isn't fair. My dad always said you play the hand you're dealt." At the confusion in Ellen's eyes, she added, "He said life is like a card game. You have to play the cards you're given. You don't always like it. And it's not always fair."

"Yeah, but in cards you can throw in your hand and get a new one."

"True. I've often wanted to throw in the cards God dealt me. Or ask for a couple of different cards. That's not how it works. Maybe we're supposed to accept what happens and try to make it right."

"How can I make things right when my mom isn't here? I know she wished I was different, more like her. Maybe if I'd been good she would still be here." Tears rolled down her cheeks.

Maggie gathered her into her arms. "The accident wasn't your fault. A drunk driver ran into her car. You couldn't have done anything to prevent it."

Between sobs, Ellen said, "She wanted me to go shopping with her, and I didn't want to. If I'd been in the car, maybe she would've gone a different way."

Wow. What guilt that poor girl had heaped on her own head.

"Ellen?" Drew came through the bathroom. He sat on the end of the bed where his daughter had been sitting before she threw herself into Maggie's arms. He gathered her into his. "If you'd been in the car, I would have lost you, too. I don't think I could have borne that."

How long had he been listening? Long enough, apparently. The anguish in his face tore through Maggie's heart. She had a notion that he'd never imagined his daughter felt that way, or carried that guilt. She eased back against the headboard in an effort to give them space. Drew murmured soothing words, much the same as he did to Maggie after the news of Jack's accident. He had good instincts.

She realized how difficult it must be for him to be both parents to Ellen. How hard it had been especially last week when she railed against him for never listening to her, for missing the planning meeting, for being late. Maggie hoped he finally told Ellen the reason.

Drew continued to hold her, even though she'd quieted. He glanced over her shoulder to look at Maggie then quirked his mouth in a what-should-I-do expression. Not wanting to intrude, she gave him an encouraging smile.

"Come on, little girl. Time for bed." He easily lifted her and carried her through the bathroom.

Maggie straightened the covers and was about to turn off the bedside lamp when she heard the bathroom door on Ellen's side close. She expected to hear Drew's footsteps in the hall. She twisted around at the light tap on the doorframe near her head. Drew stood there, looking lost. She beckoned him in.

After he closed the door to the bathroom, he came in and slumped in the chair by the window. "I didn't know what she'd been thinking about Lillian's accident. God, that poor kid."

"I guess she's never talked about it to you."

He shook his head. "Has she ever said anything like that to you?"

"Of course not. I would've told you." She sat up, sitting cross-legged like Ellen had, the covers pooled in her lap. "It's not unusual for kids to think everything is their fault. They're very ego-centric." She smiled. "When parents divorce, the kids think that's their fault, too. That if they'd been better Mom and Dad wouldn't fight and would stay together. I've seen it many times. They bargain with God, thinking if they're good, their folks will get back together."

"Or not die?"

She thought of her reaction to Jack's accident. "Yeah. Something like that. On the way over here, I talked to Tom Watson and told him about Sarah Jane and the break-in at my house. I guess Joe Pfeifer had already filled him in about the break-in."

"Eager kid."

"Good kid. I remember him well from my Humanities class. He wrote an essay about law enforcement."

"So, you weren't surprised to see him as a policeman."

"Yes, and no. I was more surprised to see he's one of our police."

"What did Watson say? Did he know about Sarah Jane?"

"Yes. He agreed that something very odd was going on. He asked what my brother could've hidden that someone wanted so badly."

"Our question, too. What else did he say?"

"He asked the same questions we're asking. What and who. He's as bewildered as we are." She paused. "Watson said one more thing. Joe Pfeifer noted something in his report that he didn't say to us. There wasn't any glass on the floor of my office. He checked outside and found window glass on the ground."

"Yes?"

"That means whoever broke the window was already in the house."

CHAPTER THIRTEEN

The scent of bacon and coffee drew Maggie out of a sound sleep. Visions of a faceless man had haunted her dreams. He smashed his way through her house, stomping on everything—her clothes, CDs and DVDs, her pictures on the piano. Each time she peered at him, trying to see who it was, his face blurred. His fury woke her again and again. When she entered the bathroom, her rough night showed on her face, in her eyes, in the dark circles under her eyes. A cold compress helped slightly.

Lured by the smell of coffee, she quickly dressed in the shorts and T-shirt she'd purchased the night before. The first thing on her agenda was laundry. Until she removed the *stain* of the invader, she could never wear any clothes in her bedroom. Thank goodness, she'd packed up her winter and fall clothes and stored them in the basement, the only place not violated in her home. Drew had checked for her.

"Morning." She forced a cheery greeting and hurried over to the Keurig at the end of the counter.

Seated at the table and dressed in khakis and a subtle plaid short-sleeve shirt, Drew glanced up from the thick Sunday newspaper. With everything that had happened the day before, he mustn't have gotten to read it.

He greeted her with a wide smile. "Can I get you a cup of coffee?"

"I think I can handle that."

A clean cup sat next to the machine. He must have set it out for her. He came over to her, putting his arms around her waist.

"How did you sleep?" He nuzzled her neck, and she arched to give him better access. He obliged. The machine sizzled and spit, indicating the cycle had finished. As much as she liked him holding her, she stepped away and removed the cup of coffee from under the machine.

"Coffee rates higher than my kiss?" He sounded offended.

"Yes. No." After a sip, she sighed. "Yes. Nectar of the gods."

Drew clutched his heart. "Done in by a coffee machine."

Maggie laughed and took another sip. "I guess so."

"I threw your jeans and T-shirt in the washer last night, along with Ellen's camping clothes. They're in the dryer now."

Maggie hadn't even noticed they were gone. "A thief in the night?"

"Something like that. I tapped on your door first, but you were out cold."

Oh, Lordy. "I hope I wasn't snoring."

"Horribly. A freight train was soft in comparison." He kept his face straight for all of ten seconds before he broke into a grin that lit his gray eyes.

"Oh, you." She batted his arm. When coffee sloshed over the cup, she grabbed a nearby towel and started blotting his shirt. "I am so sorry."

"Not a problem." Hastily, he set his cup down. He took the towel from her and looped it around her neck then used it to pull her close.

"I take it you want to wear my coffee, too." She set her cup next to his.

"Good morning." He kissed her lightly on the lips.

It *was* a good morning. She returned his kiss with a deeper one.

"Oh, no." Ellen called from the doorway. "That is so gross."

Maggie and Drew broke apart like two teens caught necking by their parents. She picked up her cup and held it like a shield in front of her heated face. "Good morning, Ellen."

The girl threw herself onto a chair. "Morning," she muttered.

Drew cleared his throat. "Good morning, Daughter. How do bacon and eggs sound for breakfast?"

Ellen grunted.

"Not a morning person, huh?" Maggie smiled. "We'll

take that response as a yes. I never fix bacon. Too much trouble for one person. What can I do to help?"

"You're a guest." Drew pulled a frying pan out of a drawer.

"Don't give me that. I can set the table if you point to the cupboard with plates."

Ellen got up. "I can do that. You don't have to."

"I could make toast then." Since a loaf of bread sat on the counter, she didn't have to ask. A quick check of the refrigerator and she found a tub of spreadable butter. "Is this okay? Or do you use something else?"

Drew reached around her for the carton of eggs. He deliberately brushed against her then gave her a wicked grin. He even snuck in a kiss on the back of her neck, exposed by her ponytail.

"Oh, God." Ellen groaned. "It was bad enough when you two were fighting. I can't take PDAs this early in the morning."

Drew stepped away. He set the egg carton on the counter then scooped Maggie in his arms, dipped her, and laid a sizzling kiss on her gaping mouth. After he righted her, he grinned at Ellen. "Now *that* was a public display of affection."

"Pul-leez."

"I think you're pushing it, Drew." Maggie busied herself with the bread and toaster.

Ellen didn't say a word. Instead, she shot them a withering glance. She stood at the slider to the deck. "It's raining. Darn. I wanted to go swimming with Beth."

"Swimming or ogling the lifeguards?" Drew asked as he whipped the eggs into a frothy mix.

"Da-ad."

Breakfast tasted wonderful. Drew zapped the bacon she'd smelled earlier in the microwave. He'd sautéed onions and mushrooms before adding the eggs and grated some cheese that melted into a yummy mixture. While she and Drew had a second cup of coffee, Ellen proclaimed she was going up to her bedroom and listen to music.

"Help clean up first," Drew said.

She was already stacking their plates. "I know, Dad."

"You might take a few minutes while you're listening to

music to clean your bedroom."

"Da-ad." She stopped at the sink. "You aren't going into work today?"

It had taken her that long to realize he wasn't wearing a suit.

"Later. I'm going to help Maggie with her house."

"Oh, you don't need to." She grabbed the silverware and took it to the sink.

"Sure, I do." He gave her a grin then turned serious. "You shouldn't have to face that mess alone."

His concern endeared him to her.

"I can help, too." Ellen rinsed plates while Drew loaded the dishwasher. They seemed to have a routine.

Drew chuckled. "You'll do anything to get out of cleaning your bedroom."

"I'll be down in five minutes. Don't leave without me." She tore up the stairs.

"I appreciate your offer, but it's not necessary. I can handle the mess." She could, even if she didn't want to.

Drew looped his arms around her waist. "I know you can. You don't have to."

She tried to edge away, but he held tighter. "Drew, we shouldn't. Not when Ellen could see us."

"She'll have to get used to the idea. I want to kiss you." He demonstrated. "And touch you." He brought her closer and slid his hand down to cup her bottom. While nuzzling her neck, he whispered, "I dreamed about you last night. I haven't had one of *those* dreams since I was a teenager."

With her face burning, she broke away. "Is that the buzzer for the dryer? My clothes should be done. I can't believe you do the laundry."

"Coward," he called as she headed toward the laundry room, guided by the buzzer. "Mrs. Boersma has enough to do. Ellen and I do our own laundry."

Ellen tromped down the stairs. "Dad, Maggie, this is so weird." She held up a compact disc. "This is that CD I borrowed. 'Maggie's Party Mix.' It won't play."

Maggie came back from the laundry room. She and Drew looked at the disc and then at each other.

Drew took it. "Let's put this in my laptop and see what's

on it." He led the way to his study, near the front door,

"It stopped raining," Ellen said. "Is it okay if I go with Beth to the pool."

Drew opened his briefcase and took out his laptop. "I thought you wanted to help clean up Maggie's house."

Her face fell. "Okay. I'll call Beth and tell her—"

"No," Maggie said. "Go to the pool, if it's okay with your dad. I appreciate your offer."

The pleading in Ellen's eyes didn't go unnoticed.

"Go. Be home for lunch. If something comes up, call me on my cell."

She raced over to him and threw her arms around his neck. "You're the greatest, Dad."

Before Drew could say anything more, she grabbed a bag stuffed with a towel that Maggie hadn't seen when she ran down with the disk. "Bye, Dad. Bye, Maggie. Have fun."

She dashed through the front door like dragons chased her.

As soon as the door closed behind his daughter, Drew smirked. "Alone at last."

"How hokey."

"We could neck now that we don't have an audience."

She was getting used to his teasing. He reached for her, but she batted his hands away. "I want to see what's wrong with that disk. It's one Jack made for me."

"Spoilsport."

He placed his laptop on his desk. Though he offered her his desk chair, she pulled up a smaller one to sit close to him and still see the screen. He popped the disk into the CD/DVD slot. And waited. When no music automatically came on, he opened File Manager to see the menu. Two files.

"Looks like one's a document," Drew said. "And the other is a video."

"Bingo," she breathed. The file was dated the day before Jack showed up at her house and scared her half to death when the garage door opened all by itself.

Drew read out loud the text on the screen:

"Maggie, since you found this, call me. If you can't because I'm not, well, around—sorry to sound morbid—you need to give this to my best friend. He'll know the password to open the next file. Tell him, it's the nickname we gave to the world's biggest pest when we were twelve."

CHAPTER FOURTEEN

"Who was the world's biggest pest when you and Jack were twelve?" *As if I didn't know.* Maggie leaned forward.

Red crept up his neck above the blue plain sports shirt. *Oh, boy.* "Jack wasn't talking about me, was he?" Campbell kept his head bent.

"He was, wasn't he? Are you going to tell me the nickname?" When Campbell's neck grew redder, she persisted. "You'd better 'fess up. I can't go after my brother, but you're right here. And if you thought I was a pest at nine, just wait until you see what a pest I can be at thirty-four."

Four short lines appeared in the box for the password. A four-letter name for the world's biggest pest. Four? Couldn't be her first name. Or her last.

While she pondered the password, she noted it was dated the day before Jack died, just like his message to her. She followed Drew's keystrokes. *Mags.* The file opened. Jack sat in his car as he recorded the video. In the background, a dilapidated sign for a closed business hung crookedly.

Tears clogged her throat as she watched Jack, alive, and as cocky as ever.

"Drew, buddy. Sorry to be so mysterious. You need to find one more thing. A tiny thing, I left at Maggie's. In her bits and bobs box." The video stopped.

"What the heck?" Drew glanced over his shoulder at her. "Do you have any idea what he's talking about?"

She swiped at the tears. "Something tiny?" She gasped. "The SD card. In my jeans. Oh my God. Did you say you washed them?"

"I did."

She backed up so he could get out of the chair. "Tell me you check pockets before you wash things."

He raced to the laundry room behind the kitchen with her on his tail. "Actually, I do. Ellen's always leaving tissues in her pockets. Apparently, so do you." He stopped in the spacious room. "I tossed everything in the trash."

Maggie grabbed the wastebasket near the dryer and pulled apart tissues until she came to the ones from her jeans' pockets. "Here." She held up the tiny black square. "I thought it was from my camera. The vandals knocked over my change box, and I found this on the floor. It's just like the ones in Jack's box."

They both ran back to his office. Sitting at his computer, Drew inserted the SD card. When Jack appeared in a video, Maggie leaned over Drew's shoulder. Her heart twisted at the sight of her brother. Still in his car, the dilapidated building in the background, he looked even more worried.

"Do you recognize where he is?" she asked, despite the lump in her chest. It hurt to see him when she knew he was . . .

"Yeah. It's an abandoned warehouse off I-96. I pass it every time I go to Muskegon."

She sniffed back tears and hoped Drew wouldn't notice. "Why did he record his message there? He could've used his living room."

"I don't know. Hang on." Drew started the video.

"New password before you can go further, buddy. Where did you break Maggie's heart?"

Drew glanced over his shoulder at her. "He knew about that?"

"I didn't tell him." She blew out a breath. "Just type in 'backyard' and see." Nothing happened. "Okay, try 'under the maple tree' with no spaces." That did it.

"Drew, old buddy. Sorry for making you jump through hoops. If you've gotten this far, that means I've gone to that great calculator in the sky. CPA joke." Jack's mouth quirked. "I wanted to talk to you face-to-face last night or, at least at the office this morning, but when I called, your secretary said you were out. Hey, no regrets, buddy. I should've tried to get hold of you as soon as I suspected something was wrong."

"I knew something was wrong."
"Shush."

"I've been doing an audit for Vander Haar Manufacturing southeast of Muskegon. The numbers don't add up. Someone is ripping off the employees' pension fund. I don't know who. Well, I have a good guess, but nothing I can prove. This company was one of Ben's clients, so I don't know all the players well enough to start asking questions.

"Vander Haar Senior started this place. About three years ago, he turned operations over to the son. Junior's a smart-ass. He's the most logical suspect. He likes nice things but according to some of the people here, he doesn't give a rip about the employees or the plant. You know how it is with the second generation. The first one sweats bullets getting an operation off the ground and making it a success. The second one runs it into the ground. Junior's had the good life and thinks the company can run itself." He blew a raspberry.

"My money's on the son, but I wouldn't put it past the old man, either. Maybe his own retirement is more expensive than he thought. Or, when the economy tanked, his portfolio went down the toilet, and he figured it wouldn't come around quick enough. I'm not sure. Junior should be smart enough to figure it out—if he's paying attention to the store. Maybe he doesn't know what Daddy is doing. Same with Daddy, if Junior is the culprit."

Jack shifted in the black upholstered front seat of the Blazer. "Maybe their comptroller is ripping them all off. I figure you'll have to sort out the players if I'm not around. I hate to sound paranoid, but I wouldn't put it past someone who stole people's pensions to make sure that information doesn't come to light. I've had a bad feeling every time I'm in their network that someone is monitoring the files I've examined—especially last night when I stayed late." Jack glanced around him, as if he heard something.

Relieved, he continued. "Sarah Jane said I should talk to you or Mags. I'm going back in tonight and start searching prior to last year to see how long the raiding has been going on.

"I've copied a file from the company's computer—not real ethical of me, so don't mention this to Ben. He's got enough on his plate recovering from that accident."

Jack took a deep breath, his brows furrowed.

"Ben. Here's my bigger worry. If the raiding of the pension plan has been going on longer than this past year, does Ben know? If he does, our company is in deep shit. I didn't want to leave this info at Maggie's, but I have to get it away from me. I don't know who to trust—except you and her."

A chart followed with employee contributions, company match, and retiree withdrawals for the year. The totals didn't match the balance in the fund.

"I told you something wasn't right."

Drew swiveled around to face her. "I thought you would be above I-told-you-so."

"Nah." She sobered when Jack spoke again.

"Drew?"

"Wait. There's more." She'd thought Jack had finished. She dug her fingers into Drew's shoulders.

"Listen, buddy. Take care of my sister. She's reckless sometimes. Don't let her know about this. I wouldn't put it past her to go after the Vander Haars. You must protect her. Don't let her go to the plant. Junior is ruthless. Senior didn't grow a one-man business into what it is now by being a nice guy."

He paused again. His mouth twisted with emotion. "Love ya, buddy." He cleared his throat. "Tell Mags I love her, too."

The video ended.

Those unshed tears poured forth, running down Maggie's cheeks, dripping on her shorts.

"Babe?" Drew spun his chair around.

She couldn't speak. He pulled her off the small chair and

onto his lap. "It's okay to cry. Let it go."

Despite her need for independence, she let him hold her as she cried.

For several minutes, Drew held her against his chest. He rubbed her back, hoping to soothe her. It had been hard enough when he watched his best friend describe an untenable situation. But when Jack said he loved him, Drew almost lost it. A rush of emotion—love, loss, despair— overwhelmed him. Only Maggie's need, more powerful than his own, kept him in control.

She hadn't sobbed in a while. A shaky breath every now and then. A hitch in her breathing. She had pulled herself back together. When she straightened away from him, he handed her a tissue from the box on his desk.

"Just give me the damn box." She blew her nose and tried to mop up. Several tissues later, she rallied. "Okay. Now, what do we do?"

"*We* do nothing. I'm going to make a copy of this then leave the original in my safe. You are out of this picture." He opened a desk drawer and pulled out a USB drive.

"You have a safe?"

"Is that the big picture?" He copied the file onto his computer then onto the USB drive. "Your brother wanted you to stay out of this."

"Now, listen here—"

"No, you listen." He stood, giving her his most menacing stare. "Jack said to get this away from you. I'm doing what he wanted. Protecting you. This is what your so-called vandal was looking for. He was so pissed he trashed your house looking for it. You didn't get the message then. Are you getting it now?"

"Whoa. Don't hold back, Campbell."

He wanted to shake her. Instead, he gripped her shoulders. "Quit being so stubborn."

She went absolutely rigid. "You will take your hands off me," she said in a deceptively quiet voice. "Right now."

Still in the grip of Jack's warning, he growled, "Or what?"

"Or," she said, again quietly, "I will smash your balls right up through your nose."

Startled, he dropped his hands. "A pleasant thought. Can't say anyone's ever threatened that before."

She backed up then leaned over, her hands on her knees. Just as he was about to ask what was wrong, she said. "Damn. I guess therapy didn't erase all my fears. Shit, shit, shit. Old Roger Dodger left his mark—in more ways than I thought."

Guilt smacked him up the back of his head. "I'm the one who's sorry. I shouldn't have grabbed you."

"You didn't. Not exactly. You see, Roger didn't stop with grabbing my shoulders."

"He hit you." And he brought up the memory. Could he be more of a jerk?

"Oh, yeah."

"And I brought it back when I yelled at you and grabbed you." More guilt seeped into his mind.

"Sort of. The self-defense class my therapist sent me to was supposed to give me the strength I needed after his second attack. I should be stronger." She wrapped her arms around her waist and rubbed her elbows. "I am stronger."

"Damn right you are."

"I overreacted. I'm sorry. I just . . ."

"No apologies necessary. I, uh, overreacted, too. I don't want to see you hurt. I'm afraid for you. Like Jack. You are in danger. He didn't know what he'd set into motion."

"Hang on. Sarah Jane. Jack mentioned Sarah Jane. Go back and see what he said."

She'd thrown him for a loop with her abrupt shift. Better than having her cry or shrink from him. Drew backed up the video.

". . . last night when I stayed late. Sarah Jane said I should talk to you or Mags."

Maggie gripped Drew's arm. "He talked to her about this."

Drew froze. "And she said something to Ben and Greg before leaving the funeral home."

"If she said she knew what they were up to . . ."

"That would be a good reason to get rid of her." He clasped her hands. "These people are dangerous, Maggie. If they suspect you know anything, I wouldn't put it past them to—" He pulled her tightly against his chest. "God, Mags. I can't lose you, too."

She let him hold her for a moment . . . or two or three. It felt right holding her in his arms. Like she belonged there. He just had to convince her to stay away from the Vander Haars. Let him deal with what Jack revealed.

"Drew? Please let me go."

"Sorry." He popped the SD card out of the machine and put it in an envelope on which he wrote "original."

She held out her hand. "Give me the original." She sounded like she was demanding cribbed notes and cheat sheets from her students.

"I will not play keep-away with you. I will lock the SD card in my safe."

"It's evidence. We should hand it over to the police."

Drew shook his head. "We need to find out more."

"Then, we should give it to Ben. He'll know what to do with it."

"You heard what Jack said. If there's a problem, he might be complicit."

"He can't be. I've known Ben for five years. He's a bit of a jerk about being in love with me, but he wouldn't do anything illegal." She dropped into the desk chair, her shoulders slumped. "Talk to me."

"Now that you're ready to listen, this is how it's going to go down. I know the senior Vander Haar. He's my client. Actually, he's been my client for a number of years. The guy is more honest than old Abe. Like Jack, my money is on Junior as the one dipping into the pension fund."

She appeared thoughtful, for a moment. "Considering my limited exposure to Junior, I'd say you're probably right. But, I'm not sure if it's because I don't like him."

"Trust your gut, my dad always said."

"Mine, too. Our dads had great instincts. I'm still waiting to hear the plan."

"Like I said before, this—" He held up the envelope with

the original. "—is going in the safe."

"Okay, I'll go along with that."

"Holy shit, you agreed with me on something." He pulled out his cell. "I'm going to write this down. On July second, two thousand and—"

"Oh, shut up, and get on with the plan."

"Follow me." He led her upstairs to his bedroom.

"Holy cow. You made your bed."

He slanted her a look. "I make my bed every day. Don't you?" He snapped his fingers. "Don't answer that. I know you don't. I remember from the day after we learned about Jack's accident. I also remember you wore purple panties when we went camping for the first time."

He loved teasing her and making her blush. "You know. The panties you kicked under her bed."

Leaving her gasping in embarrassment, he flipped on the light to his closet then shoved aside his clothes so he could reach the back left wall. A small hook was set in the drywall, on which hung a lightweight robe. When he pulled up on the hook, a square of drywall opened, revealing his safe.

"That is good camouflage."

He smiled over his shoulder. "Thanks."

After he twirled in the combination, the small safe opened. Papers and Lillian's jewelry boxes lay in back, with her handgun in front.

"You own a gun?"

"No. I don't. It's—it was Lillian's. I insisted she keep it locked up. I need to turn it in to the police. I've never liked having a gun in the house." He shrugged then put the envelope with the SD card inside. "I haven't made the time to do it."

"I know how that goes. Dad's hunting rifle is still in the gun safe in my basement. Jack was always too busy to deal with it, and I didn't make the time."

He shook his head. "We both should've made time."

As he locked the safe, she said, "Wait. Do you think we'll need a weapon?"

"*We* won't need anything. There is no we."

She blocked him from leaving the closet. "Please tell me you aren't going to keep me from discovering what's wrong at

Vander Haar, and why my brother had that *accident*."

Placing his palms under her elbows, he easily lifted her aside. "I could *tell* you that. Here's the rest of my plan. I'm going to call Senior—actually, he goes by Van—and meet him at the plant. I'll tell him it's something about the papers I'm drawing up for him."

"What papers?"

He merely stared at her.

She rolled her eyes. "I know. Client confidentiality. Okay, that sounds like a good plan. I'm coming along, of course."

He gave her the exasperated look his daughter did so well. From her expression, that didn't stop her.

"I either go with you, or I'll meet you there. Your choice."

"Did you even bother to listen to Jack's message?" He didn't grab her shoulders this time, though he wanted to. Her lack of a sense of danger infuriated him. "The part about where he thought someone was monitoring his search in the files?"

Enlightenment widened her eyes. She gripped his forearms. "You think they want to kill me, too?"

Fifty minutes later, Drew and Maggie pulled up in front of the plant. After the realization that Jack's warning about danger to her sunk in, she'd backed off arguing with Drew. Sure, she was scared. Yet, she was determined to go with him. She had to see this through. Finally, he relented.

It was a scorcher summer day, and it wasn't even August. Scanning the area, she realized they must have water restrictions here, like many communities throughout the Midwest, because what used to be grass around the front of the building had turned brown. The exposed ground had cracks a couple of inches deep. Even the hardy shrubs under the windows weren't going to make it.

"Hang on," she said as he turned off the engine of the big Navigator. "It's Monday. Where are all the cars? That one must be Senior's." She pointed to a black Cadillac CTS.

"Good question." A furrow creased his forehead. "That is strange."

The glass door was locked. After Drew's brief knock,

Vander Haar Senior pushed on the bar to let them in. "This must be some glitch you found in those papers to bring you out on a scorcher of a day. Ms. Sinclair, why are you here?"

"Call me Maggie, sir." She shook hands while he told her to call him 'Van.' "We noticed the empty parking lot. Is the plant closed?"

He chuckled. "With Fourth of July coming midweek, the employees asked to change the day off to today, giving them a three-day weekend. They'll work Wednesday instead."

"That makes sense," Drew said.

Van led them down the hall to a conference room. As they passed the room Jack had used, Van glanced back at her. "Again, my condolences on your brother's passing. I'm just sorry the accident happened while he was leaving my business."

The man, in his mid-sixties, had the kind of tan that came from golfing and water sports. His thick hair was bleached by the sun not age. And, from his athletic build, he obviously took care of himself.

"I received your kind note, sir. That was very thoughtful of you to write—even though you didn't know Jack." She remembered the shaky writing on the note and glanced at his hands. Age-spotted, slight tremor. Worry or ailment?

He sat at the end of a highly-polished conference table, while they sat next to him—Maggie closest. Van folded his hands in front of him. "What questions do you have about the contract, Counselor?"

Drew said, "I'm afraid I misled you, sir. We need to talk to you about a different matter."

"So, you got me here under false pretenses." He chuckled. "I've trusted you for how any years now, Drew? Ten? Tell me about this other matter."

"It's about Maggie's brother, Jack. Or rather, what he found while he was here. He left a message before he died."

Van raised his eyebrow.

Maggie placed her hand on Drew's arm. "Drew seems to think we can trust you. I don't know how else to approach this matter other than to come right out and tell you my brother's suspicions."

"I'm an advocate of plain speaking, Ms. Sinclair. As

Drew, I'm sure, can tell you." His mouth curved slightly.

"The employee pension fund has been raided," Drew said.

From Van's stricken expression, she knew Drew was right. This man hadn't done it.

"Show me." His voice was strained.

"We'll need to use a computer." Maggie nodded to the machine at the opposite end of the table. "Is that a digital projector?"

He nodded.

Since she'd used one at school, she quickly set it up and plugged the USB drive into the laptop. Soon, Jack's face filled the large screen in the front of the room. Her heart twisted again at the sight of her brother.

"He recorded this the day he died." Drew typed in the password.

As Jack's message proclaimed his suspicions, Maggie watched Van's reaction. The tan faded from Van's face. At the end, he slumped in his chair.

"I don't believe this." He waved his hand to prevent their protest. "I don't mean what you think. How could this happen? I can't . . ."

"There's one way to find out, sir." Maggie turned off the machine. "I'm sure you know what I mean."

"Yes. You're right." He joined them at the end of the table. Sitting down, he turned the laptop computer around to face him. "I need to get into the network."

"No, you don't."

They all turned toward voice coming from the opposite end of the conference room. A door so flush with the wall paneling that she never noticed was now open. In the doorway stood Greg Vander Haar. He propped one hand on the door, his other shoulder against the frame.

"Greg, what—"

"You know what you're going to find, so don't bother looking."

Van rose. "What have you done?"

"Sit down, old man." Greg stepped forward, his right hand in his pants' pocket.

His menacing tone surprised her. It must have surprised

his father, too, as Van dropped back in his chair.

"It's the gambling, isn't it?" Van said, defeat in his voice. "You promised to stay away from that place. You swore—"

"It's an addiction, Dad, don't you know that?" A sneer wrinkled Junior's nose. "And it never goes away."

"You promised you quit. Before I turned over operations to you. You said you quit gambling." Van rose, pleading.

"Gamblers promise and swear all the time. You should know better than to believe an addict. I needed control of the company. I would've told you anything to get it."

"We can fix this. We can replace the money. I'll get you help." The father took a step toward the son.

"It's too late for that." Greg took his hand out of his pocket. He held a small, black revolver. "Just stay right there."

"Jesus, son. What are you doing with a gun in the plant?"

"You just never know. A disgruntled employee might go postal. Or—" He shifted his weapon, pointing it at Maggie. "—a distraught woman might want to take revenge for her brother's unfortunate *accident*. After all, she has to blame someone for the fact that he wasn't wearing a seatbelt . . . or that his airbags were so conveniently stolen."

"Oh, God." The father stumbled back, landing in a chair.

"You just wouldn't give up, would you, bitch?" the younger man snarled. "You had to go sniffing around, sticking your nose in where it didn't belong—just like that brother of yours."

"You killed him, didn't you?" Maggie was surprised at how calm she sounded. She'd known the truth all along.

"Well, now, there is no proof. You couldn't even convince the sheriff to look into the matter, could you? Just your ranting."

"My brother's message will—"

"I supposed I'll have to take that." He held out his hand. "Give me the USB drive."

"Come and get it yourself," she snarled back.

"Just give me the damn thing." He motioned menacingly with the gun.

Well, now, she thought, that was a redundant thought. If

someone was motioning with a gun, it could be nothing but menacing. Oh, God, she was starting to lose it.

"Did you actually think we'd bring the original without making a back-up?" Drew pointed out.

"Oh, don't tell me you left one of those 'open in the case of my death' things," The younger man scoffed.

A small sound behind her caught Maggie's attention. Van held his right arm against his chest. Perspiration beaded his forehead and his upper lip. He was even paler now than when he realized what his son had done. She started toward him.

"Don't move," Greg ordered.

She stopped. "Your father—"

"Problems, Dad?" he sneered.

"I think he's having a heart attack," Maggie said. "We have to call—"

"Forget that. You're not calling anyone." He glanced over at his father who leaned against the table. Then Van fell to the floor, clutching his chest. "Those cigarettes you smoked all those years finally got you, hey, old man. And all those hours you worked when you didn't have time for my Little League games or—"

"For God's sake, let me help him," Maggie cried. "I know CPR." She couldn't stand there and do nothing while the man died in front of her. She leaned over Van.

The shot whizzing past made her rethink. She dropped to the floor next to Van, who lay curled up, facing away from his son and staring at her.

"Don't move, Counselor, or my next shot won't miss her. Stand up, bitch."

Van stared at her then mouthed, "Phone. Shirt pocket."

Her eyes widened. Was he faking?

"Look, man." Drew raised his hands, drawing Greg's attention. "We can work things out."

With Greg's attention on Drew, Maggie edged closer to Van. She pulled his cell phone out of his pocket and put it in his hand. He gave her an acknowledging nod.

Greg swiveled his attention to her. "What did you do?"

"I checked his pulse. It's very rapid, his breathing is erratic." She lied. Both his heartrate and his breathing appeared normal. How odd. If he was faking a heart attack, he did a great acting job.

"Your father is willing to repay the pension fund." Drew didn't move, yet again he commanded Greg's attention.

"That's my dad all right. Throw money at me and hope I'll go away." Greg rubbed his forehead. "So busy, my dad. Too busy for me. Isn't that right, old man?"

Again, he pointed his weapon at Maggie. "I told you to get up."

Using the table to lever herself off the floor, she finally stood. Van could call 911. Oh God, she hoped he got help for himself. And for Drew and her.

"Out to the plant," Greg ordered. "No funny business, either. Don't think that I won't shoot."

"You're just going to leave your father on the floor?" Maggie cried.

Greg looked down at him. "I was. On second thought, take him with you."

"What?" Drew asked. "The man needs medical help."

"You can give it to him out in the plant."

With Drew on one side and Maggie on the other, they helped Van to his feet. He leaned heavily on them as they walked out into the hall. Apparently, Drew knew the way since he turned left.

"What's in your hand, old man?" Greg demanded. "Is that your cell? Toss it on the floor." After he did, Greg waved his gun at Drew and Maggie. "Where are your phones? Throw them on the floor, too."

With reluctance, they complied. There went any chance of summoning help.

"You, Counselor. Kick them away."

Drew did.

"Keep walking."

When they reached a short hall, Drew stopped. "How are you going to explain two bodies with bullet holes in them, Greg? I assure you, you'll have to kill all of us if you plan to get away with this."

Don't give him any more ideas. Maggie glared at him, attempting mental telepathy.

"Keep moving. End of the hall. You see it's like this. The

distraught sister came for revenge, with her shifty lawyer."

Tightening her grip on Van, Maggie pulled open the heavy metal door that led from the offices to the plant. "Don't you resent being called shifty, Drew?"

"Don't think about trying to slam the door between you," Greg warned. "The door has a delayed clo—"

When his voice broke off, Maggie glanced over her shoulder. Van lurched away from them into his son. The man had to be on death's doorstep, yet he gave them a chance to escape.

Three steps led down to the machine level. She and Drew must have been on the same wavelength because as she dodged right off the top step, Drew forced the door shut. He, too, jumped right. Just in time, too. Hollow pings resounded against the metal.

"Bullets?" she asked, stupidly.

"He's not shooting blanks. Let's go."

They ran toward the outer wall, keeping machinery and storage units between them and the door to the office. She was certain Greg was going to come through any time. Drew kept hold of her hand, practically dragging her while she searched for anything lying around that she could use as a weapon against Greg.

"What about Van?"

"He made his choice." Drew urged her to hurry. "We don't want to give Greg a target if he bursts into the plant with that gun blazing. I can't believe the guy has gone off the deep end like this."

"He's trying to cover up mistake after mistake."

Keeping an eye on the door, Maggie grabbed a wrench. When the door opened, Greg stood there surveying the plant. Behind him, she saw Van lying on the floor. Poor man. She wasted precious seconds in sympathy for him. What a disappointment to discover his son's treachery.

As soon as Greg glanced to the opposite side of the plant, she threw the wrench then ducked down. A wrench wasn't anything like a baseball. Still, it got his attention when it hit his left arm. She'd aimed for the other, the one with the gun.

A shot rang out. It went wild and hit a machine across the room. Then, he pivoted in her direction and fired off three quick shots, one of which hit the toolchest in front of her.

"You bitch!" He shook his left arm. Probably trying to get feeling back into it.

She found a piece of steel on the floor. Not round, but close enough to the size of a baseball. Better than a wrench or hammer. As Greg jumped off the step, she fired the chunk of steel at his chest—a bigger target this time.

He screamed when the steel hit his midsection and doubled in pain. "I will get you, bitch. I swear I'll kill you."

He staggered toward her. Drew grabbed her hand and pulled her around a large lathe. Stooping, she grabbed another chunk of steel from discards on the floor. A bullet whizzed past.

"Damn it, Mags," Drew hissed. "That one came too close to your head. We have to keep moving."

Swearing at Maggie, Greg lurched forward, firing his gun as he advanced. The second he stopped, she threw that piece of steel and immediately ducked. From a slit between the lathe and a toolchest, she could see the result. The steel chunk came so close to his head, it nicked his ear.

He cried out.

"I've got plenty more where that came from," she yelled.

"Mags," Drew hissed again. "Don't antagonize him."

Blood dripping down the side of his face, Greg ran to the steps and leaped to the top. As soon as she saw his back, she threw pieces of steel at him. One hit his leg. Though he lurched, he swore at her and blasted through the door, ducking behind it to protect himself.

"Now, what?" she asked Drew.

Still crouched behind the big machine, he pulled her into his arms and held her tight. "I can't believe you chased him away."

"Not for long, I'll bet."

His kiss came so fast and hard she could only hang onto him. Passion quickly overwhelmed relief at escaping Greg. Desire rushed through her. Too soon, he released her. She didn't move. She couldn't. The shaking started in her hands and quickly spread throughout her body.

She clung to Drew. "I don't think I can stand."

"I got ya." Standing, he pulled her up then rubbed her back. "I always knew you should've been a pitcher instead of an outfielder."

"Nah. Never wanted the pressure." She eyed the door to the offices. "Do you think he's coming back?"

"No idea." Keeping the machines between them and the door, he led her toward an emergency exit at the back of the plant.

"Wait. Van was lying on the floor. We have to help him."

Drew stopped. "As soon as we open the door, Greg's going to fire at us."

"We'll have to be careful. We can't leave Van."

Again keeping behind the machines, she tugged his hand. This time, she led him to the door to the offices. They'd just reached the steps when the door slowly opened. Drew encircled her waist and pulled her off behind a large work bench. Van crawled through the door then sprawled in the doorway.

Drew ran to the older man and pulled him through the door. In that brief moment before the door closed, Maggie saw flames. The office was ablaze. Drew dragged Van behind the bench where Maggie waited. Van's eyes were open, his breathing shallow.

"I am so sorry." He panted. "So sorry . . . for . . . my son."

"Don't talk," Maggie said at the same time Drew said, "Where is he?"

Van obeyed Drew. "Outside. Set fire . . . to front office."

Maggie glanced up at Drew. "We have to get out of here. If we stay, the fire will get us."

"Safer in here," Drew said. "The cement walls and floor will protect us."

"Not . . . necessarily." Van panted heavily. "Oil . . . lubricating fluid . . . flammable."

"Maybe we should take that exit." She pointed to the outer door at the back of the plant.

Despite Van saying Greg was outside, they crept to the exit, holding up Van between them. Drew motioned for them to wait. "In case, he's out there waiting."

"If he has any sense," she said, "he'll wait by the cars to cut off our escape."

Drew shot her a look. "You're assuming he has any sense. Everything is falling apart for him. He's bound to do something else foolish because he doesn't have a plan."

"He's . . . scared." Van's pale face and heavy breathing frightened Maggie. He hadn't been faking, after all. If they didn't get help for him soon, he might not make it.

Slowly, Drew opened the heavy metal door a crack. Though he tried to flatten her and Van against the wall behind him, Maggie peeked out anyway. She could see bright blue sky and the relentless sun beating down on the narrow strip of asphalt along the building. She handed him a pipe to push the door open wider without showing himself.

No shots rang out. That had to be a good sign.

She hoped.

When Maggie leaned over his shoulder to look out further, he growled, "Idiot woman. Stay back. What if he's on the other side of the door?"

"Right," she said in his ear. "I'll just let you get your head blown off. Good thinking, Campbell."

He slammed the door open. The door hit the outside wall—and no soft object, like a body—then bounced back.

"Into the forest," Maggie whispered. The woods that ringed the plant were about fifteen feet away.

A bullet hit the door above Drew's head. He ducked back into the building.

Maggie grabbed his arm. "That was too close. We can't leave."

Another shot rang out.

"That was your right front tire, Campbell," Greg called out. "Only one spare? Here goes the left one."

A shot. Then, an explosion. Glass shattering. Metal clattering. A car alarm blared.

"Holy shit, Campbell," Greg hollered. "Your SUV just blew up. Sorry about that. Took out my office window and my daddy's car, too. Good thing I parked far enough away. Looks like you guys aren't going anywhere."

Maggie tugged on Drew's arm. "We need to circle round. As dry as this grass is, a spark from the fire will make everything go up faster than—"

"Oh, oops, guys." It was Greg again. "That little breeze

just picked up the fire. I do think the plant's going to go up in smoke. Well, the insurance money will come in handy."

"Little breeze, my ass," Drew growled. "The wind is getting stronger. We should stay inside the building."

"We need a phone." Maggie turned to Van. "Is there a landline out here?"

The older man slumped against the wall. He pointed to a small windowed enclosure in the right corner of the shop. "Foreman's . . . office."

"Stay with him," Drew said before running to the office.

Maggie slid down on the floor next to Van. "Drew will get help. I'm sorry we brought so much down on you."

"Not your . . . fault. Greg's." He squeezed her hand. "You were coming . . . back for me. You could've . . . gotten away."

"And leave you behind? I don't think so. We'll get out of this. I'm positive."

He fell over, his head landing in her lap. She brushed back his thick gray hair, his brow sweaty. *God, don't let him die. Send help quick. Please. He doesn't deserve to die because of his son.*

Drew ran up. "The police and fire department are on their way. I warned them that Greg had a gun, and I told them about the fire."

"Good." With her eyes, she drew his attention to Van.

Drew stooped, put his hand on Van's shoulder. "Help is coming, sir. Hang on."

The wait was interminable. Seconds seemed like minutes. Minutes dragged like hours.

"Hang on." Maggie straightened without moving Van. "Do I hear sirens?"

"I hear them, too." Drew opened the exit door. "I'll go get them."

He placed the pipe to hold the door open then ran to the front of the building and hailed the ambulance to drive around to the back. Maggie feared that Greg would shoot him or the medical workers.

In seconds, it seemed, the EMTs assessed Van's condition before placing him on the portable gurney then wheeled him out to the ambulance. They left, lights flashing, siren blaring.

"Greg?" Maggie asked.

Drew shook his head. "I didn't see him. As soon as he heard the sirens, I'll bet he took off."

"When you ran out to the front, I was so afraid for you."

"Hey, we made it," he said.

She'd been so scared that they wouldn't.

"This is another fine mess you've gotten us into." She blinked twice then burst into tears. She threw her arms around his neck and kissed him for all she was worth.

Drew's embrace took her breath away. And that was just for starters. His kiss seared her nerve endings all the way down to her toes. She wanted to tear his clothes off. His hands weren't idle. They grabbed her butt, pulling her tighter into him, where she could feel his arousal prodding her. *Oh, Lordy.* He wanted her, too.

Drew broke off the kiss, leaving her hungry for more. "Our first time will not be on a cement floor of a manufacturing plant."

CHAPTER FIFTEEN

Maggie sat on her couch, not wanting to get up. At her insistence, Drew had brought her home after his father picked them up. First, his dad had dropped them off at Drew's house so he'd have transportation. Lucky him owning two very nice vehicles, the Town Car and the Navigator. Okay, one luxury vehicle and charred pieces of the other.

Home never felt so good. Nora Oostveen, Gretchen's mother, had organized a cleaning crew. Together with Mrs. O'Malley from across the street, they'd put Maggie's house in order. They either had a large group or they'd worked through the night. She'd never appreciated her friends and neighbors as much as when she saw their work. Nora had left a note. They'd even washed all her clothes.

With Drew's arm around her, holding her tightly against him, she relaxed for the first time in hours. Call her a marshmallow, because that's what her insides felt like. All squishy and soft.

"I was really scared," she said softly.

"Me, too."

"I've never had anyone shoot at me before."

"I did. Once."

"What did you do? The first time."

"Same as this time. Prayed that all the liquid inside me didn't leak out."

She gave him a little punch on the arm. "That is disgusting."

"You tell me you didn't feel like wetting your underpants." He kissed the top of her head. "You did good, you know. Firing those pieces of steel and tools at him."

She snorted. "He sure didn't expect that."

"Looks like all that baseball practice paid off."

"Hmm. I might use that as an incentive for the girls. You never know when you need to hit what you aim at."

They sat in silence for several minutes before Drew said, "Can I get you something to drink, eat?"

"No, I'm good."

He kissed the top of her head again. "I *know* you're good." His chest rumbled with laughter under her ear.

She wasn't going to touch that. "That was really nice of your dad to come and pick us up."

"Especially since the Navigator is scattered across several hundred feet of charred grass and pavement. Better it than us, though."

"Mmm." She yawned. "You should get home to Ellen. She'll be worried."

"I talked to her while you were in the bathroom."

Maggie sat up. "You didn't tell her what happened, did you?"

"An abbreviated version. Same one Dad told her. That I we had a 'fender-bender' and had to have the Navigator towed. I left out the part about it blowing up, an idiot shooting at us, smoke inhalation—all the insignificant details." He waited for her to stop snorting.

"Seriously, Drew. Go home. I'll be fine."

"Did I mention that Ellen is spending the night at her grandparents'?"

"Uh, no. I don't believe you mentioned that."

While she was wondering when he planned to tell her, her cell phone rang. She dug it out of her pocket then checked caller ID. Muskegon County Sheriff. She turned on the speaker so Drew could hear. It was Detective Tom Watson.

"Thought you might want to know what happened to Greg Vander Haar. He ran his car off the same bridge where your brother died."

"What? On purpose?" she asked.

"Looks like it. But we won't make any suppositions like we did about your brother's accident."

"Thanks for believing in me. You were the only one who listened."

"About that. We're going to do some retraining regarding accidents. I'm glad you persisted."

She thanked him for letting her know about Greg then

hung up.

"Same bridge, huh?" Drew said. "Rather fitting, I'd say."

"Guilt?"

"I think the man was at the end of his rope. He had to do something." He shifted to face her. "About that kiss?"

Oh, she was afraid he was going to mention that.

"Uh, kiss. What about it?"

"Pretty hot, huh?" He toyed with the end of her hair that had fallen over her shoulder.

"Hot? Uh, well, scorching might be a better word."

He threw his head back and laughed. "Leave it to an English teacher to critique my romantic overture."

Heat flared in her cheeks.

"I wanted more," he said. "Back in the plant. I wanted you. I wanted to make love to you right there on that floor."

His bold words set her emotions on fire. Make that sizzling emotions. Damn, she was critiquing herself.

"What's with the smile?" he asked.

If he could be bold, so could she. She scooted closer. "I wanted to rip your clothes off."

He grinned. "Oh my, Maggie May. You amaze me."

"Then why aren't you kissing me now?" She bent closer, her mouth hovering over his.

He stood. "I was thinking about getting some dinner first."

"What?" She'd nearly fallen over when he rose.

"Dinner. You know that meal we should've eaten two hours ago."

"Oh, that meal. Okay, I guess. I'm sure there's stuff in the fridge. I don't think I have the energy to go out."

"Save that energy for later." Laughing, he leered. "Actually, I was thinking about picking up Chinese. How does that sound?"

"Chang's makes very good General's Chicken. A take-out menu is in the drawer under the phone."

He disentangled himself from her and stood. "Always prepared?"

"Hey. I'm a Girl Scout. Oh, get a double order of Crab Rangoon. Please." She gave him a pleading look. It was rather nice letting someone wait on her. Heaven knows she never got that kind of treatment before.

After ordering online, he stopped to kiss her soundly then walked to the front door. He stood there for a moment jingling his keys. "Sure, you'll be okay here by yourself?"

"Get on with you now. I'm starving." She blew him a kiss.

As soon as he left, she beat it into the bathroom. Might as well try to do something with her hair. After her shower, she'd left it to hang dry. Drew had taken a shower, too, and her bathroom still held the scent of his aftershave. She hadn't realized he had a packed go-bag in the Town Car. She refrained from teasing him about being prepared.

Poor guy. How was he going to explain to the insurance company about the Navigator? Even with the police report, they had to question the damage.

Thinking about insurance led her to Greg Vander Haar's comment about the insurance money from the plant. It would probably go for replacing the money in the pension fund. Geez, three years of—

Three years, he'd been taking money out of the pension fund.

She dropped her brush.

As soon as she finished in the bathroom, she paced the living room. If the embezzlement had been going on for three years, Ben had to know. Against her hopes, she had to admit he must be guilty. But, guilty of what? Collusion? Fraud? Cover up?

Oh, God. Not guilty of Jack's death. He couldn't be.

Lights flashed through the window, and she heard a car pull up in her driveway. Drew was back quick. Maybe too quick. He probably forgot something. She searched the room and kitchen counter for his wallet. Nope. When the doorbell rang, she ran to the front door. She had to tell him what she realized. As she pulled it open, she said, "You'll never—"

Ben Voorheis stood on the porch. "I heard what happened, Maggie. My God, are you all right?"

After what occurred to her while brushing her hair, she stayed inside the screendoor, her hand on the lever. With her thumb, she moved the lock into position. "Yes. I'm fine. What do you want?"

He was taken aback by her tone. "I found something of Jack's that you need to see."

"What?" She glanced at his hands, one empty, the other held his crutch.

"It's his computer and the case, what you wanted earlier."

"Where is it?"

"At work. I found it. He'd hidden it in the storage area."

That could be true. Jack could have hidden his computer at work. But why? A backup, in case she and Drew hadn't found his other clues?

Ben shifted. "We need to go now."

"Drew is coming right back. We can wait for him."

"We can't. Come on. We have to go."

"Not yet. I'll wait for Drew." One glimpse of Ben's darkened expression and she added, "As soon as he returns, we can go."

"We're going now." He yanked the screendoor, hard enough to break the lock and pull the door out of her hand. "We have to take care of this before the police realize how involved Jack was."

"Jack?" Maggie blocked his entrance into the house. As big as Ben was, he could plow right through her, but she wasn't going to make it easy for him. "Jack was not involved, Ben. It was Greg. And you."

"Me? No. You can't believe that, Maggie. You're right. It was Greg. That SOB."

"You've got that right. He left his father to die."

Ben's laugh sounded more like a bark. "That doesn't surprise me. He has no care about anyone but himself."

If she were a cartoon, a lightbulb would go off over her head. "He's letting you take the fall."

"Yeah, the son-of-a-bitch is leaving town. He made the mistake of telling me to get out, too."

"No. He's dead. Greg committed suicide."

An unhealthy expression crossed Ben's face. "Really?"

"Yeah. He drove off—" She stopped when she saw Ben's satisfied smirk. "Oh, God. You killed him, too."

She couldn't believe Ben could be so ruthless. That was

not the Ben she knew. Or thought she knew.

"He deserved it. My leg is killing me. I'm coming in, but I don't want to hurt you."

Because he seemed to want to talk, she figured if she let him in she might get some answers. If she kept him talking, Drew would get there and help her take him down. Despite her self-defense classes, she knew her limits. She couldn't do it alone. She stood aside.

"Thanks, Mags. Jack always called you Mags, didn't he?"

"Do not call me that." Mags was Jack's and Drew's name for her. "After what you've done, you don't deserve the privilege."

"I can't believe you could be so cruel." He gave her that hurt expression he'd perfected before hobbling over to the recliner. He sank down, an expression of relief in his eyes.

"And I can't believe you would blame my brother for what you did. You, Ben Voorheis. Not Greg. That jerk wasn't smart enough to embezzle the money by himself." Maggie sat on the arm of the sofa across from Ben.

"Shit." He scrubbed his face. "I didn't want you to know. But you figured it out, huh? Just like Jack. Greg was smart enough to siphon the money out of the pension fund."

"But not smart enough to hide it from his auditor," she said in disgust. "What did he pay you to cook the books?"

"Nothing."

She snorted. "You expect me to believe that?"

Ben propped his elbow on the chair arm then rested his forehead in his palm. "The first year, he said he only borrowed the money to pay back a gambling debt. He promised he'd replace it. He had some investments he had to sell off first."

"If he had the investments, why did he tap into the pension fund?"

"I asked him the same thing. He said he had to wait until the market turned around. Otherwise, he'd lose too much money."

"The market turned around, and he still didn't put the money back, did he?"

"No." Ben's bleak expression made it hard to look at her brother's partner—the man who'd betrayed his friend.

"I covered for Greg, but he didn't repay the money, and he didn't stop gambling. I found that out last year when I did the second audit. He pointed out that if I turned him in, I'd be in trouble for falsifying the previous year's audit. Like I didn't know that. He was my friend, Maggie. That's why he hired me to audit the books. He said he was making big changes with the company after his father turned over the reins. I thought that was why he got a new lawyer, a buddy of his from college, and why he moved the business from the firm that used to do the audit to ours. I trusted him."

"And he used you to cover up what he'd done."

"I couldn't turn him in. I'd ruin my name, the business—Jack's and mine."

After listening to him, she had to ask. "Did you help Greg kill Jack?"

He bolted upright. "Oh God, no. You have to believe me, Maggie. At first, he said he was just going to talk to Jack."

"I guess you guys did more than talk." Though she hurt inside, she had to find out exactly what happened.

Ben reached into his pocket and pulled out a blister pack then quickly popped something in his mouth. "We told him to meet us at a bar just up the road from the plant. I rode with Jack to make sure he came."

Something clicked in her mind. "Was that an antacid?"

"Yeah. My gut's all torn up. Pain like you wouldn't believe."

Good. You deserve it, you son-of-a-bitch. That was how the blister pack ended up inside Jack's car. Ben had been there, inside the Blazer. Stunned more than before, she knew he'd been that close to Jack, inside the vehicle with him before he died.

Unaware of her thoughts, Ben continued talking. "Jack kept asking how I didn't see that money was missing from the pension fund. I acted surprised. Said I had no idea."

"But you did."

He nodded.

"Tell me what happened next."

"Oh, Maggie." Pressing on his stomach, he groaned. She didn't have the least sympathy for him.

"Tell me." Her sharp tone startled him.

229

"It's all Greg's fault. Jack was going to turn both of us in. He would have ruined our lives."

"Jack was your friend. How you could kill him?"

"Not me. *I* didn't stuff him in the car, or make the skid marks, or jam the accelerator. Greg did all that. *I* didn't want to kill Jack. I just wanted the whole thing to go away. You have to believe me, Maggie. I didn't want to have anything to do with Greg's plan. I couldn't kill Jack. He was my friend. Please, believe me."

"All right. I believe you." She lied, anything to keep him talking until Drew arrived. "How did it happen?"

"Aw, Maggie . . ." He bowed his head.

"Tell me." Her demand startled him. He glanced up and then shuttered his eyes.

"Jack had to take a leak. While he was gone, Greg put a roofie in his beer. Said we had to take care of him." Tears welled in his eyes. "I had no idea he would go that far."

His tears didn't faze her. "Yet, you didn't go to the police."

"You don't understand. Greg made me help him."

She scoffed. "*Made* you? What? He put a gun to your head?"

"No." Misery swam in his eyes. "He wouldn't take no. He wouldn't listen when I said we could work it out."

"How did he make you? With your shoulder in a sling and using a crutch, what did you do?"

"He told me to disable the airbags. He even told me how. I didn't want to, Maggie. Believe me. But Greg said we'd both get into trouble. The police would think it was an accident, and nobody would know otherwise. And they didn't. The cops thought it was an accident. Nobody suspected. Not until you kept probing. You were too inquisitive. Why couldn't you accept Jack's death as an accident?"

"If I had, you two would've gotten away with murder. Maybe you didn't put Jack behind the wheel and—what?— put a stick on the accelerator?"

Again, he nodded.

"And the stick fell out when the Blazer rolled over." Though her heart ached from his tale, she pretended to muse. "So many sticks lying around nobody would notice one more?"

He nodded once again.

"Then you watched as Jack's Blazer flew over the embankment and into the river. Did you stand on the bridge? Did you see your friend die?"

"I didn't want that to happen."

Fury rose up in her. "Did you try to stop it? Stop Greg? You knew what he planned. You're an accessory the same as if you'd actually done it yourself. I suppose you killed Sarah Jane. You—"

"No." His sharp tone surprised her. "I didn't kill her. That was Greg. He was losing it. At the funeral, she told us she knew what we'd done, said Jack talked to her. Greg said we couldn't take a chance she'd go to the police. I didn't know he was going to kill her."

"Come on. You had to know what he planned. Even when I told you she was dead, you knew what Greg had done. Still, you didn't go to the police." Her mouth twisted in disgust. She remembered what he wanted her to see. "Why do you have Jack's computer?"

"Greg said we had to get the proof off the computer. He took it to some computer whiz he knew to hack in. But Jack had it too well protected. Greg's whiz gave up."

"Another screw up. The missing computer and its bag set me on the course. I wouldn't have thought anything was wrong if I'd found it in the Blazer."

"Oh, God."

"And you blew it searching his condo. You made copies of Jack's keys, didn't you? That's how you got—or Greg—got in and searched the place. You see, that was another thing that made me question the accident."

He scrubbed his forehead. "You know too much, Maggie."

"That's not all I know. The key to Sarah Jane's apartment was on Jack's keyring. Is that how Greg got in?" She saw the guilt in his eyes. "My key, too. How many times did you enter my house when I wasn't there?"

"Yes, yes. Stop. You're making my head hurt."

"I haven't even started, buster. Why did you take out Jack's emergency contact card from his wallet and replace it?"

"Jack said you never answer your landline because of all the robo-calls. We thought it would take longer for the police to contact you if they didn't have your cell number."

"I didn't get the message because I was camping, you dolt. And I do listen to messages left on my answering machine." She blew out a breath. "Why did you come here, Ben? To justify your involvement? Why did you really want me to go to the office with you?

Tears filled his eyes. "You know I love you, but I can't let you keep talking to the police."

"How are you going to stop me? Like you did Jack? Like Sarah Jane?" At his startled expression, she added, "It's going to take more than you telling me not to talk to them."

"I know." He reached inside his sling and pulled out a revolver.

"What is it with you guys and guns?" Maggie asked in exasperation. "You are not going to shoot me."

"No? What do I have to lose? They can only hang me once."

"Oh, for God's sake." Maggie leaped up, knocking into the coffee table and setting the bowl of fake apples rocking. She fisted her hands on her hips. "Quit being so dramatic. Michigan does not have capital punishment. You'll just go to prison."

"Just? Just? I can't go to prison." The gun wavered.

"Why? You don't want to be some gangbanger's bitch?"

"You don't understand."

"Oh, I understand all right. You're tying up loose ends."

"I have to. Oh, Maggie. You should've left well enough alone. You pushed me into this mess."

"Oh, right. Blame me. Just like you blame Greg. It's your fault, Ben Voorheis. Not mine."

"It is. You betrayed me by going with Drew. You were mine." His fierce expression should have deterred her.

"I'm nobody's. Not yours, not Drew's."

He ignored that. "Don't you see? I just want this all to go away. If nobody's left to talk to the police, they won't investigate further."

"I wouldn't count on that. The police are a lot smarter

than you think."

"Hey. What's going on?" Drew Campbell, bags from the Chinese restaurant dangling from his hands, burst through the screendoor.

Thank God, he's here. Please, Drew, don't try some macho stuff and get us both killed. Another forehead thunking moment—Ben was planning to kill them both anyway.

"Oh, Drew." She groaned. "He has a gun."

Ben got up, facing Drew, the revolver in his hand.

Drew edged away from Maggie. "I-I see." He sounded shaky. Still holding the bags of food, he held up his hands. "P-Please don't shoot."

What's going on? Drew never acted scared, even when Greg pulled his gun on them.

"I-I'm too young to die. Please."

What was he doing? Drew never whined.

"Oh, for heaven's sake, Drew. What's gotten into you?"

"I have a child. My baby will be an orphan. Let me go. I promise not to call the police." He edged closer to the screendoor.

Now, she knew something wasn't right. Drew wouldn't abandon her.

"Stop. Get back here. See." Still staring at her, Ben waved his gun at Drew. "I tried to tell you he wasn't any good for you. Look at how he's trying to save his own skin."

Drew would never do that. *He's playing for time, making Ben think he's not a threat. Why? How long was he outside listening?*

While those thoughts ran through her mind, he caught her eye then glanced at the bowl of apples on the coffee table. "Please. Can I put my hands down? My arms are killing me." He waved the bags of food, fumbled then dropped them.

While he held Ben's attention, Maggie grabbed one of the apples. By the feel, it was a wood one. She fired it at his head.

Ben dropped, hitting the recliner on his way to the floor, landing on his injured shoulder. His crutch and weapon landed a foot away. Crying out, he curled into a fetal position.

After kicking the gun away, Drew was on him faster than

an Al Kaline throw to home plate. "Got any zip ties? Rope?"

For a second, Maggie didn't move, stunned at what had just happened.

"Maggie." Drew's demand snapped her into action. "Zip ties. Rope."

"Yeah. Right."

She raced to the kitchen. Rifled the junk drawer. Found a long zip tie she used for luggage when she flew. Rope. Laundry room. She grabbed the clothesline looped on a hook that she used to dry delicates.

Restraints in hand, she tore through the hall back to the living room. Drew knelt on a moaning Ben's back. With quick efficiency, Drew trussed him up. At that moment, a police officer burst through the front door, weapon in hand.

"Police! Hands up. Back away from that man, mister."

Maggie stared in stunned silence as she slowly raised her hands. Drew stood, just as slowly, and raised his.

"I called you," he said in a quiet, calm voice. "Drew Campbell. This is the perp." He nodded to Ben. "The one who had the weapon."

"Ms. Sinclair, are you all right?" Officer Joe Pfeifer followed the first officer inside, his service revolver in his hand.

"You know her?" The first officer glanced at Maggie's former student.

"Yes, sir. That's Ms. Sinclair, the homeowner." Joe glared at Ben, still moaning on the floor. "He's been here before. Didn't like him then. Don't like him now."

CHAPTER SIXTEEN

Drew didn't think the police would ever leave. A backup crew hauled Ben Voorheis away. The original officer took Drew into the dining room to get his story. The other officer, the kid who knew Maggie, stayed in the living room to take hers.

Maggie.

God, he loved that woman. He recalled her stunned expression when he faked being scared. As Voorheis continued to hold the gun on them, Drew could almost hear the thoughts racing through Maggie's mind. Her face was so expressive, he knew the instant as she figured it out. Thank God, Voorheis was so self-absorbed he never realized Drew's intentions.

Maggie did.

"You were marvelous." He kissed the top of her head. They sat on her sofa, his arm around her shoulders while she snuggled in.

"You weren't so bad yourself, you wimp." She chuckled. "Ben's expression when you came in was priceless. He believed you."

"So did you. For a minute." He added the last quickly.

"Less than a minute."

"I know. If he'd watched your eyes, he would've seen when you guessed what I was doing."

"I can't believe you didn't play Macho Man and take him down. Or Super Lawyer and try to talk him into giving up." She lightly punched his chest. "Thank you."

He rubbed the spot. "For what?"

"For trusting me to handle the situation."

"After you threw tools and chunks of steel at Greg, I knew you could deal with Voorheis."

"Roger never trusted me. Not with the finances—he had to see every receipt—not with my friends or even my family.

He never would've trusted me to handle a bad guy." She paused a second. "I couldn't have handled Ben then. I didn't have the courage. Roger undermined me constantly, sapping any strength I had."

Drew squeezed her shoulder. "I never knew things were so bad. Neither did Jack. We would've rescued you."

"I know. I had to do it myself." She twisted around to face him. "I don't want to talk about that man. Or Ben." Her small capable hand cupped the side of his face. "I don't want to talk at all."

Hope rising, along with another part of his anatomy, he slid his arm around her waist. "What do you want to do?"

Her kiss told him exactly what she wanted to do. And where she wanted to do it.

He scooped her into his arms and headed to her bedroom.

"You don't have to carry me. I'm capable of walking."

"I know you are. You're a very capable woman. Could you allow me have the illusion that *I'm* capable, too?"

She grinned up at him as he entered her bedroom. "I'm sure you are capable of many things, my good man."

At her bedside, he let her slide out of his arms. He would never let on that he almost dropped her. Though trim, she was all muscle. Everyone knew that muscle was heavy. Maybe he wasn't as capable as he thought. He needed to work on his upper body strength.

"I'm scared."

Her soft revelation surprised him. He tipped up her chin. "Of me? Or what comes next?"

"What's next." She wouldn't look at him.

"Have you been with anyone since your divorce?"

"Not recently, and not anyone I really cared about."

"You care about me?"

She batted his shoulder. "Of course, I do."

"More than care?" He hadn't said the L word himself. Why did he think she would?

When she didn't respond, he said, "We can wait."

Hell if he wanted to do that. But he would. For her, he'd do anything.

She began pulling his shirt out of his jeans. "I don't want

to wait. I mean, I . . ."

"Shall we play it by ear?" He kissed the side of her neck.

"Okay. Do that again. Please."

He did. "Any time you want to stop, I will." Not that he wanted to. "Do you trust me?"

Looping her hands around his neck, she stood on tiptoe and pulled his head down. "I trust you with my life, Andrew Robert Campbell. Now kiss me. Like you did before."

He didn't hesitate.

"We never did eat." Maggie lay next to Drew, perfectly satisfied. Her bare breast against his equally bare chest, her leg resting on his. She could lie like this for the rest of her life. Until her stomach growled.

"Thinking about food at a time like this?" His chuckle rumbled under her cheek.

"I'm hungry."

"I didn't satisfy you?"

"I wasn't talking about that kind of hunger." She stretched and sighed then settled back into his arms. "You definitely satisfied *that* hunger."

"Good."

"Are you smirking?"

"Me? Never."

She propped herself up and stared at his mouth. His delicious mouth that had turned her inside out quivered, as if he were trying to control a smirk. Or a smile. Yes, definitely a smile. A satisfied smile.

A sliver of panic crept in. "This changes everything, doesn't it?" She held her breath, waiting for his answer.

"Yes." No equivocation. No asking what she meant. He knew.

Shifting, he loomed over her. "Are you okay with change?"

His gray eyes clouded in concern. He waited more patiently than she did. She thought she knew what he was asking. She'd brought up the subject of change.

"Dearest Drew. I'm here. I'm where I want to be. Where I wanted to be all those years ago when I asked you to teach me how to kiss." She looped her arms around his neck. "Boy, oh, boy. I wished I'd known how you can kiss."

He nipped her upper lip. "I didn't know how to kiss like this when I was eighteen." His expression turned serious. "Kissing Lillian wasn't like this."

His mentioning his dead wife should have turned her off, or at the very least made her uncomfortable. Curiosity got the better of her. She drew her fingers down the back of his neck but didn't meet his eyes.

"How?"

He rolled off her and flopped back on his pillow. "It's hard to say. Should we be talking about her? It feels like there's three of us in this bed."

Wow. How do go from silly to serious in a few dumb questions. "She was part of your life, part of you, and especially part of Ellen." She hesitated, unsure if she wanted to hear his answer. Still, she had to ask. "Do you still love her?"

With his forearm across his forehead, his eyes were hidden. "I'll always love her."

Maggie's heart sank. She'd started this line of questioning and deserved the answer she got. But, it hurt to hear him confirm it.

"Lillian was the mother of my child. For that alone, she deserves my love. Am I still grieving for her? No. Is she still the love of my life? I don't think she ever was. I certainly wasn't hers."

Maggie sensed he was going to reveal something awful. Something she should know.

"I wasn't enough for her." His voice sounded husky. "I wondered if she had a lover. That maybe she was on her way to their tryst when she died."

Maggie leaned over and tugged his arm down. "Her loss. Remember that. If she couldn't see what a treasure she had, then she didn't deserve you."

Gently kissing his mouth, she tried to show him he was her treasure. Her soft kisses covered his eyes, his chin, the pulse on the side of his neck. More than anything, she needed him to know she loved him. With all her heart.

He flipped her on her back, covering her. With his

mouth and wickedly delicious tongue, he set all her senses alive. When he had her quivering with desire, he stopped. Even her small moan of disappointment didn't make him begin again.

"Look at me, Maggie May. I found my treasure. She's been hanging in the background since I was eight years old. I was too stupid to recognize the real love of my life."

He said the L word. Her heart sped up. *The love of his life.* He meant her?

"Your face is so expressive. I see indecision, hope, fear. What is going through that magnificent mind of yours?" He kissed her forehead. "I love you, Maggie. I've always loved you."

They finally got around to eating the dinner he'd brought home, though it took forever to warm all the little boxes in the microwave. They sat across from each other at the table in the breakfast nook.

"How are you going to tell Ellen?"

"She already thinks we're having an affair."

Maggie dropped the box of fried rice. "What!"

"Yeah, that's what I said when she said I didn't need to make lame excuses like going to the office if I was coming over here to have sex with you."

She scraped up the rice that had fallen onto the table. "What did you tell her? I mean, you denied it of course."

He shot her a glance that questioned her intelligence. "What I was upset about was the fact that a fourteen-year-old girl even thought about something like that."

"I was thirteen when I first thought about it."

His turn to drop something—the spoon he was using to dish himself another helping of General's Chicken. "You thought about having sex at thirteen?"

She nodded.

"About anyone in particular?"

She let the corner of her mouth quirk up. "Oh, yeah."

His eyes softened to the soft gray of a wolf pelt. "Anyone I might have known?"

"Uh, hum. You might have."

He reached across the table and stroked his finger down her cheek. Little shivery sensations made her want to tell him to do it again. He rested his finger on her chin. "I probably knew all the boys you knew back then." He drew his finger upward until he touched her lower lip.

It was all she could do not to open her mouth and touch his finger with her tongue. He traced the edge of her lip. "Tell me his name."

"Why?" she breathed.

"So I can beat the shit out of him for giving a thirteen-year-old those kind of thoughts." He dropped his hand and backed away.

He appeared so smug, so sure of what she was going to say. She folded her arms across her chest. Good Lord, her nipples were standing at attention. She quickly dropped her arms but not before she caught him staring at them.

"Nick Anslyn," she said.

"What!"

She just smiled.

"Nick Anslyn? That nerd?" Drew looked like he couldn't believe it.

"I thought Nick was so dreamy. Those chocolate brown eyes . . ." She sighed.

"How could you see them through his coke-bottle thick glasses?"

"Oh, and all those pencils and pens he carried in his shirt pocket." She sighed again. "That just showed how smart he was."

"Nick Anslyn. I can't believe it. Nick Anslyn?" He shoved a spoonful of beef and broccoli in his mouth. "Nick? Anslyn?"

"You didn't think I was going to say you, did you?" She smirked.

"As a matter of fact." Leaping up, he advanced around the table like a predator. A pissed off predator. "Who did you have that teenage crush on?"

She lifted her chin and fluttered her eyelashes, a silly girl trick but effective. "You're so smart, you figure it out."

"Oh, I have." He stepped so close his leg grazed hers as he slid it between them.

Shivery sensations raced through her body. They started

at her knees where his leg touched and traveled upward. She felt his heat through the heavy cotton of his Dockers. And when he leaned over her, she felt more than that. Oh, lordy.

"I knew then, and I know now." He bent his head as if to kiss her and whispered, "Andrew VanderPloog."

He brushed past her and sauntered into the living room. She bolted after him, wrapped her arms around his throat, and jumped on his back. "You are an idiot, Campbell. A total idiot."

He carried her to the couch, a leech on his back, and casually sat down. Then, just as casually, he flipped her off his back and onto her own. He pinned her wrists to the cushion above her head and straddled her—one knee between her hip and the back of the couch, his other foot on the floor. "Gotcha."

He knew all the time. She wouldn't look at him—didn't want to see the smirk. "You can let me up now, Campbell."

"Are you going to call me Campbell when we go back to bed?"

"Guess you'll have to wait and see." She bucked and twisted to get out from under him. Well, she didn't try that hard.

EPILOGUE

One Year Later

Drew stretched and rolled his shoulders. He'd fallen asleep on the porch of Rock Harbor Lodge. The Adirondack chair left ridges down his back. He walked to the rail hoping to see the girls on their way back. For the past five days, Maggie, Trish, and six girls had hiked and camped on Isle Royale. Though they'd invited him to join them, Drew declined. He'd camped and hiked with them last summer, fall, and well into the winter. They started up again this spring and camped through June.

Trish Morrow flew in from Colorado, to a group of ecstatic girls. Maggie had embraced her friend with enthusiasm. They hadn't needed him for this trip. But, because of Maggie's condition, he needed to be close. She'd insisted that her five-month pregnancy shouldn't keep her from camping and hiking. He trusted her to a certain extent, even though Trish—a registered nurse—could handle anything.

Selfishly, he wanted to be close when she and the crew returned. He had to see for himself that she was all right.

Singing caught his attention. He smiled at the sound of "This Old Man" as the girls came closer. It reminded him of an old Ingrid Bergman movie *The Inn of the Sixth Happiness*, a film his dad watched each time it came on television. The children had sung that song to keep up their spirits as they marched across the Chinese countryside.

Now, his girls sang to announce they'd returned.

After snatching up his duffle, he rushed off the porch and onto the trail. Ignoring their leaders, the girls broke rank and charged him. Ellen flung herself into his arms, while the other girls all talked at once.

"You should've come with us."

"We saw a moose in the water."

"She had a baby moose with her."

"And a snake crawled across the trail."

"Gretchen saw a sandpiper."

"A *semipalmated* sandpiper," Gretchen corrected.

Since he didn't know the difference between a semipalmated sandpiper and a regular sandpiper, Drew just smiled and nodded.

"We heard loons all night long."

"Yeah, they sounded weird."

When their voices trailed off, he asked, "Did you have fun?"

Their resounding "yes" nearly knocked him over.

"Okay, girls," Trish called them to order. "We need to get down to the harbor to catch the ferry back to Copper Harbor."

The six girls—minus Susan and Janie who'd dropped out last summer—followed Trish. Maggie caught his eye. "Did you have fun?"

He helped her off with her backpack, worried again that she carried too much, then wrapped his arms around her. "Not as much fun without you."

Her eyes twinkled. "You could have come with us."

Reaching down, he grabbed his duffle then slung it and her pack over one shoulder. "This trip was for you, Trish, and the girls. You didn't need me horning in."

They strolled toward the dock where the girls and Trish waited for the ferry. He let her set the pace.

"You wouldn't have horned in, as you put it. The girls love you. I think they were disappointed you didn't come."

He pressed his finger to her lips. "We've been over this before. I was fine here." More than fine. No tent, no sleeping bag, no bugs.

"Okay." She looped her arm through his. "Let's get back to the mainland. I desperately need a shower."

With a dramatic sniff, he grinned. "Yes, you do."

She punched him in the arm. "And I need a bed, a real bed."

"That can be arranged." He thought about what they could do in that bed. They had reservations for the night at a hotel in Hancock before the long ride home.

"And a good night's sleep. With no interruptions." She sighed. "Other than using the bathroom. You wouldn't believe how annoying it was to get up every two hours to pee in an outhouse."

Despite the fact that carrying his child added to her misery, he made sympathetic noises. "You're right. Annoying."

She stopped before they reached the dock. Before he could ask what was wrong, she looped her arms around his neck. "I missed you."

He dropped their packs and held her tight. "I missed you, too, love."

As he ducked his head to kiss her, laughter and whistles broke them apart. The girls jumped up and down, still full of energy. They whooped and shouted for them to hurry up and kiss. The ferry was docking.

Drew kissed her nose. "I'm ready to go home."

"Me, too." Her kiss landed on his mouth and told him all he needed to know.

Maggie May Campbell loved him.

Turn the page for a quick look at

The Case of the Bygone Brother:
An Alex O'Hara Novel

by Diane Burton

An Excerpt from *The Case of The Bygone Brother:*
An Alex O'Hara Novel

She had trouble written all over her.

Like a scene out of *The Maltese Falcon*, a beautiful woman begs the P.I. for help. Shades of Sam Spade, with a slight difference. The elegantly-dressed woman pounding on my plate glass window was more than twenty years older than me and, even though my name is Alex O'Hara, I'm not male. But I am a PI —O'Hara & Palzetti, Confidential Investigations since 1965. Not that I've been around since 1965.

As soon as I unlocked the outer door, the woman burst through, a few maple leaves stuck to her Manolo's. Frankly, I was surprised she wore only a sweater. She must have been freezing out there. In spite of the fact that it was mid-October, the temp had dipped that afternoon to the low forties. We might even get frost.

"Ms. O'Hara, thank God you're still here. I was so afraid—" She broke off on a sob. Taking a small, white, lace-edged handkerchief out of her Louis Vitton purse, she dabbed at her eyes.

Now I'm not one to belittle a person's worries. However, I thought she switched a little too quickly from imperious knocking to damsel in distress.

Damsel? Not quite. I pegged her around fifty-five, give or take a few years, and well-preserved. Even in her Manolo's, she only came up to my chin. Next to her I felt like a hulking giant. Since I'm five-ten in my socks, I look down on most women. Despite her elaborate up-do, from my angle I could see her roots. A visit to her hairdresser might be in order. But I digress.

"What can I do for you?" I tried not to sneeze from her overpowering perfume. An oriental scent. Shalimar or Opium. I never knew which was which. I tried them on at the perfume counter at Macy's. That's the closest I'd ever get to wearing expensive perfumes.

"I need your help." Her breathy voice reminded me of Marilyn. As in Monroe, not Manson. "My brother is missing. I must find him."

About the Author

Diane Burton combines her love of mystery, adventure, science fiction and romance into writing romantic fiction. Besides the science fiction romance *Switched* and *Outer Rim* series, she writes romantic suspense and cozy mysteries (The Alex O'Hara Novels). She is also a contributor to the anthology *How I Met My Husband*. Diane and her husband live in Michigan. They have two children and five grandchildren.

For more info and excerpts from her books, visit Diane's website: http://www.dianeburton.com

Connect with Diane Burton online

Blog: dianeburton.blogspot.com/
Facebook: Diane Burton Author
Twitter: @dmburton72
Pinterest: dmburton72
Goodreads: Diane Burton Author

If you would like to know when a new book is released, sign up for Diane's newsletter. http://eepurl.com/bdHtYf

Thank you for reading **Numbers Never Lie**. I hope you enjoyed my story. It would be great if you let others know. Authors love reviews. If you have time, please consider leaving a review at Amazon and/or Goodreads — even just a line or two about what you thought of the book would be so appreciated.

www.ingramcontent.com/pod-product-compliance
Lightning Source LLC
Chambersburg PA
CBHW072217170626
46813CB00003B/984